SMOKE AND MIRRORS

A copycat killer makes a cold trail run hot

DENVER MURPHY

THE
BOOK
FOLKS

Published by The Book Folks

London, 2019

© Denver Murphy

ISBN 978-1-7986-2738-9

www.thebookfolks.com

Smoke and Mirrors is the third book in a trilogy featuring retired detective Jeffrey Brandt. Details about the other books can be found at the end of this one.

Prologue

They say that time is the great healer and, with Brandt dead, and consequently her sole remaining purpose in life having now gone, Stella Johnson had plenty of time on her hands. Yet in the weeks since Brandt's second visit to her house, only her physical wounds had healed. The doctors had told her that she was lucky she would only suffer a couple of discreet patches of long-term scarring; but they were only talking about what they could see.

Far more damaging had been the injury she suffered the first time Brandt visited her house: the death of the man she had started falling for.

On that occasion, PC McNeil had saved her from former Chief Superintendent Jeffrey Brandt, the serial killer they had hunted for months, but in so doing he had been fatally stabbed.

McNeil's death and Brandt's subsequent escape weren't the only causes of her pain; equally bad was the knowledge that she was responsible for them both being there that night. In her desperation to catch Brandt, she had instigated the publishing of a newspaper article that suggested he had been preying on young women to hide that he was a closet homosexual. He had tracked Johnson down to prove to her first-hand that the allegations were untrue, stripping her and tying her to the bed. He was about to rape her when McNeil arrived.

McNeil had been to her house just once before, and that was only because she was driving with him to Canterbury to see whether a murder there was linked to the killings they were investigating in Nottingham. But it was in Canterbury where their association had begun crossing over from professional to personal. Had it not been for some crucial evidence being discovered as they made their way back into the hotel that night, it was highly probable that Johnson would have slept with her younger colleague. Her determination not to lose focus in her pursuit of Brandt had made that moment the closest they'd ever come to becoming physical.

Brandt denying her the blossoming relationship with McNeil had seen Johnson return to work far sooner than she was mentally ready. She may have successfully lied her way through her Occupational Health interview, but her boss, DSI Potter, had not been fooled. Resolutely keeping her away from the hunt for McNeil's murderer, and leaving it to DI Fisher, who appeared to be falling for the false trail left by Brandt, Johnson decided to go it alone in her search for justice.

After tracing him to the Spanish seaside resort of Benidorm, but failing to lure him into a trap there, she found herself with little option but to revisit the strategy that had drawn Brandt out the first time. Coercing his ex-wife into agreeing to an interview that would seemingly confirm the earlier rumours, she lay in wait for his return to Nottingham. But just as her past actions had inadvertently led to the death of another, Brandt had lured her out under the pretence that she could save his ex-wife when, in reality, he had killed her hours before.

Johnson had eventually awoken in her kitchen, tied to a chair and with Brandt pouring petrol around the room. She had derived little satisfaction from managing to escape the resulting blaze as he perished within. Although nothing would bring McNeil back, Brandt denying her the revenge she craved had left her feeling empty.

The thought of killing Brandt herself had been the one thing that had kept her going. As far as she was concerned, all she was now left with was a destroyed house and a career she no longer wanted.

What Johnson didn't know was that Brandt had left her with less than that. The charred remains of the body dragged from the house weren't his.

Chapter One

As the bus from Canterbury swept down the hill into Whitstable, and with the blue-grey sea now visible beyond the houses on his left, Jack pushed thoughts of everything else to one side and concentrated on the task at hand. With no experience of murder, either directly or indirectly, Jack knew his greatest chance of getting away with it would be to make himself as unnoticeable as possible. This wasn't just in terms of the location of the killing itself but his movements in the surrounding areas.

He had alighted at the stop before the odd industrial unit turned into the main thoroughfare of shops. Jack knew little about the deployment of CCTV but suspected a quiet seaside town such as Whitstable was unlikely to have much coverage outside the very centre. That his route to the beach would take him close to his grandmother's old house was a coincidence. He wondered how his parents and, most of all, his grandmother would feel if they could see him now and knew what he was planning on doing. It wasn't too late to change his mind. He could simply turn around and catch a bus back home, putting all this behind him.

But Jack knew the truth.

On what should be a day for celebration, with less than an hour passing since he finished his final A Level exam, Jack couldn't look to the future with this still hanging over him. He was certain he could find the strength to turn around, but equally knew it would merely postpone the inevitable.

This had to be done.

Jack carried on walking and, instead of thinking of his family, he turned his attention to the man who had inspired him.

Brandt.

Had he ever experienced such doubts? Jack liked to believe that he hadn't but even if he had, he had managed to overcome them, a fact which to Jack was a source of strength.

Not that Jack felt he would have to worry about this. He had no intention of making a career out of murder. This was to be a one-off, just something that would enable his mind to settle and allow him to focus on the long summer ahead, so he could begin looking forward to his adult life. He reassured himself that, much in the same way he had quickly lost interest in his internet searches years ago, he would be able to put thoughts of death behind him after this. Having delivered it first hand, his previous fantasies would sufficiently pale by comparison to render them pointless.

Feeling much better, Jack found himself able to concentrate solely on the present; a discovery that coincided with his arrival at the short alleyway that took him directly onto the beach. He slowed his pace, enjoying the narrow view his confined sight gave him of the water. From here, the sea seemed infinite and Jack found the expanse comforting in its vastness. It made him feel small and, by the same virtue, so too the act he was about to perform. He had read recently that with a global population now well in excess of seven billion, a person dies in the world every half a second. In this context, what he was going to do was wholly insignificant. In fact, Jack didn't really believe it was adding to the statistic. Given he knew he couldn't move on with his life until the deed was done, it wasn't so much ending someone else's life as trading theirs for his. He wouldn't know the background of his victim, but he felt confident his life was worth more than theirs. Not only was he young and should be allowed to look forward to many happy years ahead, but he was an able and intelligent person who could well go on to make a valuable contribution to the world. Whoever he was going to find walking aimlessly along the beach, when they should be at work, was clearly not as important as him.

Taking a deep breath, he emerged from the alleyway; the crunch of the shingle underfoot signalling his arrival at his destination. Reaching into his shoulder bag, he touched the knife for the first time since placing it there that morning. It was one of the smaller blades from the wooden block that stood proud on the marble work surface, and was the closest he could find in size to the steak knife used in the attacks in Nottingham and Canterbury. A serrated edge would have added to the authenticity of the experience, but Jack reassured himself that he was only seeking to take inspiration from those events.

He was going to bring it out and attempt to hold it discreetly, perhaps the handle reversed so it would sit up his forearm, but as soon as it was exposed to the sun's rays the reflection shone in his eyes. He cursed himself, knowing that his hero wouldn't make this kind of mistake. It mattered not to Jack that there wasn't anyone within sight, schoolboy errors like this would see him caught.

'Stop pissing about,' he muttered to himself and continued to trudge along, the sound of his footsteps matched only by the gentle tumbling of the waves and the gulls calling out overhead. This was not at all the experience Jack had been expecting. He thought he would be feeling pumped; energised by the sheer thrill of finally experiencing a death he had created. Instead, he felt out of his depth and, despite the familiarity of the setting, lost and far from home. He still wanted to kill but this was more about getting the deed over and done with than any kind of watershed moment in his life. It would have to be the very first person he encountered. Any notion of selecting his victim would only give him more time in which to lose his nerve.

Jack stepped over the wooden groyne and spotted a person headed in his direction. All he could make out from this distance was that they were male and seemed of average build. Jack would have liked a woman, and not just because of the synergy it would create with the other attacks. He felt it would give him more of a chance to overpower his victim, if things didn't go smoothly. However, his own physique was strong – if not overtly muscular – and he reassured himself that a man would be less wary of a stranger approaching. Similarly, selecting this particular man gave Jack one significant advantage – he was alone. Jack wasn't intimidated by dogs, but he knew that some breeds could be very protective of their owner and, even if they weren't, the sort of barking that his actions may provoke could draw unwanted attention.

Even though luck had seemed to bring him a suitable person, Jack didn't like the speed with which their travel was converging. A few minutes earlier it may have seemed like his whole life had been building up to this point, but now it was upon him, it all felt too rushed. As Jack stepped into the groyne field the man had entered a few moments before, he became convinced that the best course of action was to merely pass him and take the next turn off back towards the main road. It no longer mattered that he would regret this action to the point of finding himself drawn to kill at a later date, at least today he could try and continue his life as normal. It may torment him, but he could attempt to deal with the pain, perhaps seek counselling.

Maybe he should just tell his parents. He knew the revelation, which wouldn't include anything about this visit to Whitstable, would deeply disturb them, but it was their job to support him. Rather than help him secure a summer job so he could raise extra cash for going to university in October, they could send him somewhere that would allow him to get over these thoughts. And that's all it was at the moment – just thoughts, irrespective of what he was about to do. Jack had read about plenty of celebrities going into re-hab for drink or drug related problems; perhaps there was something similar that could help him.

He stopped walking. He knew exactly what that place was. His parents would send him to a mental hospital. If he went home now and waited for them to return from work, only to tell them that he wanted to kill someone, they'd first laugh nervously as though believing he was cracking some kind of dark teenage joke they didn't understand. But once they realised he was serious, they would have him sectioned. They would convince themselves they were being supportive, but really what they would do is what they had always done when faced with a problem; they would have someone else deal with it and preferably quickly enough so that neither the neighbours nor their friends at the rotary club would notice.

'Are you okay?'

The question startled Jack and he raised his head to see the man staring at him with a look of concern. Like with most young people, Jack was pretty useless identifying the age of people comfortably into adulthood but, with no signs of grey in his dark brown hair, nor any prominent wrinkles, he guessed the man to be somewhere in his thirties.

'What are you doing here?' Jack asked.

'I was just walking past and you seemed a little... troubled,' the man replied.

'No,' Jack said calmly. 'Why are you here?' He could see his question still wasn't understood and so decided on a different approach. 'Why aren't you at work?'

'Excuse me?' The confusion in his voice was matched by the couple of steps he took away from Jack.

'Don't you have a job?'

'Well, I guess I could ask you something similar but, if you must know, yes I do, and I'm going to it now.'

'What do you do?' Jack asked, reaching into his bag.

'I work at the Cross Keys,' he replied impatiently. 'I'm running late so, if you don't need help or anything, I had better get going.'

'Wait! Hold on!' Jack cried, causing the man to turn back. 'I do need your help with something.' He withdrew the knife, a little unsure what to do with it next. Fortunately for Jack, the sight of the blade only caused the man to pause and look at him with bewilderment.

The moment of inactivity was brief but felt an age to Jack. There was no going back but his arm wouldn't move. It was as if the knife was a dead weight.

'Look, whatever it is, it can't be as bad as all that.'

Jack opened his mouth to ask him what he meant but closed it again. He could feel a rare emotion building inside him. Anger. This man just viewed him as some unstable kid. An unstable kid who has skipped school and was threatening suicide as some pathetic cry for help.

'I bet he never had to deal with this shit. I bet he never had his victims patronising him,' Jack muttered.

'Who are you talking...?'

Jack had silenced the man before he could complete his question. They both stared at the knife's hilt protruding from his chest. Jack found the bloom of blood that was spreading out mesmerising, especially the way the material of his white T-shirt was greedily soaking up the moisture. It was proving an effective sponge. He looked up to see the man's eyes wide with disbelief and could feel his manners compelling him to apologise. But this was no error. It may not have been planned, but Jack had come to this place in order to do something specific; something that had yet to be completed. He reached for the handle.

'Don't!' The man gurgled, and blood bubbled on his lips.

Jack smiled. Any reassurance it conveyed was not designed to bring the man comfort; instead it was a surety that blasted away his earlier reticence. This was not only right but what he was meant to do.

As Jack withdrew the blade, his smile turned into a grin. The material of the man's top couldn't cope with the increased flow and blood started dribbling in rivulets. The grin turned into a laugh, as Jack plunged the knife repeatedly back into the man's chest until the man's knees buckled, collapsing him onto the beach.

Jack swung around to check he hadn't been observed. Satisfied, he wiped the back of his sleeve across his face, mopping away the blood that had showered him. He looked down and was disappointed to see that the man's head was facing the ground. Using his foot to lever him over, Jack wasn't surprised to find sightless eyes staring back at him. He knew the man was dead; he had felt his life pass from him.

But still he waited, watching the blood drip from the end of the blade, splattering the pebbles below. He stooped to wipe it on the small section of the man's shirt that had remained white and carefully, almost reverentially, placed it back in his shoulder bag.

As Jack continued walking in his original direction, he could feel the calmness descend.

Chapter Two

'Ma'am, take a look at this.'

DC Stepford stood patiently whilst DCI Marlowe carefully read the document he had just placed on her desk. He knew from past experience not to interrupt her when she was concentrating.

'What do you make of it?'

He couldn't resist asking the question.

'In terms of what?' Marlowe replied coolly.

'Do you think it might be...?' From the very moment he had arrived at the beach in Whitstable, Stepford wondered whether their killer was back in business. It was nearly three weeks since the person attacking women in Nottingham had decided to target their city, only to seemingly disappear once more. No one had said it, but he was sure he wasn't the only one who had been hoping he may strike again so that they would have more evidence to go on this time.

'The same man?' Marlowe finished for him, her eyebrows raised. She let out a long sigh. 'I really don't see it. Look, I understand why you are looking for the link though. I had a quick catch up with DCI Johnson earlier in the week and she was talking about a murder in St. Albans, claiming that to have been done by our guy. She shared the details with me but, to be honest, I don't really buy that either.'

'Do you think he just stopped?' Stepford tried hard to prevent any impertinence coming through in his tone. Nevertheless, he waited for some form of rebuke.

Instead, he received a simple shrug from Marlowe. 'I don't know, but perhaps that's just the very thing. Whoever this guy is, he's committed four attacks that are definitely attributable to him but has left us very little to go on. For whatever reason his deliberate disposal of the murder weapon was perhaps a sign that it was to be his last kill.'

'This DCI Johnson doesn't seem to think so.' Stepford had been out interviewing local residents when she had come down to check on the investigation, but that hadn't stopped him hearing about her. In the short time Johnson had been at the station she had caused quite a stir, managing to put a fair few people's noses out of joint.

'Are you suggesting I should call her about this?' A hint of menace had crept into Marlowe's voice. 'Perhaps you would like to go and visit the DSI and share your concerns about how I am leading this case?'

DC Stepford suddenly felt very uncomfortable. 'I'm sorry, ma'am, I wasn't suggesting…'

'Then sod off and find out who really killed this man.'

Chapter Three

The room looked familiar, but Johnson knew the chances of her being in the same one as when she was admitted to the hospital before were slim. Even so, she was still wary that one of the nurses from her previous stay might enter. She tried to sit up, which took some effort, not helped by the effects of the drugs still in her system, but she felt remarkably okay. Johnson guessed it wasn't just because her injuries were lighter than before, the bandages on various parts of her body indicating where she had received burns, but because things were very much different this time. Before she was having to deal with the death of McNeil, and the knowledge that his killer had got away.

As Johnson reached out with an unsteady hand towards the cup of water on the table next to her, she contemplated how she really felt about what had happened this time in her house. In many respects it was a mixture of relief and regret. Relief that she had survived it and that the sadistic serial killer, Brandt, was no longer at large, but also regret for how things had played out. For the third time, her plan to outwit him had failed. Even if she hadn't learned from what had happened when he first came to her house, the events in Benidorm should have taught her that Brandt would always remain one step ahead. She wanted to believe her actions had been the result of desperation but knew, deep down, there was an element of arrogance. Throughout her life, Johnson had viewed failure as a temporary state. If she was unable to do something, she had always shown resilience – resolving that she need only try harder to then succeed. Most of the time she had been right and every successive reversal in fortune had only strengthened her belief that she could achieve whatever she set out to do.

Johnson viewed this personality trait as a quality, but recently it had been leading to the death of others. This time there had been Susan, Brandt's wife. Johnson had yet to receive confirmation that he had killed her, but she knew better than anyone what he was capable of. The other death she was aware of was Brandt's own. This took up the large proportion of the regret she felt. The outcome she had sought may have been the same, but it was meant to be on her terms, not his. She took little satisfaction that his plan to kill them both in the house fire had failed; what he had done was to steal her opportunity for retribution. In a way, it was the final insult.

And what had he left behind? Johnson knew she should be grateful to still be alive but what life could she look forward to? McNeil was still gone; her house was now destroyed and the career she had held so dear was in tatters. Even if none of her actions could be viewed as criminal, she still had a lot of questions to answer, not just in terms of what Brandt was doing there, but also why she had chosen to return to her home rather than remain anonymous and safe in the flat she had rented.

Her thoughts were disturbed by the door opening. The flash of a smile confirmed that this nurse was neither the one who had her pinned down and sedated before, nor the one who had refused to get her some clothes when determined to leave.

'Do you think you're well enough for a visitor?' she asked in a soft, soothing voice.

'Come again?'

'It's fine, I'll just tell him he'll have to come back at another time.' The nurse turned to leave.

'Who is he?' Johnson called out and was surprised to find her question wasn't answered directly, more seen as an indication that she wanted to see whoever it was waiting outside. Without reply the nurse was gone and the door was about to close again when a male hand caught it.

'Hello, Stella.'

'Guv?' It was DSI Potter. Not only had he come to visit her the first time she had been admitted to hospital, but he had helped her leave, collected items from her house, and booked her into one of the city's many hotels.

However, much had changed in the last few weeks.

All the apparent kindness seemed to have evaporated on her return to work. He had shown a complete disregard for how she had been feeling; her overpowering need to catch McNeil's killer. Instead, he had put her on some bullshit drug related case whilst DI Fisher had continued to fuck up the investigation.

'How are you doing?'

Johnson ignored the kindness in his voice. 'Why are you here?'

He recoiled from the sting of the accusation. 'I… I wanted to see how you are. I care about you, Stella.'

'Huh,' she huffed. 'Fat lot you care.'

'If this is about what happened when you returned to work…'

'This is exactly about what happened,' she said. Johnson wanted to tell him that because of his cruelty she had been forced to hunt for Brandt herself. If he hadn't made her take things into her own hands she wouldn't be lying here, her body covered in burns. But she couldn't. She didn't understand why he had been so cold towards her, but he wasn't responsible for what she had done. If nothing else, there was the possibility that if she hadn't made her suspicions known to Brandt in Spain, he may not have evaded the police following the murder of the woman in the caravan.

'This is the last thing I wanted for you.' Potter seemed genuinely distressed.

'I suppose you're going to tell me that's why you kept me off the case.'

'Exactly,' he cried out. 'After what happened to you last time, I wanted you as far away from that madman as possible. I was trying to protect you. I was trying to be your friend. Put yourself in my shoes; you would have done the same thing.'

'But that's the trouble though, isn't it, guv? You blurred the boundaries. Your desire to protect me was as a friend but you used your position of authority to carry it out. That's not fair. That would be like me…'

'Like you using your position of authority to keep a young officer you were attracted to close by?'

Johnson recoiled as though slapped. The look of horror on Potter's face did not make it any easier. 'It wasn't like that,' she hissed.

'I know, and I'm sorry I said it, but I wanted to show you that things are not as straightforward as you make out.'

'Just go.' Johnson could feel the tears beginning to well up and wouldn't give Potter the satisfaction of seeing them again. The last time he had held her and told her it would be okay, now she didn't want him anywhere near her.

'I'll check in to see how you are getting on in a couple of days. I'll try and hold off on you being questioned.'

Johnson didn't ask him what he was referring to. It wasn't just that she didn't want to delay his departure, she knew exactly what he meant. What she wondered was whether he was telling her this to ensure she used the opportunity to get her story straight. At the moment she couldn't give a toss about how the police perceived her actions, especially not Professional Standards, but equally she knew there was little to gain from giving them anything to be suspicious about.

Her exchange with Potter had left her exhausted and she was contemplating finding the switch to recline her bed and get some more rest. She was considering whether it would be best to wait for her next load of pain medication, in the hope she may fall into a sufficiently deep sleep that she would not dream. It was rare that the events of Brandt's first arrival at her house didn't revisit her in the night, and she was sure that things would only get worse in the short term as her brain tried to come to terms with what happened when he returned there. She had been around enough officers in her time who had suffered with PTSD to know that it would not be a fast recovery.

And yet even whilst sitting up, she could feel her eyelids growing heavy. It was only when she heard a polite cough that she noticed the nurse had returned to her doorway. 'It seems like you're quite the popular one today. Got enough strength for another visitor?'

Johnson was genuinely curious who it might be this time, even if she didn't fully believe Potter's claim that he would keep officers away from her until she was feeling a little better. She nodded, which was all the encouragement the nurse needed.

The woman who entered was instantly recognisable, even if Johnson had only met her once. 'Claire?'

'Oh, I'm so glad to see you,' McNeil's sister said, immediately approaching the bed. Her expression was one of genuine worry and in complete contrast to the stony determination she had shown in the graveyard.

'Look, Claire, I wasn't ignoring your messages. I just… I just didn't want to…'

'Shh,' she soothed, reaching out for one of Johnson's bandaged hands. 'I'm the one who should be apologising to you. I should have had more faith.'

Johnson didn't know how to respond. Instead she continued to stare at her visitor with wide eyes.

'You did it, Stella.' Hearing her first name come from Claire's mouth was almost as alien as hearing McNeil referred to as Darren. 'You did what was needed and you got him.'

'But… but I didn't…'

'Yes, you did,' she responded firmly. 'Nothing will bring my brother back, but I can try and move on now that sick fuck is dead. We both can.'

The tears that had threatened to spill when Potter had been there were back again, and this time nothing would stop them falling. Through her blurred vision Johnson could see Claire had also started to cry. She wondered whether hers were also for fear of what moving on meant. With thoughts of revenge no longer providing a purpose to her life, all Johnson could look forward to was emptiness.

Chapter Four

As far as Brandt was concerned, this was his first legitimate trip to Wales. Any previous visit had been years before and purely so he could get to the ferry at Holyhead to visit his family in Ireland. He was usually running late, and the main focus had been on driving as fast as possible through it.

In many respects, it was for this reason Brandt had chosen Wales as somewhere he would try and settle down. Its relative unfamiliarity meant that he felt far removed from what had happened in Nottingham, not just in terms of avoiding the glare of the authorities, but also separating himself from his deeds. This was another reason why he hadn't sought to return to the continent. Not only would he be pushing his luck for the third time at passport control, but also his attempt to impersonate someone else may require killing again; something he wanted to avoid.

Now that he had brought his dealings with DCI Johnson to a conclusion, and the source of much of his pain, Susan, had gone, he just wanted to have a stab at trying to move on. The intermittent thoughts of suicide hadn't left him, but there was no way he was going to set fire to himself. He didn't fear the agony of burning, it was just so far removed from the plummeting from a great height that he had fantasised about since staring up at the 10m platform at Westminster Lodge as a child learning to swim.

He would see if he could settle in North Wales. His existence now wasn't about trying to find redemption for what he had done; he still believed he had been acting in the public's best interest. But his snap decision to spare Johnson's life necessitated an end to the killing. What he hadn't expected in the moment he decided to loosen her restraints, was the feeling of freedom that faking his own death would bring. He no longer had to be former Detective Superintendent Jeffrey Brandt, a man who had become so disillusioned with society to have turned to murder. He may not have been as successful as he had intended, but he had tried his best.

Now it was time to move on.

Certainly, his final act had caused a media frenzy. Even days later, he might no longer have been headline news, but he was still taking up column space. Believed to be dead, pictures of him had reverted to formal ones taken whilst he had still been in the force and didn't reflect the look he had cultivated in Spain. The temperature in Rhyl may not have been anywhere like it had in Benidorm, but it was sunny, and he was keeping his tan topped up, as well as growing out his new beard once more.

Perhaps it was a sense of fatalism that prevented Brandt from becoming as concerned about being spotted as before, but he also knew that no one now expected to see him alive. Any similarities between him and the pictures that had been plastered across the newspapers and on television would be quickly dismissed.

Most of all, Brandt felt safe in his privately rented static home in a quiet caravan park away from the livelier and more popular sites closer to the seaside town. The campsite backed onto a stretch of beach that, at the beginning and end of each day, was deserted except for the occasional dog walker. Strolling along the sand and staring out to sea, he could feel an inner peace that had escaped him for so many years; this soon became his favourite place.

But along with the belief that he could find some semblance of happiness, was also the knowledge that his limited funds would not enable him to stay there indefinitely without finding some form of paid employment. Once the children went back to school and the off-season began, he intended making the owner an offer on a longer-term rental; one that would be considerably less than what he was currently paying but would provide them both with a degree of security. Nevertheless, even if it was accepted, taking into account his living costs, Brandt's money would dry up before the winter was over.

Immigration had always been an issue that preoccupied the British public, no more so than since the Brexit referendum. Brandt knew that if he were to survive in a country obsessed by national insurance numbers and tax codes, he would have to think like an illegal immigrant and find the sort of work that paid in cash and asked few questions. He had considered enquiring if the campsite owners would offer him odd maintenance jobs. The idea of being able to gain employment so close to home was attractive but also the reason why he decided against it. If they did request any form of identification, it may lead to a situation where he felt the need to leave, something he didn't want to risk just as he was starting to feel settled.

Instead, Brandt chose the most stereotypical of seasonal work. One synonymous with immigrants because it was a job that few Brits would be willing to do, with its low pay relative to the effort involved: fruit picking. The last time Brandt had done any work that could be considered physical was 30 years ago when he was an officer walking the beat, but the idea of being out in the

open and using his body rather than his mind held a
certain attraction.

Chapter Five

Jack knew he needed to try and secure a job for the remainder of his time in Canterbury before heading off to university; the destination to be determined when he collected his A Level results in a few weeks' time. However, any pressure from his parents had now faded seeing as his mood had improved. Yet Jack didn't know how he was feeling. Killing the man in Whitstable was meant to have been a calming experience, to allow him to move on from the thoughts that had dogged his childhood; enabling him to concentrate on the future. But the past few weeks had been the most tumultuous Jack could ever remember. Whilst his friends were enjoying the long summer days and trying to put their exams at the back of their mind, Jack was unsettled.

The guilt that followed realising Brandt hadn't cheated him quickly faded, and he became obsessed with being ready to find out about Brandt's next exploit as soon as it happened. That his idol's next action was to be his last, left Jack confused. He had never envisaged it ending like this. Childish as it may have been, he had expected his hero to go on forever. In the hours that followed the news of Brandt's suicide in the house fire, Jack had felt numb.

When feeling started to return, it was one of loss. It seemed such a waste, but he drew strength from the fact that Brandt had intended it. It had been on his terms and he had denied anyone the credit for catching him.

What Jack entered, even though the concept would be alien to him, was a period of mourning. Although he had never expected to meet the man who had given him so much inspiration, the knowledge that he now never would, gave him great sadness. Whilst trying to maintain a relatively cheerful persona in front of his parents, Jack started to consider how he could honour Brandt; both in his work and his sacrifice.

* * *

Jack had lied, claiming that his trip to London was to meet a school friend and spend the day visiting some key attractions. The train he boarded at Canterbury West early that Saturday morning was heading to the capital but only for the purpose of allowing him to change to one that would take him north and to Nottingham. He may have already visited the spot where Brandt had killed the girl on countless occasions over the last few weeks – a small road just off the main high street and only a few minutes' walk from Jack's own house – but Jack still needed to go to where it all started. He found it fitting that his walk to the station took him past the garage where Brandt had disposed of the murder weapon and along the route where their paths may well have crossed that day.

Catching the 06:25 train, the ride into King's Cross took less than an hour. Although the change of line meant only a platform switch, Jack had fifty minutes to kill and went in search of some breakfast on the concourse. Unbeknownst to him, he passed the bar where Brandt and Franklin had met prior to the Arsenal game. Instead, Jack found an upmarket café with a menu not dissimilar to the one he had worked at just a short time ago. But he was too nervous to stomach anything fried and elected to have a pastry to go with the coffee he ordered.

The remainder of the journey was long and boring, with most of the places they passed through towns Jack had barely heard of. Nevertheless, the excitement inside him built, especially after Loughborough, the last stop before Nottingham. That he would arrive at the scene of the very first attack on Sarah Donovan was a particular thrill. Given what he had been through in Whitstable, he wondered whether Brandt had experienced the same kind of apprehension as he approached her just outside the station. Maybe that explained why his attack hadn't been sufficient to end her life. Jack felt uncomfortable any time he thought back to the repeated stabs he had delivered to the man, because the crazed way in which he had dealt those murdering blows was out of sync with the calmness he believed Brandt to have approached his victims with. However, in Sarah's case he had perhaps been too controlled and self-assured, and had learned from the experience that he would need to inflict multiple wounds in order to ensure the kill.

With it now being mid-morning on a glorious summer's day, it wasn't surprising to find the area busy with people. Not only could Jack loiter without drawing attention to himself, but he enjoyed the similarity with what he had experienced outside King's Cross in London. He had been aware of Nottingham's existence prior to news of Brandt's actions there, but only because of the role it had in tales of Robin Hood he had enjoyed as a child. Yet the bustling city that greeted him was as far removed from those as one could get.

With the stabbing receiving only local news coverage at the time, Jack had no photographs he could use to identify the precise location, but he had read that Sarah hadn't been a passenger, merely passing the station on her way to the shops that Saturday. Whilst he would have loved to stand on the very spot on which she had collapsed, just being on the same stretch of pavement was sufficient for Jack to feel exhilarated.

Much as he could have spent ages there, drinking in the same sights, smells and sounds that Brandt would have experienced, Jack had much to do before he would make the long journey home that day. So, to make the most of the limited time he had available, he walked away from the station in the direction that Sarah had come from and followed the signs for the City Ground and Trent Bridge. The route was initially disappointing with the buildings becoming increasingly plain and often dilapidated. Things perked up as he neared the river and it seemed the area had gone through a degree of regeneration, not least indicated by the typical English boozers giving way to trendier waterfront bars. Jack enjoyed the modernity it offered – a contrast to the traditional surroundings of Canterbury.

Jack had memorised the location of where Brandt had committed his second murder long before he had thought about coming to Nottingham, but as he left the main road behind him and set off along the water's edge, he checked his phone just to be sure. He needn't have worried because after he went around one of the river's natural meanders, he could see up ahead a few bunches of flowers marking the spot. It didn't escape him that most had long wilted. Jack had the urge to reach out and touch one to see if it would crumble in his fingers, but he was disturbed by a voice from behind.

'Awful isn't it?'

Jack turned to find a middle-aged woman stood there, her Border Collie sat patiently next to her, wagging his tail and panting with his tongue hanging out of his mouth. He didn't remember passing her on the path, nor had he heard her approach.

'Er, yeah, terrible,' he mumbled, not sure exactly whether he was supposed to be agreeing with what had happened there, or the fact that people had soon forgotten and stopped laying fresh flowers.

'Know her did you, duck?'

The question sounded innocent, but Jack was disturbed nonetheless. 'Er, no,' he responded before he managed to will his brain to get into gear. 'But I pass this way now and again and it just feels strange to think what happened here.'

The woman nodded, the action causing her generous double chin to wobble in time. 'Absolutely. But for the grace of God, it could have been either of us.' She paused thoughtfully. 'Although more likely to be you than me I reckon.'

'How so?' Jack asked. He had been anxious to get rid of her as quickly as possible but found her last comment intriguing.

'Well, from what I heard he wasn't just into young girls like this poor one, but also into young boys as well.'

'You what?' Jack didn't consider himself homophobic and had been well aware of some of the speculation in both the press and on social media as to Brandt's motives, but he didn't like the implication that he had been driven by anything other than a need to create death.

The woman continued, 'Indeed, they say he was doing it to try and prove something to himself, when all the while he was fancying men.' She stopped a moment to give her dog a quick pat on the head and ruffle of its coat. 'Not that I have anything against them queers. What they do in the privacy of their own home and all that, is up to them.'

'I had better be going,' Jack muttered, setting off before the woman could share her thoughts on any other groups in society. He regretted being unable to scour the ground for any signs of blood stains, but he doubted he would have been allowed the peace to explore the area whilst she had a captive audience.

Jack consoled himself with the thought that Brandt had trodden the very same path he was taking. He didn't know from which way he had approached, but it made no sense to Jack to think Brandt would have doubled back and risk being noticed by people he may have passed on his route. He imagined that Brandt probably chose this direction because, like Jack, he would be heading away from the hustle and bustle of Trent Bridge and be looking to slip quietly away into a residential area.

And it was a particular house Jack was looking for now. He estimated it would take him the best part of an hour to walk there and he would need to stop for some lunch on the way. Unless he had ample time before needing to catch his train, he would skip the alleyway where Brandt had made his first kill. It was off route and if his experience in Nottingham so far was anything to go by, he would not be afforded the peace to enjoy the spot properly. Besides, Johnson's house was the purpose of his visit. Brandt had not only been there twice, spending considerably longer on each occasion than he had at any of the other sites, but it also marked the place of his own passing.

Jack sensed he had found the right road even before he saw the street sign confirming this was where Johnson lived. The address hadn't been divulged after the first attack, but Jack assumed the police were less bothered about keeping it a secret now that Brandt was dead, and the house burned down. The pictures he had seen on the internet had shown the extent of the devastation, provoked, he had read, by the gas boiler exploding; but seeing it up close, and with the unaffected houses mere metres either side providing an alarming contrast, was something entirely different. He wondered what it must have been like inside, with the searing heat and flames all around.

As much time as Jack had spent thinking about death, he had rarely touched upon suicide; far less thoughts of his own. But whilst he might not have given it much consideration, he was sure he could never set himself on fire. He pondered how much pain Brandt had experienced before he died, but also how Johnson had managed to escape. Brandt may have made a mistake with Sarah Donovan but that had been because it was his first attempt. With everything he subsequently went on to do, Jack was surprised to think that he would go on to mess something up that was seemingly so simple. But, then again, Jack had never tied someone up. He imagined that DCI Johnson would have to be strong and fit if she were allowed to be in the police force. Moreover, he had read stories on the internet about amazing feats of strength during times of crisis. One had particularly struck him where a mother had supposedly managed to rip a car door from its hinges in order to save her child.

Jack was saddened that there were no flowers or notes of despair laid by the house. Brandt's death was not being acknowledged. He would have liked to have read the messages left in Brandt's wake, just as he had on the canal path earlier that day.

With one final gaze at the cremated shell of bricks and mortar, Jack turned to make the walk back to the station. He was pleased he had made the trip. It might not have provided him with the sort of connection with Brandt he had hoped for, but he had seen the place first hand where his hero had chosen to make his final stand.

And yet, as his train sped through the countryside on its return journey to London, the key emotion he experienced was one of sadness. In that anonymous street, Brandt had ended something that was so pure, so inspiring. It didn't seem right, and Jack began to develop the notion that it was his responsibility, his duty even, to redeem whatever mistakes had led Brandt to believe the best course of action was to take his own life.

Chapter Six

The hearing went as Johnson had expected. She knew she should have prepared better, or at least been more rested, but she had been enjoying her time with her sister and nephew so much that she had only returned to England on the last available flight. Now that it was over she could go home, at least to the place she currently called home: the flat she had been renting since Brandt had first visited her house. Between her ill-fated trip to Benidorm and her holiday at her sister's place in the south of France, she had spent longer away from the apartment than she had in it. At least this time the insurance company were paying for her rental, even if they were beginning to press her to decide what she wanted to do with her old house.

The truth was Johnson had no idea what would come next. The inquest had not resulted in any charges being brought against her, and she was free to resume work as soon as she completed another one of those bullshit evaluations she'd had to do the last time. The psychological test would be more thorough this time, with the hardest questions at the inquest not being reserved for her but fired at the doctor who had cleared her for active duty. Apparently, it didn't matter that the events which led to Brandt's attempt to murder her had come when she had supposedly been taking a break from work; the panel viewed her being given the all clear as a mitigating factor behind her subsequent actions.

Regardless, Johnson had no intention of returning to the police. What she resented far more than the steps she would need to take in order to resume her old position, was how she had been treated by the department. She wasn't sure she could trust her team. It wasn't just that they had done little to find Brandt and been duped by the bogus suicide note from Franklin. The man who had been asked to stand in for her in her absence, DI Fisher, was also a problem. During the time he had spent under her command, Johnson had managed to keep him on a sufficiently tight leash, but her concerns that he might now be actively working against her were largely confirmed at the hearing. Not only had he provided answers suggesting Johnson had always been a loose cannon, but he even went so far trying to twist proceedings to fit his agenda that, in the end, the chairperson had cause to silence him early, but not before she delivered a few words of admonishment.

If Potter couldn't see what a problem Fisher was to the department, that was his problem, not Johnson's. He had hardly come out of the whole affair smelling of roses and if he wanted to persist with Fisher's poor leadership of the team, it was for him to regret at a later date.

As she walked back to her car, Johnson considered whether all this meant a change of location was the best way forward. She had never contemplated switching careers before and a fresh start in a new constabulary might be what she needed. However, she knew that she wouldn't be able to leave all her baggage behind. Her fame was close to notoriety and whilst many on the job might see her as something of a hero, there would still be others that viewed her with suspicion. She had felt it at the hearing when one woman had questioned how, when she was tied to a chair in a burning room, she thought she was able to escape. Johnson had dismissed the question with the simple truth that she didn't know, all the while resenting the implication that her not being burnt to a crisp was somehow curious. Fortunately, nothing had come up to suggest anyone knew about her trip to Benidorm, and to prevent them digging any further Johnson volunteered the information that she had been the one to put Brandt's ex-wife up to the interview with the journalist Gail Trevelly. Whilst this raised some eyebrows and led to questions about her motive – with some of them so impertinent as to suggest she may have predicted what would then go on to happen to Susan – there was nothing she had done that was criminal.

As she approached her Audi TTRS, its red paintwork looking resplendent in the summer sunshine, she regretted once again her decision to go for the hard top over the convertible. In an effort to get herself as far away from the hearing as possible, she hadn't even thought to light the cigarette that her body now craved. In an effort to try and get her habit back under control, she had reinstated her ban on smoking in the car; something she would feel less guilty about reneging upon if she were able to lower the roof and allow the elements to banish all evidence of her filthy addiction.

But today would have to be an exception, and at least the warm weather meant she could have the windows down. As she reached into her handbag to retrieve her packet of Marlboro Lights, she shook her head about how petty her concerns were these days. In the aftermath of McNeil's death, she had chastised herself for dwelling on anything of a trivial nature but knew now they were the product of a highly-strung person who no longer had a demanding career to monopolise her thoughts.

A tap on her shoulder immediately roused her from her musings and she spun round with the unlit cigarette still poking from her lips.

'I didn't mean to startle you, ma'am.'

'What is it, Hardy?' Johnson hadn't meant to sound so impatient with the man who had assisted her when trying to track down Brandt, but the last thing she wanted to do was make small talk with one of her former colleagues.

'I wanted to apologise for what went on in there.'

Johnson was genuinely confused by this statement. Hardy had been present but hadn't been called on to provide any comment. She shrugged. 'Not your fault.'

'Perhaps not,' he agreed timidly. 'But I just wanted you to know that's not how we all feel about… well, about how things happened.'

'You mean what Fisher said?'

'Er, yes… exactly.'

'So how do you feel?'

'Well, a little guilty, if I'm to be completely honest. I allowed Fisher to convince me that Brandt wasn't the key player in all this when I really should have listened to you.'

'Not your fault,' Johnson repeated but with more feeling this time. She could see that this wasn't sufficient to allay Hardy's concerns. 'Look, you're just starting out in your career really, and are relatively new to the team. If you had stuck your neck out and championed me whilst I was just sitting on the side-lines, all you were likely to wind up doing would be getting your head chopped off.'

He was nodding, but the slow manner in which he did it suggested he wasn't fully following what she was trying to say.

'Look, Hardy, you're a good detective, and I don't just mean good at your job, you're a decent person too. But in your position, there is only so much you can do. If you do feel guilty then the best thing you can do is keep your head down and your eyes open.' Johnson couldn't believe she was about to say the next bit. 'DSI Potter is a good man too. If you have any concerns about what is going on, you take it to him, but you make sure you have your ducks in a row first, because I have met ambitious pricks like Fisher before. If he sees you as a threat, he'll hang you out to dry as soon as look at you.'

'Understood, ma'am. And thanks,' he added.

Johnson felt there was no more to be said and opened the door to her car, her cigarette long forgotten. That conversation alone was enough to tell her that she was better off out of it.

Chapter Seven

Brandt hurriedly read the newspaper for the second time. His break was nearly over but he wanted to check that he hadn't missed anything. Not that the article offered much detail, merely confirmation that the hearing into the events at Johnson's house had taken place, and that she was free to return to work. Brandt was pleased by this and hoped that she would be able to move on in the same way he had managed. He remembered reading once about the power of forgiveness and merely saw it as a load of Christian crap. However, the decision not to kill Johnson had marked a total change in his attitude towards her. He felt somewhat benevolent, and there was no point granting her life, if she couldn't now go on to use it. McNeil wasn't meant to die. He hadn't been chosen, and his death was not part of what Brandt had set out to do, he was just a stupid cop on a glory mission. Albeit inadvertently, McNeil had fucked up his plans and ruined everything. Or maybe he hadn't. Maybe Johnson was always meant to live, despite her vicious attacks on him in the paper.

Given what she had been through, Brandt wondered whether she would take the opportunity to go back into the police. Able to view things dispassionately now, he acknowledged that Johnson had all the qualities needed for a successful detective, even if her determination to win in his case had led her down a dark path. But he also knew there was a fair chance she would turn her back on her career, in much the same way Brandt had done. It still might only be a matter of months since he retired, but the truth was he had given up caring about what he had been doing years before. He didn't like to think it either coincided with or was a contributing factor in the breakup of his marriage, instead choosing to focus on how he felt society had become so fractured that the people he had sworn to protect were no longer worth saving.

'Gregori, we've had a coach load of people arrive and we need you back at the counter.'

It had been weeks since Brandt assumed his new identity, one that had allowed him to fit in with the rest of the Eastern Europeans who, despite Brexit, still seemed to be arriving to find work. His employers had been more fastidious than expected and asked for his documents, but when he spun a tale about fleeing his native country of Georgia to escape oppression, they hadn't bothered to chase them up. Moreover, it provided him with a useful cover story when asked about his background. He would feign great sadness and give the impression that to speak about it, even only a little, would be a source of great pain. He knew his fellow co-workers suspected something, especially because he had done everything he could to avoid them. However, nothing had been said, and he reasoned that quite a few of them had their own past they were trying to keep hidden.

Things moved on quickly for Brandt. The orchard where he worked was owned by a man called Samuel Jones, who made a fair proportion of his money running a Welsh food market just north of Betws-y-Coed. Unlike Rhyl and the other nearby coastal towns that seemed exclusively frequented by Scousers, this region was very middle class, appealing to hikers in their expensive gear.

An unexpected absence among Jones' staff had led to him recruiting one of his fruit pickers to make up for the shortfall. With Brandt's English being the best, he was selected.

Brandt had enjoyed his day there and impressed sufficiently to be offered a switch from his former occupation. He had jumped at the chance, not only because it would be easier work than the exhausting manual labour he was still struggling to get used to, but he genuinely enjoyed being there. Throughout his life, Brandt had reserved a fair proportion of his contempt for a particular brand of wealthy: the nouveau riche. Working in the cities, he tended to have little contact with the landed classes but had plenty of experience with this group. The source of their newfound wealth had changed over the years, with the 1980s seeing many of them emerge as a result of the stock market boom and thankfully slink away again after Black Monday. Today it all seemed to do with the internet. Brandt was certainly no Luddite and had made effective use of computers both in the police and his exploits post-retirement, but he had no idea how people in their 20s and 30s could make the sums of money he read about.

And it was these people he enjoyed serving the least in the large tearoom housed in the food hall. The older clients he saw merely as lonely people who used their visit as a chance to get out of the house and be sociable. They tended to make a pot of tea last an hour and view the purchase of any of the various cakes and pastries as a particular treat. However, the young breezed in and bought far more than they ever intended consuming; as long as it was local and/or organic they hoovered up the stuff, and it seemed like the more expensive it was, the better they liked it. Brandt knew how much the case of blueberry granola muffins cost Mr Jones and the sale of just one of the cakes covered it.

The children of the nouveau riche offended him the most. They would bowl in noisily, demanding all sorts of food, only to then just sit there and pick at it, whilst complaining that they wanted to go outside and play on the swings. Yet he reserved a special kind of hatred for their mothers. Desperately trying to hold on to a physique that was proving challenging since childbirth, they would ask for all manner of hot beverages. It turns out that good old tea and coffee isn't sufficient for them. They want skinny lattes, frappuccinos, macchiatos or whatever new complicated beverage they can think of.

'Gregori is coming!' he called in response to the request to get back to work. He knew that the endless supply of contemptibles would dry up once the holidays were over, but he hoped that, unlike the fruit picking which was most definitely seasonal, he could convince Mr Jones to keep him on through the winter. It wasn't as though there weren't plenty of opportunities to make the most of the produce available in the different months. Halloween was big here, but he supposed that as soon as that was over they could concentrate on Christmas. If the shop that sold expensive tat was anything to go by, a line of supposedly handmade decorations was likely to go down a storm.

'Mrs Hardcastle,' he called in the Georgian accent he was slowly allowing to drop, as soon as he emerged from the back. 'If you were wanting on having the second pots, I should be now getting that for you,' he continued, gesturing towards the window at the steady line of elderly people making a beeline for the tearoom.

'Oh, thank you Greggy,' she called in reply. It seemed that few people beyond the age of 55 could cope with pronouncing a foreign name correctly, especially if it was similar to the English version. But Mrs Hardcastle was still one of Brandt's favourites. She was fairly typical of their regulars, albeit one of the younger ones, but managed to tread the fine line between using her visit to strike up the sort of conversation that largely eluded her since her husband died, and attempting to monopolise the staff's time when they were busy serving other customers. Brandt always ensured she got the largest slice of whatever cake she was going for that day and she would wait until he was the one clearing tables before leaving her standard tip of a £2 coin. 'Besides,' she added. 'I'm always pleased when people like them arrive because it makes me seem so much younger.'

Brandt's good-natured laughter wasn't entirely false.

Chapter Eight

Jack knew this wasn't going to go well and it wasn't as if he could share with them the reason why he was far less disappointed than they were going to be. Emerging from his bedroom, he found them waiting expectantly on the landing.

'I didn't get in,' he stated flatly.

'I… I don't understand,' replied his father.

Much as Jack found his apparent incomprehension an irritation, he knew that his father had struggled with the concept that the university application process was different to his day. At some point early in the morning of A Level results day, the Universities and Colleges Admissions Service updated with whether your universities had accepted you.

Jack knew that being rejected by both his firm and insurance offers was a bad thing in terms of what he could expect for his exam results, but he wasn't despondent, having regretted the university choices he had made since his trip to Nottingham.

'I suppose there's always Clearing,' his mother said hopefully.

'That's the spirit!' Jack responded cheerfully. 'We knew that both offers were high and with there no longer being a cap on the number of places that universities can provide, there should be some good courses and decent places still available.'

'Just hurry up getting ready so we can get to school early and see what the bloody damage is.' Jack knew the subtext to the snappy order. Whilst it made sense to find out as quickly as possible what his grades were, what his father really wanted was to get this over and done with before suffering the ignominy of seeing the delight on the other parents' faces as their children revealed how well they had done.

An hour later they were back home again. Jack's Head of Sixth Form had clearly already known what his results were, because he was only too willing to open the study area early and give him the envelope. He had suggested Jack stay so he could receive advice as he trawled through the various courses still available, but Jack had politely declined, claiming he didn't want to get distracted when all the other students arrived. That Mr Gower did little to try and convince him otherwise, showed he shared a similar view to his father; a view evidenced by the fact that the speed at which he had been driven to school wasn't matched in their return journey.

Not that Jack had needed any advice. He knew exactly what he was looking for when he logged back on to UCAS. He didn't know what everyone was so disappointed about anyway, three Bs and a C was a perfectly acceptable haul and one that should make him an attractive applicant in the Clearing process. Within a few minutes, he had found what he had been looking for, even if it left him with an awkward dilemma: Nottingham has two universities. In his father's language, there was the proper one and the ex-polytechnic. Jack had known that he would be able to find courses still available at Nottingham Trent, and indeed a few of them were science related – what he had been looking for. However, despite being high-ranking and as good as the institutions that had rejected him, the University of Nottingham also had a couple of places available. There was nothing for Science or Maths, but Jack could go for the one in Politics and International Relations off the back of his B in History. That Jack had never really enjoyed history, much less the political aspects of the topics he'd been made to study, wasn't an issue for him at that point. The fact of the matter was that this could provide the perfect compromise between going to the city of his dreams and ensuring his parents were happy with the outcome. He was sure they would be sufficiently delighted that he was going somewhere prestigious and similarly fail to see the implication of signing up to three years of studying something he had little interest in.

A phone call to the admissions area, followed by a quick chat with the head of the department guaranteed his place and it wasn't long before Jack was confronting his parents once more. Whilst his father slumped on his kitchen bar stool in relief, his mother couldn't contain her excitement.

'Politics and International Relations at the University of Nottingham. Did you hear that, Malcolm?' she said, turning to her husband. 'Jack might go into the United Nations or NATO when he's finished.'

The proposed job opportunity seemed to rouse his father. 'Yes, son, you could become a diplomat, perhaps even work in a foreign embassy. You could be the ambassador!' He paused, looking at his wife. 'What are you doing, Gwen?'

'Oh, I'm posting the good news on the family WhatsApp group.'

Jack allowed a satisfied smile to escape him. There was nothing like the fear of something awful happening to make something acceptable seem great. He left them to bask in their collective glory and went back upstairs to start researching where he was going to live.

Chapter Nine

He knew he shouldn't, but Brandt couldn't help checking from time to time whether there was any further news about DCI Johnson. There had been nothing in the papers but that wasn't to say she had not returned to work on something not high profile enough to trouble the press. The temptation became so strong that he considered seeing if he could break into her social media, but the discovery of someone hacking her accounts may raise unnecessary suspicion.

Brandt had accepted that the faking of his death could easily be uncovered. It would only have taken a checking of the dental records to confirm it wasn't him. He had hoped that Johnson's testimony would be enough to avoid such steps being followed but, if he were in charge, he would have taken every opportunity to ensure he had the right man. But that was because Brandt had never been interested in the political side of the job. He had never seen the distinction between the right result and the correct one. He supposed, especially since he had gone on to murder again after the authorities had allowed him to escape the country, it was simply too convenient to want to believe that he had killed himself in Johnson's house fire.

With it now being well into September, the body would have long been buried in an unmarked grave. He knew enough about these matters to be able to fathom the whereabouts, and it would give him a perverse sort of pleasure to go and visit the place where he had supposedly been laid to rest. But he wouldn't, because that would be like admitting that he hadn't moved on. Life wasn't exactly rosy and, with the temperatures already starting to dip significantly in time with the tourism tailing off, his caravan wasn't quite as cosy as it had once been. Yet Brandt felt an inner peace that had escaped him for so many years. At night time when he had trouble sleeping, thanks to the rain drumming on the metal roof above him, he found himself wondering whether his peace had something to do with Susan no longer being alive. She had been killed as a punishment for her collusion with Johnson to spread more lies about him. In some respects, he believed she had it coming for choosing to abandon him in the first place. Not that he regretted the death of any of his victims, but perhaps if she had stayed she could have worked to convince him that he needn't take such drastic action. What was most interesting about his arrival at her place, was that she hadn't seemed entirely surprised to see him. If that was meant to somehow convince him to spare her, it spectacularly backfired because she knew what the consequence of her actions would be, and yet she went on and did it anyway. Susan had no one else to blame but herself. At least in Johnson's case, when she had the first newspaper article, in which it was suggested he was bi-curious and potentially impotent, she hadn't anticipated that his next step would be to track her down. Similarly, as misguided as Johnson's dealings with Susan had been, again she had underestimated the result of her interference, much as she had done with her arrival in Benidorm.

But the main reason why Brandt never regretted his decision to allow Johnson to live, whilst Susan had needed to die, was because Johnson hadn't owed him any degree of loyalty. Not only could Brandt understand her desire for retribution, but she had never sworn to love, honour and obey him. Even if they were no longer together, Susan should have honoured the years they had spent living with each other by refusing to throw him to the wolves. He hadn't expected her to understand the reasons behind his actions, but she should never have abused her unique position to cause him harm. At least in Susan's case her pain was fleeting and long since over, whereas Brandt would have to continue with those cruel words in the newspaper article still etched on his mind.

The main difference between Brandt and Gregori was that everyone seemed to like his new persona. On some days, the subservience he needed to maintain in his job grated, but it was nice to be genuinely popular. Brandt had always commanded a great deal of respect whilst he was in the force, but that was more in spite of the way he came across rather than because of it. With little more to offer people than a slightly larger than normal slice of cake, and a warning to get their order in before the next coach load of thirsty punters walked through the door, he had needed to rely on charm. It was alien at first and merely there to make himself seem indispensable to Mr Jones, but it soon came more naturally. Brandt even started looking forward to certain customers popping in and they, along with the work in general, provided a routine that kept him occupied; so much so that his least favourite days were those when he didn't have a shift.

With the summer holidays finished, there was no suggestion of overtime and, although Brandt still enjoyed his walks along the beach to mark the start and end to each day, he found the intervening hours harder to fill. He hadn't touched a drop of alcohol since he had returned from Spain. Initially, it had been so that he could keep his wits with his cover story, but the longer he went without drinking, the more it felt that he was transforming into a different man to who he had been before. That's not to say he didn't often think about alcohol; especially on those long, boring days stuck in his caravan with nothing to do except watch daytime television. He supposed he would drink again at some point, but he was anxious to leave it until he felt sufficiently settled in his new life that it wouldn't provoke his demons to return.

Chapter Ten

Jack's ability to put to one side the thoughts of death and killing that had occupied his teenage years had only been temporary. His desire to honour Brandt would go far beyond just visiting the place of some of his murders. He would kill again and this time he would do it, not for himself as he had done in Whitstable, but to carry on Brandt's great work. From the absence of any further news since the days after his death, it had seemed to Jack that people had been quick to forget about the man. He would ensure that Brandt's name would live on in the minds of the people of Nottingham.

With all of them having now turned eighteen, Jack and his peers were free to go where they chose. The evening of their last day in Canterbury before heading off to university began with most of them boasting about their exploits that summer.

With nothing worth sharing on any of the topics for discussion, and not sufficiently competitive to bother making anything up, Jack concentrated on nodding in the right places and drinking his lager. However much of their stories might have been made up, it would seem that many of them had spent a proportion of their summer increasing their tolerance to alcohol because, as they made their way to the third bar, Jack felt considerably further along the line to drunkenness than his merely raucous companions.

The new venue was much livelier and with talking in a large gathering hard to maintain over the thumping music, people had started to split into smaller groups, with the main focus being on consuming shots of spirits and bothering the women who were occupying the dance floor. What Jack liked least of all was that the majority of the people there seemed to be the new Freshers for the University of Kent. The fact that the local university was already underway was even more of an indication to him that it was high time he moved on, not just from this bar but his home town altogether.

Jack slipped away unnoticed. Any more alcohol would be a bad idea, especially when he had a long car journey in the morning.

But although he managed to leave the venue without any of his so-called friends succeeding in preventing him, he didn't go straight home. Without the fear of having to consume any more drinks, Jack could enjoy his current level of intoxication. As desperate as he was to make the leap to the next phase in his life, there was a certain apprehension about moving to another part of the country. For many of his friends, alcohol seemed to increase their bravado, causing them to say and do things they would ordinarily be too afraid to. For Jack it was allowing the doubt he had kept buried within to surface. Trying to convince himself it was mere melancholy, he went to say goodbye to the places that held the greatest memories. As he stood outside the café, he felt regret, not for the fact he was sacked and hadn't managed to raise the sort of money he had hoped would supplement his student loans, but that he had never gone on that date with Emily, the waitress. He knew that starting university would open up a wealth of opportunity, but the summer may have panned out very differently if they had started dating.

Jack passed through the archway of the West Gate and headed for the hill that would lead him up to his old school. It was a walk that he typically resented for its steep incline, but he was enjoying the fresh air and felt that, even if his time there hadn't ended with the glittering A Levels his promise had shown, it was still worth commemorating this huge influence in his life.

However, passing the garage where Brandt had deposited his knife only served to remind Jack of the part of Canterbury his current destination was trying to avoid. It didn't matter that he had spent seven years at St. Edmund's, the spot that held the greatest influence on him was a small side road, just off from the high street; somewhere that Jack must have passed countless times over the years, but only recently had become the most significant place in his entire life.

In that instant, Jack knew the root of the apprehension he was feeling. It was one thing to imagine carrying on Brandt's work but, as he found out when he went to Whitstable on the day he had completed his last exam, quite another to be able to live up to that ideal. Although his underperformance in his A Levels had necessitated him finding an alternative institution, he knew that living in Nottingham and finding he didn't have either the courage or the resolve to carry out the tasks he had planned would be torture. At least if he were at Warwick, if he found himself lacking the necessary fortitude, he wouldn't have to be reminded on a daily basis of his unworthiness.

Having barely managed a few paces past the garage, Jack turned around. He knew what he needed to do if he was going to be able to set off tomorrow with any degree of confidence. What's more, he now viewed it as entirely essential if he were to be able to settle there without being immediately drawn to testing whether he was capable.

Having made the decision, the main thing troubling Jack was that he didn't possess a knife and, without going home first, which would add a multitude of other complications, he couldn't see how he was realistically going to be able to get hold of one. His concern was such that he considered abandoning the whole endeavour, hoping that he would wake up tomorrow and feel differently; being able to chalk this up to the effects of the alcohol and the typical trepidation of leaving the place he grew up in.

But a single thought stopped him from turning tail and slinking back home.

Brandt.

Jack considered the challenges he must have faced, not least when he had needed to flee the country following his attack on DCI Johnson. There must have been many occasions when conditions were not at their optimum, and yet he had always found ways to overcome them. Moreover, to use not having a knife as an excuse to chicken out wasn't acceptable. It may have been Brandt's preferred weapon, but neither of his killings in Spain had involved a blade. He had used his hands to strangle his victims and there was an argument to suggest that this had shown an evolution in his methods where he felt comfortable to use a more intimate approach. It would be a bold step for Jack, given his relative inexperience, but if the whole purpose of this was to demonstrate his capability, then its success would be all the more meaningful.

Realising he could spend the whole night stood there debating the best thing to do, he set off back the way he had come. Jack had considered many times the route Brandt would have taken from where he killed the girl. It would have been as direct as possible, whilst avoiding the CCTV cameras positioned in the city centre. When his identity was revealed, and it transpired he lived nowhere near Canterbury, Jack assumed that he didn't have local knowledge and so settled on a path he felt most logical under those circumstances. Jack had retraced the assumed route, the sense of being out of his depth which had marred the experience in Whitstable lessening with each step. There were many ways in which his actions could lead to him being caught, but using the same location as Brandt was much more than merely honouring what he had done. The knowledge that he had escaped detection for his actions there, removed some of the variables that had been such a concern with Jack's first killing. Furthermore, if tonight were to prove a success, this could be a blueprint for Nottingham, where Jack could gradually feel his way towards filling Brandt's shoes by using the relative safety of replicating his initial murders.

Walking down the residential road, with only the odd noise drifting over from the high street and the occasional babble from a television escaping through an open window, now more than ever Jack understood why Brandt had chosen this location. It struck the perfect balance between being somewhere secluded and a place where there were likely to be passers-by. However, whilst the darkness and time of night aided the former, Brandt might have had a number of people to choose from, whereas Jack had none. It had not occurred to him once on the journey there that he may arrive to find himself presented with no potential targets. He cursed himself for drinking quite so much that he had dulled his senses, but as much as this offered an unwelcome challenge, he'd come too far to abandon his plan now. This was something that simply had to be done.

Jack slowed his pace to enable him time to consider his options, of which he believed there to be two. He could either pick a looping route that would continue to avoid CCTV and see him pass here every five minutes or so, or he could try and find a place to hide out until a suitable victim came by. With the bars in Canterbury being as busy as they were, it was just a matter of time until someone came home this way, but he didn't know how many loops he would need to make until that happened. It would only require one resident to notice him passing for a second occasion for them to potentially remember enough of his description for the police to be able to track him down. Therefore, it was better for him to wait somewhere. Ironically the best place would be somewhere that, were he to be spotted, would arouse the most suspicion. Waiting in the street wouldn't cause one of the neighbours to contact the authorities until after he had committed his crime, but lurking in a car port or one of the few garages would reduce the chance of him being seen and, crucially, if he was, his dubious whereabouts would lead to him being challenged before he settled on a target.

Glancing around to make sure no one had installed their own cameras since Brandt's visit, he found a covered spot behind some wheelie bins and sat on the tarmac to wait. It didn't take long before he heard footsteps and he resisted the urge to emerge from his hiding position to see who they belonged to. He became convinced that the sound was from a single pair of shoes, but an accompanying voice caused him to hesitate. Between the gap in the bins he saw the man walk past, his mobile telephone pressed to his ear, a woman audible on the other end of the line. Jack knew that he still had time to come out and strike whilst the man was distracted, but he was reluctant. Jack was undoubtedly strong but what if the man was able to wriggle free or, worse still, beat him off and leave him unable to escape before the police got there? He would only be charged for an attempted robbery but there was a chance his fingerprints or DNA had been left on his victim in Whitstable.

Settling back down, he reasoned it was far safer to wait for a woman and he liked the fact that, considering the absence of a knife, it would at least provide some similarity with what Brandt had achieved.

Jack spent the next hour huddled behind the bins, becoming increasingly cold; during which people passed on four occasions. Twice he was encouraged by the sound of a woman's voice; both times their hoydenish laughter being carried to him on the still night air. But in each instance, it became clear they were not alone, and he was forced to wait for the next opportunity.

He heard the distinctive sound of high heels clipping along the pavement. They were approaching slowly, but their irregular beat caused Jack to think they might belong to more than one pair of feet. The sound that began to accompany them, a murmur at first, seemed confirmation. As Jack contracted himself to become as small as possible, a scraping sound followed by a thud and a giggle caused him to re-evaluate what he had heard. Daring himself to risk a look, he stood up and peered around the corner.

A lone woman was struggling to regain her feet following a fall. If what Jack had overheard before wasn't enough to suggest she was inebriated, the short dress that was currently riding up around her midriff and displaying a black lace G-string underneath, established she was returning from a night on the town. He had to act now, before anyone else came along; this representing the best opportunity he was likely to receive that night.

'Hey… you!' she hollered drunkenly.

Jack could feel a prickle of fear sweep across his skin, causing his flesh to come out in goose bumps. He wasn't so much concerned that she had spotted him, but more that someone in one of the houses may have heard her and was about to switch on a light. A nervous glance around as he approached her seemed to suggest otherwise. Even if the residents had heard the fall that preceded her calling to him, they were probably used to such antics late at night and had learned to tune them out.

'Can I help you up?' he whispered, hoping that his apparent desire to be of assistance would prevent the woman from recoiling at his advance. Bathed under the orange glow of the sodium street light, he could see that under the smeared make up and, despite the unfortunate crust of vomit to the right of her mouth, she was attractive. A little old perhaps for Jack but, with her long brown hair and curvaceous figure, appealing nonetheless.

As she looked up at him with dark eyes, glassy and struggling to focus, he reached out as though to help her up, diverting his hands to her throat at the very last moment. His application of pressure was not met with the immediate resistance he had anticipated, and it took a few seconds for her brain to register what was happening. The resultant flailing of arms and kicking out of legs appeared alarmingly loud to Jack, but there was no turning back, especially as her movements did not threaten to dislodge him.

The whole process was much quicker than he expected, but with the woman now hanging limp from his grip and her tongue lolling lifelessly from her mouth, he still clung on just to make certain. He wasn't sure whether it felt quite as dramatic as seeing the man's blood fly from his chest on the beach, but he knew then that his thirst for death had merely remained dormant for a while, and even after tonight would never entirely go away.

Noise in the distance caused him to finally release the woman and she slumped awkwardly back onto the pavement where he had found her. He allowed himself a final scan of the surrounding houses to ensure that no one had witnessed his actions before slipping quietly away in the direction he had come.

Chapter Eleven

'Well, obviously it's not Brandt but I really don't like where it is,' DCI Marlowe said thoughtfully.

'Do you think it might be a copycat?' DC Stepford asked, unable to hide the enthusiasm in his voice.

Marlowe got up and walked slowly to her office door, slamming it shut. She waited until the silence became so uncomfortable that Stepford turned to face her. 'I don't want to hear any of that shit, either from you or the rest of the guys. It's bad enough what the press are going to make of this without you feeding them stuff that's going to put them into a frenzy.'

'But, ma'am,' he pleaded, still reeling from the uncharacteristic rebuke. 'You've got to admit, it's all a bit odd.'

'Yes, as I said the location is disturbing and, before you ask, I am going to phone Nottingham so they are aware but, even if there weren't any clear distinctions between the crimes, the last thing we need is to blow this out of all proportion.'

'Look,' she said, unable to avoid the sigh that accompanied it. 'You're doing a good job out there and I don't want you to stop looking for inferences and patterns.

What I'm saying is that we cannot allow anything to cloud our objectivity. Am I making sense?'

'Yes, ma'am,' he nodded.

'Whilst I don't want us to rule anything out at this stage, it would be wrong to jump to any conclusions just yet.'

'Agreed. I suppose it might be her boyfriend unhappy about her flirting with other guys when they were out,' Stepford offered.

'Exactly,' Marlowe replied with false enthusiasm. Not only did she not believe in coincidences, but she also didn't like the unintended implication that this poor woman somehow did something to provoke it. It was one thing for the smug lawyers to be always searching for mitigating circumstances when they had a suspect bang to rights, but she didn't like her own team allowing their misogynistic attitudes to guide their lines of enquiry. Just because a woman chose to go out in a short skirt doesn't mean there is any sense of promiscuity. However, she did have to admit that most attacks against women were committed by someone they knew.

DC Stepford remained motionless with an expectant look on his face.

'So if you could look into that…'

'Oh yeah, of course, ma'am,' he said, having got the hint and now retreating back to his own desk.

With her door shut again, Marlowe lifted the receiver but then put it back down. She needed to work out what she was going to say first. The last thing she wanted to do was cause any alarm, especially when they still knew so little about what had happened, but she knew from experience that it didn't pay to delay the inevitable.

'This is DCI Marlowe from the Canterbury Constabulary, can you put me through to DCI Johnson, please?'

'I'm sorry, ma'am, DCI Johnson is currently… currently on leave at the moment. Can I put you through to the person who is leading her cases at the moment?'

This revelation came as something of a shock. Naturally Marlowe had heard of what had happened to Johnson, but she had met her and saw in her the same steely determination that had driven her own career. And from the uncertain response she had received, it didn't sound as though she were merely taking an overdue holiday.

'Ma'am, are you still there?'

'Yes, yes, just put me through to whoever then, please.'

'Yes, hello?' came the impatient response after a short time on hold.

'Hi, this is DCI Marlowe from Canterbury. To whom am I speaking?' She was sure her introduction would elicit a warmer tone now.

'DI Fisher, what is it you want?'

Covering for Johnson or not, she out ranked this guy and was irked by his continued brusqueness. She had two choices. There was the strong temptation to immediately slap him down, but she didn't know who this DI Fisher was. Therefore, she would go with the other, more subtle and pernicious option which was to feed his impatience by being slow to come to the point. That way he would have to backtrack of his own volition when she finally dangled something of interest in front of him.

'You may recall we had reason to combine our efforts a few months ago following an incident here.'

'I'm well aware of that.'

'Okay, sure, well, clearly things have changed now that the perpetrator is no longer at large.'

'Yes. Clearly.'

'However, it would be remiss of me not to inform you of something that happened here overnight that, whilst unrelated, may be of interest.'

The awkward silence that followed suggested this DI Fisher was going to prove a harder nut to crack.

'Something that bears similar hallmarks.'

'Look, just spit it out. We're all very busy here even if you lot aren't.'

That was it, enough messing about. 'Now you listen to me, Detective,' she left a deliberate pause to emphasise that, unlike her own title, there was not going to be anything to prefix the word that was coming next. '...Inspector. I have no doubt you're busy, especially as you try and fill the shoes of someone far more capable than you are.' She stopped for a moment to see whether he would choose to argue back and allowed herself a brief smile when it was clear that he was too stunned by her sudden change of tone to do so. 'I can assure you we're very busy here as we deal with the aftermath of a brutal murder. Now I am ringing you purely out of courtesy,' Marlowe took delight in carefully sounding out each syllable. 'The murder here last night is at the same location as Brandt's. There is nothing at this stage to suggest this is more than an unfortunate coincidence, but I wanted to share this with you nonetheless. I'll have my DI send over the relevant details.'

With a smile at that last insult she put the phone down. Now that the unpleasant phone call was out of the way, it was time to get the latest information from her team before she went and briefed the DSI.

Chapter Twelve

Killing that woman the night before he left for Nottingham did serve to allow Jack to concentrate on settling into his new surroundings and courses. The first week was a blur where, unlike that evening, he was unable to avoid being dragged into consuming far more alcohol than he felt comfortable with. But Jack was young and able to sleep off his hangovers and start drinking again afresh, meeting lots of people along the way and forming the beginnings of some friendships.

It wasn't as though things completely settled down when his lectures and seminars began, so he spent far less time reading the texts he had been assigned than was probably wise, especially since he had little background in the sorts of topics he was studying. But in his first week he had received a portion of advice from a final year student that he was seeking to hold on to. His first year wouldn't count in terms of his overall degree classification and he was told it was about being able to strike a balance between doing enough to pass the year and getting enough partying out of the way that when it was time to knuckle down he wouldn't feel as though he'd missed out.

On this particular Sunday morning he had awoken early, despite not returning to his room until the early hours. In truth, it had been a bit of a tame night with many of his fellow Freshers using the weekend to either go home or visit old friends. Jack had no reason to leave Nottingham and he had no plans for the day, other than to make a start on a rather lengthy tome on the history of the Cold War. Despite his inability to sleep in, he knew that he wouldn't be able to concentrate, much less be bothered to make notes, unless he did something to liven himself up.

He had only been to the centre of Nottingham a couple of times since his arrival, and it had been in a taxi late at night in order to frequent one of its various clubs. Jack wasn't into dance music but the sheer size and popularity of Gatecrasher had impressed him. That evening he had not only snogged a fellow student but, towards the end of the night, when things had really started to get messy, he had tried to chat up a woman who was clearly a few years older than him. In his drunken state, he had been attracted to her bottle blonde hair, fake tan and ample cleavage but when he had grabbed her bum whilst dancing, she had told him that she was a police officer and what he had done constituted assault. Jack assumed she had been joking but took that as his cue to beat a steady retreat and reunite with his university acquaintances.

However, rather than dwell on that occasion as he walked towards town, Jack found himself thinking about his trip to Nottingham in the summer. The weather may have been considerably different, with him now having to wear a jacket to combat the dull and overcast effects of a typical October morning, but walking along unfamiliar streets conjured the same images. It had not been his intention when he set out, but he found himself calling up the web browser on his phone so he could check on the whereabouts of the one destination he had failed to take in that day. As he suspected, it would need only a very slight detour to find the alleyway that Brandt had used for his first murder.

Almost instantly Jack could feel his pace quicken and all thoughts of hangovers and boring reference books were cast from his mind. Throughout the remainder of the journey he considered how exciting it would be to just arrive, wait for the next person to come along and kill them there and then. But the nearest Jack had to a bladed weapon was a butter knife as part of the, as yet untouched, small cutlery set that his mother had bought him along with some basic pans and other utensils. Even if he had thought to bring it with him, he wouldn't feel confident trying to impale someone with such a blunt implement.

If he were to do anything that morning, it would have to be with his bare hands and, despite the temptation to give in to the urge, he could see two clear reasons why it was a risk not worth taking. His efforts in Canterbury could not be seen as conclusive in terms of him having the necessary strength to overpower his victim, because the woman he'd killed couldn't even stand, let alone effectively defend herself. The other matter was that he didn't know what evidence he had left on her body. He wasn't sure whether one could really leave fingerprints on another person's skin, but he did remember watching the film Red Dragon a few years ago where the FBI agent found the killer's fingerprints on one of the victim's eyelids. It may have only been fiction, but it was enough to warn Jack that the impulsivity driving his murders so far was liable to see him caught if he didn't curtail it. He might have been confident that there was no record of his DNA or fingerprints on a database somewhere but offering a link between the murders in different cities was best left to professionals like Brandt.

Nevertheless, as he wandered down the alleyway, stopping at where the body was found, thanks to it being marked by more dead flowers, Jack did not feel any regret at being able to do no more than observe. The absence of any other walkers in the entire time he spent there indicated that it was too early to expect to find a suitable victim, but also allowed him more time to drink in the scene. He found a mark on the ground he hoped was the remnants of the blood stain. It may have been sufficiently faint that he was unable to get anything on his fingers despite using his nails to scrape the ground. But that didn't stop him putting them to his lips in the hope that he may be able to detect the slightest coppery tang.

He wondered what sort of a thrill Brandt had got from seeing the young mother lying there. Jack felt better able to empathise now that he had killed a second time. Had Brandt waited, as Jack had in Canterbury, to make sure the woman was dead before continuing on his way or had he, as he must have done outside the station, completed it all in one fluid motion, hoping this time he had done enough? More than anything, Jack wanted to get to the stage where he could perform his tasks in the same cool and calculated way he imagined his hero had done.

Leaving the scene, Jack didn't bother to continue into town as per his original plan. Visiting there had given him lots to think about and being in a deserted shopping centre a good couple of hours before anything was due to open would just be a waste of his valuable time. There was much for him to decide. Now that he was in Nottingham, it was important he plan carefully, and first he needed to decide on an appropriate course of action.

In effect Jack considered himself at a fork in the road. Going back was not an option and both routes forward would allow him different ways in which to honour Brandt. One of them see him forge his own path where he would, as with his killing in Whitstable, merely take inspiration from Brandt. The other would see him pay a far closer homage and seek to recreate the very murders that Jack felt had defined him.

As Jack closed his bedroom door, grateful that it was still too early for those students who had remained on campus over the weekend to be up, he stripped off his clothes so that he could climb into his bed and plan in comfort; he reached a decision. He intended spending at least the next three years in Nottingham and, as much as he was supposed to be a student of Politics and International Relations, he also considered himself a pupil of the greatest serial killer in British history. Maybe not the most prolific, but the greatest nonetheless. He would allow himself to continue to learn and use the methods and destinations carefully selected by Brandt to guide him and keep him safe, as he had done in Canterbury, until he was ready to branch out on his own like the true disciple he aimed to be.

Chapter Thirteen

'Morning, boss, is everything okay?' Brandt winced at his perfect English but judging by Mr Jones' unchanged expression, he hadn't detected anything remiss. It was always the same following a day off; with no one to talk to, Brandt struggled to get back into the character of Gregori straight away.

'Yes, everything's fine,' Mr Jones replied, but in a manner that was far from convincing. Brandt knew when people were lying, and he knew when they were hiding something, but what he also had learned early on in his career in the police was that the best way of getting people to confess wasn't always to challenge them. It would often lead to them pulling the shutters down and, partly out of a sense of pride, make them even less likely to admit the thing they had been trying to conceal.

'Sure thing, boss,' Brandt said cheerily, walking out from the counter to check that everything was arranged correctly for when they opened.

'No, hold on a second Gregori, there is something I have been meaning to speak to you about.' If that wasn't enough to concern Brandt, his next statement was. 'Let me grab us a coffee and a slice of cake and we can have a nice chat. You take it black, don't you?'

'Er, yes,' Brandt responded, trying to think what on earth he was soon to be told. Mr Jones had been kind enough to give him a job picking fruit and then to move him into the tearoom permanently, but he never made a show of being generous. Brandt suspected it was not so much out of meanness and more through fear of being accused of favouritism and, in all the weeks he had worked there, he had never once seen him offer anyone a free anything.

The couple of minutes it took for Mr Jones to fiddle with the unfamiliar controls of the barista machine felt like an eternity to Brandt and, by the time they eventually sat down, he didn't have much of an appetite for the Victoria sponge placed before him.

As it transpired, Mr Jones wasn't one for bottling things up very long because he decided the best course of action was now to simply come out with it.

'I had been hoping to last until after Halloween and maybe then the interest before Christmas might be enough to justify keeping you on longer,' he said, 'but I'm afraid the tail off since summer has been sharper than I expected.'

'I understand,' said Brandt. Much as he had tried to convince himself otherwise, he had found things particularly quiet over the last couple of weeks.

The look of relief that spread over Mr Jones' face was nauseating and, although Brandt knew part of it was a case of sour grapes, he saw him as nothing but cowardly in that moment.

'Really?' he responded. 'Oh, that's very good of you Gregori and I have always said that you are a decent man. Very decent in fact. Believe me it's not about capability and certainly not about popularity amongst the customers but, you see, it's only right and proper for it to be a case of first in, last out. Do you understand what I mean?'

'I understand,' Brandt answered, unable to keep the anger out of his voice entirely.

'Of course, I'll let you work out the rest of the week to give you a little bit of time to try and find a new job somewhere.'

Brandt just wanted him to shut up now rather than offer him any more of his bullshit. They both knew no one in North Wales would be looking to hire staff at this time of year, especially someone who claimed to have only recently arrived in the country. The old Brandt, the one who wasn't pretending to be the thoughtful and subservient Gregori, would have enjoyed taking his cake fork and jamming it in Mr Jones' eyeball. That would surely give him a different take on what was right and proper. But, if for no other reason, Brandt couldn't afford the prospect of missing out on another week's worth of wages. The caravan owner may well have agreed to a longer term let in exchange for a massively reduced rental charge, but every penny would count if he were somehow going to survive the winter. Now more than ever, Brandt wished he had used the opportunity presented by being around at Susan's house to relieve her of all the jewellery she had insisted he should buy her over the years. He could have made quite a tidy sum pawning it off, enough to tell Mr Jones where to stick his entirely ungenerous offer of working the remainder of the week.

'Look, I totally understand if you would rather just go now if it would be too painful for you to carry on.'

Too awkward for you more like, you cowardly little shit. What's more I bet you'd only be too glad not to have to stump up the pittance of a wage you pay me.

'No, I want to stay,' Brandt responded, his voice almost a whisper. 'But if you don't mind, I think I have lost my appetite.' Fuck trying to put on a stupid Georgian accent, he thought, pushing his plate away and standing up.

Chapter Fourteen

The room was familiar but somehow different. Were it not for the fact that he was lying on the floor, it might have taken a bit longer to realise that the furniture looked the same but the other items around them were not his own.

Jack sat up with a start; suddenly aware of his nakedness. More shocking was that the bed he had somehow missed, the same narrow single as the one in his own room, was currently occupied. The covers were pulled around her and he didn't need to observe the jumble of clothes at the bottom of the bed, a mixture of his and hers, to remember that he had sex for the second time in his life the night before.

With his body stiff from his uncomfortable sleeping position, he got up to stretch, but as quietly as possible so as to not risk waking her. Delicately easing himself into one of the room's two chairs, the supposed lounge chair to match the stiff-backed wooden item that went with the small desk, he felt very satisfied with his work. That he had ended up having a far better physical experience with this girl than the one at Henry's house nearly 18 months previously, had been a fortunate outcome of the evening.

Mandy was on his course and he had got talking to her one day as they waited for their seminar room to be unlocked. Her contributions the previous week had suggested that she was not only well read, but also had a keen interest in the subject. Jack had calculated she was someone worth knowing because she may be able to help him compensate for his lack of preparation and general apathy towards politics. She was also reasonably attractive, with her short blonde hair a match for her oval face and with eyes like chips of emerald ice.

After his decision to ease into Brandt's shoes slowly, Jack wanted to recreate the attacks as faithfully as possible. In order to do that, he needed a blade and not just the blunt butter knife his mother had bought him. To be truly authentic, it had to be a steak knife and Jack assumed that Brandt's decision to use one of his as the weapon of choice was because of its ubiquity. It would have given the police little to go on and, for all Jack knew, Brandt had a set of them lying around at home.

But Jack's parents hadn't. His mother may have owned every kitchen contraption and utensil under the sun but, for some reason, that hadn't extended to steak knives. Similarly, as an 18-year-old student, it wasn't something he would be expected to have and the university wouldn't stock them in their various cafeterias and canteens. He had settled on the idea to simply purchase some but had felt uncomfortable at the prospect of doing so. The sale of knives was restricted and, although he was old enough to buy them, he knew that his doing so would seem unusual for someone his age. If it wasn't bad enough that the people of Nottingham were well aware of the implement used in the murders that shocked their city, when another would suddenly happen a few days later there was a chance, however slim, that the shop assistant might remember him and provide the police with his description.

Playing the role of Brandt wasn't just about replicating his murders but also learning from the care and preparation they must have involved. Jack was a very different person; as were his circumstances. Appreciation of the disparities was key to ensuring that he didn't allow complacency to force him into a mistake. The knives were a case in point, where Brandt's ease of obtaining them didn't match his own. Jack had come to the conclusion that stealing one was a far better idea, and that was where Mandy became involved.

Mandy had willingly helped him fill in the blanks of his knowledge prior to their tutor arriving. The seminar had gone well, and Jack had made a number of contributions, not least so that he could build up some credit should he find himself back to barely keeping up with what was being discussed in subsequent sessions. Afterwards, he had made a point of catching Mandy before she disappeared, to thank her for the help. He had known that asking if he could show his gratitude with buying her dinner that evening was uncharacteristically forward, but he surmised that if she declined, as long as she wasn't entirely horrified with the idea, at least she might choose to help him out again in the future.

Jack need not have worried because Mandy accepted. She had laughed and called him old fashioned, but had claimed it a refreshing change to just being asked for a drink. His initial delight was suddenly met with fear that she might be a vegetarian. To Jack it had suddenly all added up. The short hair and the interest in politics that seemed to stem from a left-wing position meant that she was bound to be a vegetarian; most likely a vegan too. With a sense of dread, he had asked whether there was any type of food he should avoid when settling on their destination for that evening. Nervously waiting her consideration of the question, he had been unable to stifle his own laugh when she finally said that she was getting a bit bored of going to Nando's but, other than that, she was happy to give anything a go.

Delighted, Jack had gone back to his room to complete some research and book a table. He knew plenty of chain restaurants with steak on the menu and therefore likely to provide the appropriate cutlery. There were some issues though. Even if Jack could convince himself that the likelihood of not being provided with the correct knife for his selection from the menu was slim, he worried that its absence would be noticed when their table was being cleared. To minimise the chance of that happening was to go somewhere that saw the majority of the customers ordering steak, perhaps even Mandy herself. That way there would be lots of the knives knocking about and taking one away with him would be easy.

The rational part of Jack's brain knew that he was overthinking what was, in reality, quite a small thing but, rather than it trouble him, he drew comfort from the depth of his preparation. Brandt had benefitted from the luxury of being retired when planning his murders; presumably with nothing to distract him from ensuring every last detail was considered. That Jack was going to such lengths to secure a murder weapon in the safest way possible made him feel worthy of following in his hero's footsteps.

His preparation had been rewarded by a thoroughly enjoyable, if expensive evening. Rather than be put off by the upmarket steakhouse Jack had chosen, Mandy had been both impressed and excited. Having already moved onto her second Pornstar Martini by the time they ordered food, she'd matched his choice of a ribeye.

The longer they spent talking in the restaurant, the more he had found his date intriguing. Mandy was driven and wanted a political career so she could tackle the inequalities she saw in society. Whilst on the face of it her feelings were in stark contrast to his own privileged background, Jack could see a certain similarity between the two of them, even if the reason behind it wasn't something he could share. He too had found his purpose in life and he drew inspiration from her seemingly unwavering commitment to hers.

Their different upbringings and outlook on life didn't stifle the chemistry between them. They spent the evening discussing common interests. It turned out they liked many of the same movies and Jack's eclectic taste in music overlapped with some of hers.

In fact, the evening was progressing so well that Jack almost forgot about the main purpose for them being there. If it hadn't been for Mandy excusing herself to use the toilet after they had finished eating, Jack might have missed his chance altogether. Watching her confidently ascend the steps to the restaurant's upper floor, he had concluded that he did find her physically attractive, and decided to spend the remainder of her absence planning how he could act on this knowledge. It was only when he was distractedly playing with his napkin that he noticed the steak knife sat innocently next to his fork.

The next few minutes had been extremely uncomfortable for Jack. Maintaining interest in Mandy's conversation upon her return had been a challenge when, all the while, he had expected her to suddenly notice and comment on the sole item of cutlery left on his plate. However, that was nothing compared to how he felt when the waiter finally came to clear their table. It may have only taken a few seconds, but it was agonising nonetheless. When he didn't immediately leave and opened his mouth to talk, Jack was ready to take the knife off his knee and theatrically look under the table for where he had supposedly dropped it.

'Come again?' Jack had responded, not sure of what he had been asked.

'I said can I bring you the dessert menu?'

The question was so unexpected as to leave Jack flummoxed.

'I'm not sure I could manage another thing,' Mandy confessed.

'Perhaps another drink?' The waiter offered, but whilst Jack welcomed the calming influence additional alcohol would provide, more than anything he now wanted to get out of the restaurant altogether.

'Just the bill, please.' Jack's gratitude for Mandy voicing his own desire, was quickly met with concern why she was similarly keen to leave. He may have only asked her out so he had a reason for being there, but he had started to like her and didn't want her to have found his behaviour odd.

With the waiter now gone, Jack summoned up the courage to ask. 'Is everything okay?'

'Yeah, look you've spent enough on me this evening. Let's go somewhere else and I can buy you a drink instead.'

* * *

Sat naked in her bedroom chair, Jack remembered the relief he had felt. He had gone to the pub willingly, steering Mandy away from the sort of bar where the doormen were likely to search him and find the steak knife deposited in the lining of his coat. That it had meant going somewhere quiet had proven a bonus because, with little else to entertain them, Mandy had soon suggested heading for home.

Much as he enjoyed his evening out with her and what had followed, Jack now couldn't wait to leave. He thought about writing her a note but didn't want to be accused of being old fashioned again. Besides, hunting around for a piece of paper might only serve to wake her and he was anxious to get going.

Chapter Fifteen

Becky liked this route to work. It might not have been the most direct, but it allowed her to have some head-space. When you spent all day speaking to members of the public it was nice to see as few of them as possible either side of office hours. After what had happened, Becky had taken her mother's advice and stuck to the main roads but now he was dead – that sick pervert preying on women in Nottingham – she had started using the river path once more. She hadn't told her mother because she knew what she would say and, besides, she wouldn't use it once the nights had drawn in and her journey home was in the dark.

What Becky liked most about her walk to the office, where she worked as a receptionist for a large company of recruitment consultants, was how it allowed her to spend time looking at the river. Water had always fascinated her. In a world where she knew she was just a cog in a very small wheel, it was a reminder of the power of nature. Whatever the weather, this particular stretch flowed with immense power and it gave her a strange sort of comfort to know that, if she were to fall in, she would be swept away to places unknown.

Becky had wondered from time to time whether she was unusual. It was a fear she had shared with her mother whilst still at school but had been told in reply that it was normal for teenage girls to feel a little lost. Becky guessed she had now found her place in life. Having received few qualifications, she knew she was lucky to have obtained such a steady job and was currently enjoying the stability of a long-term boyfriend. Like much of her life, it wasn't quite how she had imagined it as a child. It certainly wasn't love at first sight, nor had Kyle swept her off her feet. Instead they had met in a chatroom discussing video games. She had been used to, had courted even, the attention one of the few girls in there had received. Hidden behind her keyboard she had developed a confidence that could never be replicated in the real world. In amongst the usual requests for her photo, along with boys sending inappropriate images of themselves, Kyle had stood out as someone more interested in what she had to say about the topics for discussion than the fact she had breasts. What's more, once they had been chatting for a few weeks, it was Becky who had finally suggested they meet up. She took his hesitation as a sign of his continued respect for her but when he finally agreed to send her a photograph, so she would be better able to recognise him, she understood why. He looked like a typical computer nerd. From her experience, these people came in two flavours, they were either terribly skinny with a bad complexion to match their greasy hair or, as was in Kyle's case, self-consciously overweight.

But Becky didn't mind. She liked that it kind of made him look strong and, in a world where she experienced a number of anxieties, that was important to her, along with the fact that he was generous and thoughtful. Becky could tell from the moment they met up that he considered her way out of his league. She found it flattering but believed it to be symptomatic of his own self-image problems, until one day he declared that the thing he loved about her most was the way she had no clue how truly stunning she was.

Yes, life was much better for Becky since she had found Kyle and, although he lived a few miles away in Chesterfield, she hoped he would soon suggest they find a place together. She was loath to give up her job because the company she worked for had always been kind to her, but she now had enough experience to hope that she could pick up something similar anywhere. Not only did Becky know that she could bring up the idea of them renting their own place, but she also knew from the way Kyle doted on her that there was little chance of him turning her down. However, she was a traditionalist and a romantic at heart. Life might not have turned out to be quite as magical as she had hoped, but she was prepared to wait for Kyle to build up enough courage to ask her himself.

Becky smiled as she took out her phone. Just because she wanted him to take the lead in this, it didn't mean she couldn't start sowing the seeds that would compel him to search for some privacy. His parents were quite liberal and seemed to have no issue with them sharing the same room when she stayed over, but her mother was more conservative with her values. When Kyle came to Nottingham, they would have to make do with a kiss and a cuddle in his car before returning to her place, whereupon they would head to their separate bedrooms. Becky had never been confident with her appearance and much less herself as a sexual being but trying to assist Kyle with his own body-image problems had not only seen her address that, but also become far more daring than she would have ever previously thought possible.

With the River Trent glinting in the weak autumn sunshine, she started typing her opening gambit. Now was always a good time to catch Kyle. He started his job as a web designer an hour before she did and rarely seemed busy first thing. Typically, she could expect his undivided attention at this time of day.

> *– Hi babe. Really looking forward to this weekend. Would you mind if you came over again? It's proving to be quite a hectic week and I'm not sure I fancy the coach ride. B xxx*

Becky wasn't used to being manipulative and was sure this would somehow backfire. Kyle would either look to cancel altogether or suggest she use her meagre savings, which unbeknownst to him were there purely to help with the deposit on a flat, to buy a car.

> *– Morning gorgeous! I don't care as long as we're together although we do get more of a chance to be alone at my place… Xxx*

She could feel her heart flutter. This was typical Kyle. She knew exactly what he meant about being alone.

> *– That's true ☺ but I do feel a little self-conscious with your parents sleeping close-by xxx*

Becky's pace slowed as she waited for the reply. The time between texts was much longer than before and caused her to consider whether she had said something wrong. She hoped he hadn't taken her claim that she couldn't completely relax as a sign that she didn't enjoy the sex. Not only would that not be true, but she would hate the potential impact on Kyle. He was really starting to come out of his shell and when she had last been round he had suggested they try a couple of new positions.

Becky was almost too scared to read the message, its arrival heralded by a sharp ping.

> *– I completely understand. Why don't we go away for the weekend – my treat? I could come and pick you up and we could head to the Peak District or somewhere? Xxx*

She knew she needed to respond straight away to save him the same agony she had experienced but found herself too excited to type properly. Her fingers were hitting the wrong keys and the phone was autocorrecting her mistyped words into nonsense. The nervous giggle this provoked only served to make her hands shake more and prompt a fresh round of laughter at the ridiculousness of her situation.

'Something funny?'

The sudden and unexpected voice caused Becky to spin round with shock, her phone slipping from her grasp and dropping to the pavement.

'Oh, I didn't mean to startle you,' the young man replied, bending down to pick it up. 'Thank goodness the screen didn't crack. Of course, if it had, I would have got it replaced for you, seeing as it was my fault you dropped it.'

'Er, thanks,' replied Becky taking back her phone, unsure what she should say in the circumstances. The man in front of her, little more than a boy, sounded sincere, but there was a strange look in his eyes that suggested he found the whole thing entertaining despite his concerned words. She turned to leave. Her message to Kyle would just have to wait until she got to the office.

'You know it's sad really, isn't it?'

Becky could feel herself involuntarily turning back to see what the man was referring to. But he was no longer looking at her. Instead he was gazing at the withered bunches of flowers tied to a tree. Her skin began to prickle as she realised the exact spot along the river where she was. She wanted to turn and run but that would be crazy behaviour. She didn't know who this lad was, but she prided herself on at least appearing normal.

'How quickly people seem to forget what happened here,' he continued. 'At first, I thought you had stopped to pay your respects but then I heard…'

The unfinished sentence was left hanging in the air. 'I'm sorry, I didn't mean to offend you,' she said. He wasn't acting affronted but it seemed the right thing to say in the circumstances. When he didn't respond but remained stood there with his hands in his pockets, she decided to add more, by way of an explanation. 'It's just my boyfriend had texted me and I was trying to respond but my phone…'

'I have a girlfriend,' he interrupted, turning back to face her; his tone matter-of-fact. Becky was starting to wonder whether this man had some sort of disability. 'Well, I think she is. I didn't wake her to ask her because I needed to get down here as quickly as possible.'

Now it all suddenly made sense to Becky. He didn't have learning difficulties or something similar. It also explained why he commented on the dead flowers and had spoken to her when he had found her laughing. 'I'm so sorry. You knew her.' More a statement than a question.

The man smiled, to Becky it didn't look sad but cruel instead. She supposed it must feel cruel to see the place where someone you were close to died, the tributes now forgotten and people passing like normal. 'No, I didn't know her.' The pause that followed was just enough for Becky to consider that this conversation was getting stranger by the second. 'But I did know the man who killed her.'

'What?' So shocked was Becky but this, surely false, claim that she neither noticed that the lad had taken his hands out of his pockets nor that one of them was not empty.

'And you're about to meet him,' Jack cried, plunging the blade into her stomach.

Chapter Sixteen

'I'm sorry, Mr Jones, I just… well, I can't…'

'I understand, Gregori, really I do. I'll still pay you until the end of the week and, of course, am happy to provide you with a glowing reference for your next job. You take care now.'

The phone line went dead. Even if it wasn't for the relief he could detect in Mr Jones' voice, the speed at which he hung up demonstrated he wasn't exactly disappointed that Brandt didn't feel up to working his notice.

Yesterday was hard. The feelings of anger that Brandt had experienced when hearing the news he was to be let go hadn't, as he had feared, lingered. At least rage had a certain power to it, whereas what followed was merely debilitating. Sadness had never been an overriding emotion in Brandt's life but, as he tried to carry out his duties that day, he had felt close to tears at a number of points. His new life wasn't much, and certainly on paper didn't look anywhere near as good as what went before, but he had built it from nothing and it was something he was proud of. It wasn't the work itself that he was going to miss, but the relationships he had built up. He liked the other staff there but the resentment that they were to be kept on whilst he was to be cast adrift prevented him from feeling too sorry that he wouldn't be seeing them again. It was the customers he would miss. He still held the tourists in contempt, not least now because their absence was the root cause of his departure, but he had grown fond of a number of the regulars. His relationship with them was small in the context of their overall lives, but it still felt real.

All Brandt had ever wanted to do was to serve the people. What he was doing in the tearoom in the quiet Welsh food market, was on a much smaller scale to what he had been trying to achieve when he had been in the police, but the difference was that here he had made a success of it. The people appreciated what he did for them. Of course, the expectation was there, given that was what he was paid to do, but the fact he went above and beyond the call of duty to make them feel welcome was keenly felt. None of the apathy he had experienced with society as a whole had set in.

Seeing them arrive the day before not only served as a reminder about how far he had come, but also was an indication of what he was soon to lose. The job had been purely about ensuring he had the finances to survive, but had become much more than that. Ironically if he had stayed fruit picking until the inevitable lay off there, he might not have realised that he would be unable to live in solitude. And that's why Brandt had broken his abstinence and spent some of his dwindling reserves of cash on whisky. It wasn't just that his circumstances had forced him to purchase the cheap stuff, the knowledge that it represented the enormous setback he had suffered had served to make every drop of it taste sour. But he had persevered in search of the temporary oblivion it offered.

Brandt had known the moment he handed over the money at the local shop that he wouldn't set foot in that tearoom again. In his later years in the police he had gone to work plenty of times suffering the effects of a night's drinking, but he knew a stonking headache and acerbic gut would erode any last resilience he felt.

He uttered a bitter laugh at the irony of him still wearing yesterday's uniform and headed for the bathroom. Brandt tended to use the campsite's communal washing facilities because he found the caravan's shower cubicle too small and the water temperature too erratic. But today he didn't want to run the risk of bumping into anyone and, having washed, he plonked himself in front of the daytime television he so detested and allowed himself to drift off into a troubled doze.

A knock at the door awoke Brandt some time later. He struggled to hang onto the wisps of his dream and the second, louder rap, roused him so he could only remember that it was his long recurring fantasy of plunging to his death. The interruption caused him more confusion than irritation because he hadn't received a visitor since agreeing to the long term let with the caravan's owner.

'Mrs Hardcastle?' The surprise in his voice masked the absence of any semblance of an Eastern European accent.

'Oh hello, Greggy, I'm so sorry to bother you. Do you mind if I come in?'

'Er, sure,' said Brandt, casting a quick, nervous glance around the contents of the interior. He usually kept the place neat and tidy but last night's escapades had served to create something of a mess.

He managed to clear some space for his guest to sit before she had fully entered.

'Is there something the matter, Mrs Hardcastle?' He may have no longer been employed but it was hard to deviate from the nature of the relationship he had built with one of his favourite customers.

'I'm so sorry,' she repeated, just about managing to sit down before bursting into tears.

All thoughts of his own pathetic situation evaporated from Brandt's mind and he knelt before her, clasping her hands with concern. 'What is wrong?'

A faint laugh interrupted her sobs. 'That's so typical of you, Greggy, I've come here because of you and all you're concerned about is how I'm feeling.'

'I don't understand,' Brandt confessed truthfully. 'Can I make you a cup of tea?'

Mrs Hardcastle laughed again but waited until she had regained full control of her composure before trying to speak once more. 'I knew something was wrong yesterday,' she said finally. 'Don't get me wrong, you were perfectly pleasant and everything, but I could tell something wasn't quite right. I wondered whether you were a bit under the weather so I came back in today to check if you were feeling better.'

'But it is Wednesday, Mrs Hardcastle.'

'Yes, I know, Greggy, but I was worried about you and so I told the ladies at bowls that I would just have to skip this week. Obviously, I didn't tell them why; they would have thought me foolish, but I just knew something wasn't right.'

Brandt didn't know how to respond. This changed nothing and, if anything, her loyalty only heightened his feelings that he was missing out on something pure.

'When you weren't there I asked Mr Jones if you had phoned in sick. He said you had but there was something about his manner that made me think he was hiding something. I wasn't going to say anything; I'm not one to pry but I suddenly thought, what if you were really sick? I mean, like really ill. I just couldn't drink my tea and so I confronted him. It took a lot of pushing but eventually he told me.'

Mrs Hardcastle had stopped and was staring at Brandt; he knew that she was waiting for him to say something. But what could he possibly tell her? That it was okay, and he would find himself another job? If she had any grasp of reality, she would know that wasn't true and why should he make it easy on Mr Jones anyway? At least that would be better than the truth; what was the point of shattering her illusion of him by admitting that he had wanted nothing more than to shove the cake fork into Mr Jones' eye? She might laugh nervously at first, like when someone tells a joke that's a little too close to the bone, but then see the seriousness in his eyes and her reaction could turn it into situation similar to Benidorm, where the only option he had was to shut her up.

'Er, how did you find me?' He knew it was a stupid question, but it was a relief to try and deflect things away from his feelings.

'I hope you don't mind but I was so shocked by the idea of Mr Jones sacking you. Of course, he claimed he hadn't and that your work there was only ever meant to be temporary. But I told him, I said if there's anyone who wants letting go it's that Gloria girl. It's not that I'm racist, in fact my nephew once went out with a half-caste, but she doesn't even know how to make a cup of tea properly. I even caught her putting the milk in first the other day.'

She paused, having lost her train of thought. Brandt had to stifle a smile because this was classic Mrs Hardcastle. She was always at pains to point out how liberal and open minded she was but always seemed to say something in her attempted justification that unwittingly contradicted the notion.

'Where was I? Oh yes! So, I said to Mr Jones I don't give a flying fig about last in, first out or whatever blather he was spouting. I told him that I have connections and if I wanted I could show him what off-season really meant.' Her voice was now raised with excitement to match her pomposity. 'And do you know what he said to me, Greggy? Do you know what he said?'

'Er, nothing?'

'Exactly!' she shouted. 'He just shrugged and went into the back room. I mean, how rude is that? I always knew that the act he put on was just to try and sell more stuff. In fact, I said to Mrs Hewlett just the other day, I said, behind that smile there is a shrewd man.' Mrs Hardcastle paused again in an attempt to let her brain once again catch up with her mouth. 'Oh yes! So, do you know what I did?'

'Followed him?'

'Er, no I didn't because the back room is clearly marked "Staff Only". But I jolly well waited for him until he finally emerged.' Brandt lifted his hand to his face in a gesture that he hoped would appear to suggest he was deep in thought, rather than trying to hide the smile at the juxtaposition between Mrs Hardcastle's supposed militarism and her keenness not to break the smallest of rules. 'I said to him, that's just not good enough. I said, if you're not willing to help this kind man who has been through God knows what in Russia or Poland or wherever, then give me his address and I will.' She stopped again. 'And, er… here I am.'

'Well, I really appreciate your concern but honestly…'

'If I didn't take any nonsense from Mr Jones, then I'm not going to take any nonsense from you either.'

'I'm sorry?' Brandt was genuinely taken aback by this latest outburst.

'Look, I know that your past, and don't worry I don't expect you to start telling me about it, must have been hard to leave you here.' She looked round the room, but Brandt could see it was more for effect than to be unkind.

'It's not normally quite like this.'

'Yes, yes, but what I'm trying to say is I want to help you.'

'How?' Brandt sincerely hoped she wasn't about to offer to tidy up and clean the place.

'I… I don't know,' she said in a muted tone. 'I tried to think of it on the way over. I almost turned around and went home until I could come up with something, but then I thought of you all alone here. No job, no family. I just need you to know that you're not alone and I'm going to find a way to help you. I know lots of people and if I ask around I'm sure one of them will need some help or something. Even if it is just the odd day here and there, something to get you through the winter until we can find you a more permanent position in the spring.'

'Thank you, Mrs Hardcastle,' Brandt said, and he meant it. He wasn't convinced that she would be able to do anything for him, but he appreciated the thought nonetheless. He had long given up on humanity and this one act of kindness, however small, held some true meaning. 'Can I get you that cup of tea now?'

'Oh no,' she laughed, standing up. 'I finished mine whilst waiting for that little weasel to come out from hiding. I had better get on, and I hope you didn't mind the intrusion.'

'Not at all, Mrs Hardcastle, and thanks again for thinking of me.'

'Kath,' she said, taking the steps carefully onto the soggy patch of grass between the caravan and her car. 'Please call me Kath from now on.'

Chapter Seventeen

The day had started for Johnson much like any other. She had awoken early with her body not needing the length of sleep it used to when she had been far more occupied. Sitting in her kitchenette, with the first rays of light starting to emerge on the horizon, she was finishing her small breakfast. She had taken to running in the morning knowing it was odd seeing as she visited the gym each day but didn't like to go there until everyone else had gone to work.

Running through the streets of Nottingham was different. She would blank out the commuters in their cars through a mixture of dogged determination and the loud music she played through her headphones. It had the effect of pushing her far more than the comfortable surroundings of the gym and she would return home exhausted; glad of the opportunity to gain some rest.

Having washed as soon as she got back, she settled down in front of the television to carry on with the box set of the American drama she was steadily working through. She prepared some lunch around midday, despite not feeling truly hungry yet, because she wanted to give herself time to digest before heading off to the gym.

Johnson was picking through the last of her salad and wondering whether she should just do a circuit of the weight machines and go for a swim in the pool instead of anything more vigorous, when her mobile rang. She glanced at the display as she raised it from the coffee table, the action of bringing it up to her ear stopped abruptly by the name on the display. Claire.

Johnson only knew one person called Claire. Not only hadn't she spoken to her in a while, but, following her visit to the hospital, she had never expected to encounter her again.

'Hello?'

'Oh, thank God you're there. Have you been told? Do you know what's happened?'

'Hold on, slow down, I'm struggling to understand what you're saying.' Johnson was trying to sound calm, but the speed of Claire's delivery was only heightening the anxiety she was experiencing from hearing from her again.

'It's him. Well, it can't be him, but it was there, the same as before. The same place; same everything.'

'You're making even less sense now. Claire, please just take a breath and tell me what it is you're talking about.'

'Shit! You don't know, do you?'

'Know what, Claire? You're starting to worry me now.'

There was an audible sigh on the other end of the line but not one through frustration, more in an effort to regain composure. 'There's been a murder. This morning. By the river, in the same spot as before. I thought it was him when I heard about it, especially as it's a stabbing. A young woman too.'

Johnson froze with shock. What Claire was saying was now clear, but her brain was struggling to accept it. 'Jesus Christ,' was all she could utter.

'I couldn't believe it. I heard it on the local radio but had to go on the internet to check. There wasn't much on there but...'

'I know, there wouldn't be at this stage. Look, do you mind if I go now? I'll call you back later, I promise.'

'Er, well,' Claire hesitated, sounding not at all sure.

'I should have some more details for you then.'

The cold delivery and implication that Johnson may be able to find out information before it was put in the public domain seemed enough to convince Claire. 'Yeah, look if I haven't heard from you by this evening I'll phone back.'

'Fine,' Johnson responded, ending the call immediately thereafter.

But she didn't place the phone back on her coffee table. Instead she was hunting through her short contacts list.

'Hardy, it's me.'

'I'm sorry, ma'am, we're a bit busy at the moment.' His protest didn't hide the lack of surprise in his voice at who was suddenly contacting him.

'Obviously that's why I'm calling. I need the details.'

'Ma'am?'

'Let's not start doing all this bullshit, shall we? I haven't got the patience for it and you just said that you're busy.' Johnson then waited quietly whilst DC Hardy confirmed everything that Claire had just told her.

'What type of knife was it?' she asked as soon as he stopped.

'We don't know yet. The pathologist is still…'

'Was the blade serrated?' Johnson interrupted, doing nothing to disguise her irritation.

'Er, we believe so. Yes.'

'And was there a swipe on the victim.'

'A what, ma'am?'

'A swipe, Hardy. A fucking swipe of blood on the victim somewhere? You know, not directly related to the blood that would have escaped the wound.'

'Er, hold on a second,' he replied nervously, rustling through some papers. 'Not that's been found so far,' he said eventually.

'Okay, good. Keep me posted.' Johnson ended the call rather than wait for Hardy to protest once more.

Chapter Eighteen

'What are you doing here?'

'I came to see you,' said Jack, ignoring the resentment in Mandy's voice.

'Where have you been?'

Jack bowed his head plaintively.

'You could have left me a note. Sent me a text or something. I knocked at yours when you didn't turn up for the lecture after we… after…'

Jack had known Mandy had attempted to visit. He hadn't long since arrived back from his walk along the river and was still buzzing from the kill. He had wanted to open the door to her. He had wanted nothing more than to pull her inside and fuck her right then and there. As he observed her through the spyhole, his curtains drawn to prevent a change of light alerting her to his presence, it had taken Jack all his strength not to turn the handle. But there were too many questions for which he hadn't thought up answers at that stage. He wouldn't have known how to explain why he had simply left her that morning, where he had gone and why he suddenly needed to devour her.

There was another reason too. Aside from his enormous sexual urge, a feeling that had been entirely absent from his murders back in Kent, he immediately wanted to plan his next killing. The power he had felt, as the woman begged him not to thrust the knife back into her, had been intoxicating. Jack had suddenly felt important, as though he really mattered, and he couldn't wait to experience that again. As he had stood over her body, he knew that finally Brandt would have been proud of him.

'I'm sorry. I didn't want to wake you that morning. Seeing you lying there, you just seemed so… so perfect.' Today Jack did have the answers that meant he could act on his urge. 'I just needed some space to think. That's why I didn't go to the lecture.'

'Oh, I get it,' Mandy sighed. 'You've got a girlfriend. I should have known it.'

'What? No!'

'You woke up feeling all guilty, so you scurried away but, deep down, you think you're a decent person, so you've come here to explain it. But it's simply to make yourself feel better and I can bet you one thing. I bet you haven't thought to tell her, have you?'

'Who? What are you talking about, Mandy?' Jack was confused. Even more concerning was that the buzz he was feeling was wearing off. Perhaps it had been a mistake coming here. His answers might have been well-rehearsed, but he hadn't legislated for how hurt Mandy had been by his disappearance.

He turned to leave. If he wanted to, he could try and deal with this later, but what he needed most of all was to preserve the feeling of power his trip to the alleyway had given him. It had been perfect; more so even than his well-timed meeting at the river. If his first murder in Nottingham hadn't been enough to convince Jack that what he had chosen to do with his life was the right thing, today had. Although he knew there were a number of key differences between his woman in the alleyway and the one Brandt had killed, there were too many similarities for it not to seem like fate. He knew she was the right one the first moment he clapped eyes on her, and his only regret was that the speed at which their paths were crossing might fail to make him fully enjoy the moment. The only chance he had was to somehow strike up a conversation but, what about, he hadn't had the slightest clue.

But then luck had been in his favour once more. Just as he was contemplating whether offering something complimentary about her son would sound odd coming from someone his age, the boy dropped his soft toy dinosaur out of the buggy. Better still, his mother hadn't noticed; providing Jack with a far less awkward reason to speak to her.

'Excuse me! Your son just dropped this,' he had called, after waiting for her to fully pass so that she would have to turn back around in order to face him.

'Oh great,' she had replied enthusiastically. 'He's forever losing it but thank goodness it always turns up because I doubt he'd be able to sleep without it.'

'I completely understand. I used to have a bear I took with me everywhere,' Jack had lied. 'Well, that was until Mum decided one day that I was too old for it. I was devastated.'

'Ah, you poor thing,' she had said, reaching for the toy.

Hold on a minute, Jack had thought, ever so slightly pulling his arm away from her. Not only had he not liked the absence of any real feeling in her tone following his tragic story but, given how precious she had claimed the dinosaur to be, it didn't seem right that she should be trying to dismiss him so quickly.

He had read the slight look of unease in her eyes. 'Do you mind if I give it back to him myself?'

A slight shrug. 'Erm, sure. Go ahead.'

'There you go, little fella,' Jack had said to the boy. Any discomfort shown by his mother was not replicated in her child, his arms excitedly outstretched to be reunited with his companion.

'Nice kid,' he had commented, standing back up. 'What's his father like?'

A bitter laugh. 'A complete shit if you must know.'

'Well, he's going to need to step up to the mark pretty fast.' Jack had waited, enjoying her look of confusion turn to apprehension. 'Aren't you going to ask me what I mean by that?'

'Erm, well, thanks again. We'd better be going now,' she had answered, attempting to turn the pushchair around as fast as possible.

Jack had quickly glanced back down the alley to check that they remained unobserved. 'Hold on, there's something I need to show you first.' He had tried to keep his voice calm despite his heart now pounding in his chest…

Remembering what had happened next caused Jack to unconsciously feel for the comforting weight inside the lining of his jacket.

'Bought me some sort of cheap gift, hoping that might make you feel better?'

'What?' he asked, quickly withdrawing his hand as though scolded.

'I think you'd better go.' Mandy moved to close the door but found its movement blocked by Jack's foot.

'What the fuck?'

'Look, you've completely got the wrong idea here. Just give me a minute to explain and I promise that if you still want me to leave then I will.'

She stared at him intently. 'Go on,' she said, the coldness in her voice betrayed by the way she stepped back to allow him to enter.

'There's no girlfriend.' Jack blurted out. That he also shook his head was less about adding emphasis and more frustration at how it seemed harder to talk to her than it had either of the two women he had recently murdered.

'What I said about you that morning was true. I fancied you; of course I did. I wouldn't have asked you out otherwise, would I?' Lies no longer felt uncomfortable on his lips. 'But we have so much in common and it was brilliant. Not just going out for dinner but afterwards when we… you know. I just woke up and saw you and got a little freaked out.'

'But why?' Her tone had softened considerably.

'I don't know. I've only just met you, but it felt so right.' He lowered his head, realising that power came in many forms and not just through domination. 'I guess… I guess I got a little scared.'

'And now?'

'And now I just knew that I had to come and see you. The truth is, I'm not used to all this sort of stuff and I'm sorry if I hurt you.'

'Shh,' she said, pulling him inside and allowing the door to close behind him. 'It's okay. I understand. We can take things slowly if you like.'

'Slowly?'

'Yeah, we don't have to get all serious and stuff.'

Jack could feel his heart hammering once more. 'But does that mean we can't...?'

'No,' she whispered, letting go of him so that she could pull her top up over her head.

Chapter Nineteen

'Hello?' Johnson recognised the number as being the generic one from the station, but she didn't know who would be calling her. Most likely it was DC Hardy, but so far she had always needed to chase him if she wanted any information.

'Hello, Stella, it's Steven.'

She hesitated for a moment, whilst her brain put together the voice with the unfamiliar name. 'Guv?' Similar to McNeil, she had only ever thought of her immediate superior as DSI Potter. She supposed it was a sign of their extended parting that he thought it appropriate to drop the formalities.

'I'm pleased I caught you. I need to speak with you.'

'Okay. Go on.'

'Are you at… home? I'll send a car round.'

'What is it, guv? Tell me.'

'It should be there in a few minutes. We'll speak when you come in.' Johnson didn't see that there was any point arguing but, at the same time, she wasn't going to sound like she found this bizarre request acceptably normal. 'Oh, and one other thing,' he added. 'Don't wait outside. The driver will buzz up and give you my name by way of clearance.'

The anxious wait that followed wasn't helped once the car arrived, because the officer seemed reluctant to reveal why he had been sent out.

'I've already told you, the call came down for me to come and pick you up. I don't know why you're wanted at the station,' he said as he closed his door, having first ensured she entered the car safely.

Johnson believed he was speaking the truth in that he didn't know specifically why Potter wanted to speak to her, but she could tell he was holding something back. 'But you think you know what it is to do with.' Not a question but a statement.

'I'm sorry but I had better not say.'

She had already grown tired of this jobsworth. The station was full of people like him, so afraid of putting a foot wrong that it rendered them impotent. Time for a change of tack. 'Am I under arrest?'

'I'm sorry?'

'Am I under arrest?' Johnson repeated, more slowly this time. 'Because if I am, you haven't read me my rights.'

'No, you're not under arrest,' he sighed.

'Good, then stop the car please,' she said calmly.

'What?'

'I said stop this fucking car and let me out!'

'I... I can't.'

'Oh yes you can, PC whoever the fuck. What's more, if you don't stop the car right now, I'll have you arrested for abduction.'

'Please,' he cried, gradually slowing the vehicle nonetheless.

Johnson waited until they came to a halt. 'Now that's better. Okay then, where were we? Oh right, you were going to tell me exactly what I am doing here, otherwise I am going to get out and walk home.'

'I told you, I don't know exactly!'

Johnson sighed theatrically and reached for the door handle.

'But I think I know what it's about.'

'Go on…' She allowed the impatience to remain in her voice, despite knowing that victory had already been achieved.

'It must be connected with what happened earlier.'

'And what did happen earlier?'

'The murder.'

'What murder?' As much as Johnson had loved Nottingham, the city wasn't without its fair share of problems. One of its more unfortunate nicknames was Shottingham, meant to reflect the gun crime people in other parts of the country believed to be rife here. The truth was there were far too many shootings, but they tended to be localised to particular wards and were usually limited to the elements of the criminal underworld who lived there. 'Where?'

'In an alleyway, close to…'

Johnson didn't listen to the rest. It suddenly all made sense. She had spent the last couple of days hoping what had happened by the river was just some sort of sick coincidence. Although news of another hadn't come as a complete surprise, for it to come so soon was a shock.

'Put your foot down,' she ordered.

'But…'

'But what? We've already wasted enough time here. Get me to the station!'

* * *

'Wait! I'll open the door as soon as I park up.'

'I know the fucking code,' Johnson shouted, slamming the car door. As soon as the gate to the secure car park had retracted she had got out. It wasn't just that she was in a hurry, she wasn't about to be escorted into her own station as though she was some kind of guest or, worse still, a suspect.

'Ma'am,' Sergeant Andrews greeted her briefly before returning his attention to his log book. Johnson was grateful he didn't question her arrival as he would have been entitled to under the circumstances. She reflected that she really had got him wrong and he was a decent guy despite his usually officious exterior.

As if she needed further encouragement to scale the stairs up to CID without further delay, she could hear the back door opening in the corridor behind her. She would do the man who had driven her here a favour and not wait until he said something that required her to slap him down in front of his superior.

Yet she couldn't help but feel a little apprehensive as she approached the door leading to her old unit. She assumed that her failure to gain entry at the first attempt was through her punching in the wrong code, but her more cautious second effort yielded the same result. She was about to bang on the glass when she noticed someone approaching.

'How come it's not working?' She demanded as DC Hardy opened the door.

'Fisher changed the code,' he whispered in reply.

'Why?' The shrug that greeted her question implied it had been done on a whim, but Johnson suspected something more sinister. 'So, where is he?'

This time she didn't wait for a response as she had already spotted Fisher's lanky frame over by the case pin board. It seemed convenient that he had found something to do which meant he wouldn't have to face her.

'DI Fisher,' she called, emphasising his rank, as she strode over.

'Ah hello, Stella,' he said in return, the warmth he had put into the words belied by him selecting her forename in speaking to her for the first time ever.

'What have you got for me?' Time to make this smarmy shit play his hand.

'For you? Nothing. You're not on active duty anymore,' he scoffed.

She stood there, hands on hips with a smile to match her raised eyebrow. 'So, now you've got the keys to the playhouse you've decided you don't want to share any of the toys?'

Johnson waited, enjoying the way his mouth flapped open and closed as he tried and failed to think of a cutting retort. 'Just remember, Fisher, you're merely the caretaker here so you'd better try and enjoy it whilst it lasts.' And with that she spun away and headed towards Potter's office.

Johnson considered knocking but decided there was no point breaking the habit of a lifetime. In addition, she liked the thought of Fisher, who was bound to still be watching her, seeing her do something he would never have the balls to try himself.

'Guv,' she said by way of greeting. Despite how much she had grown to dislike him following McNeil's death, she couldn't help but smile at the way DSI Potter didn't even seem in the least bit surprised by her method of entry.

'Thanks for coming, Stella, do sit down.'

'Not that I had much choice,' she muttered sufficiently loudly as she took her seat.

'I'm sure you already know what this is about…'

'But you didn't tell me anything,' she interrupted innocently, amused by his resulting expression suggesting he knew full well that she would have got what she needed out of the officer he had sent to collect her. But the thought of the circumstances of her return caused her to forget the office politics and reassert her authority. 'I take it there are links to the one the other day.'

'Yes, similar kind of serrated blade, if not the same actual knife.'

'Copycat?'

'Probably. Although…' Potter left the sentence unfinished.

'Although what, guv? What else could it be? Surely you can't think it's just a coincidence?'

More silence.

'You don't think it's coincidence.' Johnson was stunned. She had been certain that the reason for asking her in was because they wanted her back. As soon as this got out, there would be a media frenzy and they couldn't allow the same kind of fuck ups they'd had following the identification of Brandt. She hadn't worked out whether she had been going to agree, but had planned on enjoying being asked nonetheless.

'Like I said, it's probably a copycat.' Potter had that same calm tone that had always managed to infuriate Johnson when she was trying to get him to admit something.

'But?'

'Tell me, Stella, how sure are you that it was Brandt who died in your house?'

'How sure?!' she shouted. 'I watched him burn to death. I saw his body whilst I lay in my back-garden choking on the fucking smoke!'

'But did you actually see him set light to himself or recognise that it was specifically him when you saw the body?'

'You know I didn't,' she replied bitterly. 'But the examination of the dental records would have confirmed…' Johnson stopped, instantly seeing the guilt in Potter's eyes. 'Please, tell me you checked them,' she implored.

'It would be inappropriate for me to discuss the details of an investigation…'

'Look, you don't need to tell me whose fuck up it is. I think I can guess, but I suppose it's a good thing for both of you that Brandt is dead, and this is just the work of some sick copycat.'

'How can you be so sure?' The desperation in his voice was clear.

Johnson thought for a moment. All this may have been distressing on some level, but it was still nice to see Potter squirm. She had no idea why he was covering for Fisher but now was the time to remind him she was eminently more capable.

'There are a number of reasons. Firstly, what would be the point of faking his death only to then go on and indicate he was still alive? But even if he was mad or stupid enough to do that, why would he just recreate his old murders rather than continue to evolve as he had done? Moreover, if for some reason he did want us to know, then he would have used the same method of indicating the link as he had before.'

'Hmmm,' Potter responded, considering what had just been said. 'But they are so similar, right down to the weapon used.'

'Tell me something, guv, was there a swipe of blood on either victim?'

'No. Why?'

'Because that was Brandt's calling card. He used it to show it was the same man committing the first murders and he did it again with that guy in Milton Keynes because he wanted us to know it was him, hoping we would continue to dismiss what had happened in St. Albans. What you have got to ask yourself is this: if he wanted us to know he was alive and killing again, he would have given us his tell-tale link and if he didn't, would he be stupid enough to commit more murders in the exact same spot as he had used previously?'

'Okay, supposing all that is true, there is another possibility here.'

'Go on, guv…'

'Maybe it wasn't just Brandt and Franklin. There could be a third person out there who had been lying low and has now come out of the woodwork.'

Johnson put her head in her hands. 'No, no, no! There was no Brandt and Franklin. I tried to tell you this before. I don't know the exact nature of their relationship and what sort of a hold Brandt had over Franklin, but this was his own work. I was sure of it after he… after I first spoke with him and am absolutely certain it was having met him again. You know the suicide note was bullshit; it was Brandt just trying to cover his tracks. To think there might be a third party is just… just…'

'Just what?'

'Just desperation.' Despite the breakdown of the relationship, Johnson still felt uncomfortable delivering such a damning assessment of the person she had looked up to for so long. She wanted to continue before he could respond.

'I'll tell you another reason why this is the work of the copycat rather than Brandt or someone who was acting with him. The similarities that you find so compelling between these murders and Brandt's are there because it is someone trying to recreate them. What they have done is recreate them as they understand them. But not only will you find some key differences that are distinct to this particular person's motivation for the attack, but the lack of a swipe proves it's someone who only knows the details in the public domain. Otherwise they would have done that too in an effort to be as authentic as possible.'

'So, your theory hangs on a swipe of blood?' Potter had never been prone to sarcasm and his use of it now was just a further indication to Johnson of how desperate he had become.

She stood up. 'Obviously, you can just ignore everything I have told you but then why bring me in here if you didn't want to know how I saw it.'

'I brought you in to try and protect you. If Brandt really is still out there…'

'Ha,' scoffed Johnson, swinging open the door. 'It seems like you're the one who needs protecting. From yourself.' And with that she slammed it shut and marched across the open plan office of CID. Much as she wanted to, she decided that she wouldn't seek to engage Fisher but would leave them to their catalogue of mistakes – her head held high in the knowledge that there was nothing more she could do to help them if they didn't choose to help themselves.

Chapter Twenty

The knock at the door wasn't a complete surprise this time. Even if Mrs Hardcastle hadn't promised to return with news, whilst reading his morning newspaper Brandt had heard her pulling up in her Kia Sportage. The events in Nottingham had reached the national press and he was keen to keep a tab on things. He was still extremely concerned about how he was going to last the winter without a regular income but supposed the reigniting of interest in him that the copycat killer had provoked was better whilst he was more isolated from the public.

As to his feelings that someone was going around seemingly recreating his murders, he wasn't quite sure what to make of it. On the one hand, it was flattering and certainly fitted the purpose he had been trying to achieve of provoking fear. But he wasn't sure he felt comfortable with someone he didn't know, in effect, acting in his stead. The body he had left in Johnson's house was long buried so he wasn't especially concerned about people thinking he was alive and back in business once more, particularly because he could see no logical reason for people to think, even if he had still been alive, that he would choose to revisit old murder scenes rather than move on to fresh pastures.

Before heading to the door, he flipped the kettle on. He hoped that Mrs Hardcastle had something good to tell him but, regardless, he was grateful for her continued concern and would not allow her to leave this time without being suitably refreshed.

'Hello, Greggy,' she said as soon as he was stood before her. She appeared a little nervous and for the briefest of moments Brandt wondered whether she might also have been reading the newspapers and had somehow realised that Britain's most notorious serial killer of the 21st century was the man who had been serving her a particularly generous slice of her favourite lemon cake twice a week for the past two months. A voice in his head that had never quite gone away told him it would be best to kill her now rather than run the risk of detection. But whilst Brandt may have been unable to rid himself of its unwelcome contributions entirely since he came to Wales, he fully understood them for what they were and would do his utmost to ignore them.

'Hello, Mrs Hardcastle, it's good to see you again,' he said, ushering her in. Irrespective of the voice's motives he would soon be able to determine whether her visible anxiety was purely because she was unaccustomed to entering the lodgings of men she barely knew, or if there indeed was another root cause.

'I told you to call me Kath,' she chided, but not unkindly.

'Of course, Mrs Hardcastle,' Brandt said in response, the wink that he followed it up with causing them both to laugh. 'And to what do I owe the pleasure on this fine day?' he continued, looking past her and out of the open door at the steady drizzle that had commenced before dawn.

'Well, it's about what I said the other day, about finding a way to help you out of your current… circumstance.'

This was good. Brandt was pretty sure that she was telling the truth, and this was the purpose of her visit. Besides, if she even for one moment suspected his actual identity, it would be utter madness for her then to choose to come along to confront him in a, now near-deserted, caravan park in the middle of nowhere. Surely not everyone was quite as bold and reckless as DCI Johnson had been.

'Oh, great,' he responded. 'I really do appreciate this. Honestly, when Mr Jones told me he was letting me go I never imagined that someone would be so kind as to…'

'Please, Greggy, I have something to tell you,' the seriousness with which she delivered her interruption not only caused Brandt to stop talking immediately but also to sit up straight on the banquette designed to be the equivalent of a living room sofa. 'I'm afraid it's not good news. I have been asking around everywhere I can think of, really I have, but it appears that no one is looking to take on new staff at this moment. Or at least…' She paused, seemingly unable to conclude her sentence.

'Someone foreign,' he finished for her.

'Well, er… yes,' she confirmed with a sigh.

Brandt got up and moved into the kitchen area to attend to the kettle, which had just finished boiling. He didn't know why he was quite so disappointed with Mrs Hardcastle's news. It was nothing less than he would have expected and yet he had clung onto that shred of hope over the last few days. It had kept him going and had even seen his drinking the night before her first visit become a mere blip on an otherwise exemplary track record.

'How will you manage?' she asked, breaking the awkward silence that had descended.

'Oh, I'll be fine. Really,' Brandt replied, heading to the fridge before remembering that Mrs Hardcastle liked her tea to steep for at least five minutes before the milk was added.

'No honestly, Greggy. How will you manage?'

Brandt sighed and re-joined her in the lounge area and sat down again. 'Honestly, Kath, I don't know. I think I have enough to last me until Christmas but if I can't get a job until then I'll have to find somewhere else. Perhaps if any of the fruit pickers have decided to stick around, I can share with them.'

He got up again. The tea bag might not have been in the water long enough for her tastes but, under the circumstances, it would just have to do.

'Sit down please, Greggy.'

Brandt complied with her request. He had assumed that their conversation was drawing to an unsatisfactory close, but it seemed she had something more she wanted to say.

'There was something else I needed to ask you…'

Here it comes. She's clearly not convinced but she at least suspects it's me. What she really wants is for me to deny it, so she can try and cast it from her mind. But what if my reassurances aren't enough? What if she's here, not to hear whether it's me, but to see if it is? Has she been studying the photos of me in the newspaper and wants to see my face one last time, so she can be sure? Sure enough so that the first thing she does once she pulls away in her car is to phone the police?

'Go on…' Brandt encouraged her, flexing his fingers so they were ready to squeeze the life out of her, should the need arise.

'Well, everything you've told me is how I imagined it would be and so I've been thinking… thinking whether you would like to come and live with me.'

'What?' Brandt exclaimed, unable to hide the shock from his voice. This turn of events was entirely unexpected.

'Oh, good God, I didn't mean like that,' she responded in distress. 'I didn't mean live with me as in… I meant come and stay with me. For a while. Just until the new year and things start to pick up again.' As if thinking that this was still not enough to confirm that her suggestion was purely platonic, she continued. 'It's a large house. I'm just rattling around it on my own. You would have your own bedroom. Of course you would,' she added, still flustered. 'But what I mean is that the house is big enough that it wouldn't even be directly next to mine. You could come and go as you please. It would be like you were my lodger. Erm, except that you wouldn't be paying me. Although, if you wanted you could repay me in other ways. Oh, good God, I didn't mean like that, I meant doing some odd jobs. It's not quite the place it once was before my husband passed away. You could do some of the things he used to do. Around the house I mean.' She stopped abruptly, perhaps realising that the more she tried to justify herself the more she seemed to be tying herself up in knots.

'Kath, I really appreciate you offering but you don't need to do this.'

'I know I don't,' she responded, a steeliness entering her tone. 'But I said I would help you because I want to, and this is the best way I can.'

The voice came back telling Brandt that this was just a trap. All women are the same and Mrs Hardcastle was just trying to lure him back to her place like that slut had in Benidorm. As soon as she got her wicked way she would cast him back out onto the street.

'I don't know what to say,' he admitted. He looked into her face and could see the kindness within. Was he really going to refuse her offer and remain here in this increasingly cold and deserted caravan park, and just wait for his money to run out? He had come to Wales to make a fresh start and Mrs Hardcastle was giving him a way of ensuing the setback dealt to him by Mr Jones wasn't incurable. He knew he didn't deserve such generosity considering what he had done, but then part of him believed he did. Her desire to help had been borne out of the relationship he had forged with her in the tearoom. Had he treated her as just another customer she would not have felt compelled to come to his aid. Perhaps this was a sign that his actions in his former life weren't irredeemable; that he wasn't beyond redemption.

'As long as you promise to put me to good use around the house then I shall accept your gracious offer. But I have one question for you first…' He allowed the tension to increase once more before continuing. 'Where is it that you actually live?'

'Oh, Greggy,' Mrs Hardcastle squealed like a schoolgirl. 'You are going to love it. It's a converted farm house overlooking Betws-y-Coed and…'

Brandt tuned out her excited ramblings about the property and the grounds on which it sat. He was keen to leave some details as a surprise and, instead, just wanted to bask in the warm glow of finding companionship for the first time in years. He didn't know if he would like living under someone else's roof and having to abide by their rules, but he was keen to find out.

Chapter Twenty-one

'Look, guv, I told you there's nothing to worry about but if it makes you feel any better I haven't told a single person my new address. I'm perfectly safe here.'

'Stella, that's not why I called... Brandt is still alive.'

'What?' Was this some kind of sick joke? She didn't know how this was meant to be a suitable lead into begging her to return to work, but Potter had better justify himself, and quickly.

'I thought carefully about what you said the other day and you were right to be shocked that standard procedure hadn't been followed. To tell you the truth, I had only just found out that Fi... that no one had seen the dental records cross referenced. I know I should have checked it had been done but... well anyway, I made the right decision and had the body exhumed.'

'Who... who is it then?' Johnson still couldn't believe she was hearing this.

'It was the husband of a couple who went missing after returning from holiday.'

'Let me guess, returning from holiday in France. By car.'

'Yes, that's about the size of it.'

'Fucking hell!' Johnson cursed quietly. Having got over the realisation that Potter had been calling her for a different reason to what she had expected, she realised what a monumental cock up they had made. Now it dawned on her the true meaning of his revelation.

Former Detective Superintendent Jeffrey Brandt, the man who had killed McNeil, along with eight others that they knew of, in fact, make that ten given the couple returning from holiday, was not dead. He had faked his own suicide and was out there somewhere thinking he had got away with it.

Johnson had the sudden urge to throw up but strangely she didn't feel in immediate danger. What had occurred at her house hadn't been the crazed final stand of a dangerous man believing himself backed into a corner. He must have planned it all along. To lure her out, under the pretence his ex-wife could still be saved and then use the time when she had been unconscious to set the stage for his elaborate escape.

But why then would a man who meticulously tried to avoid leaving anything to chance, not only kill himself before seeing Johnson burn in the flames, but allow something as basic as not securing her bonds tightly enough to see his plan fail?

'I know what you said about no one knowing the whereabouts of your flat, but remember he found you once before and I assume you're still driving around in that red sports car he traced you in.'

'He's not coming for me, guv.'

'What? How can you say that after he hunted you down, not once but twice?'

'But that's the whole point. Admittedly, the only reason why he didn't kill me the first time was because of McNeil suddenly arriving,' Johnson was unable to say that last bit without an involuntary change to her voice as a lump formed in her throat. 'But if he had wanted me dead the second time he would have done so.'

'I don't understand, Stella. Are you telling me now that you're not surprised he's still alive? But when I asked you in the station whether…'

'It's not that at all!' Johnson didn't know why she was being so defensive of her thoughts and, more crucially, Brandt's actions. 'It's just I truly believe if he had wanted me dead, he would have made sure of that last time, or at least, what with him still being alive, he would have finished the job in the months since then. And before you ask why I think he decided not to kill me, I don't know. Although, now I come to consider it, perhaps he didn't see that he needed to anymore, seeing as he was about to make a clean getaway. Believing him to be dead, I obviously wouldn't still be looking for him.'

'Are you sure you wouldn't feel safer staying somewhere else? Just say the word and I'll have something arranged.'

It wasn't so much the repetition of the same concern that irritated Johnson, more that Potter didn't even seem to want to acknowledge her thoughts on Brandt's motives.

'Listen, guv, I'm staying put. And like I said, it doesn't really change anything.'

'How do you mean?'

'It's still not him who's done these two recent killings. There's still a copycat out there.'

The silence that followed was worse than the denial she had expected her assertion to receive. It meant that Potter was so unconvinced by it that he didn't see the point of challenging her. It was just like when they found Franklin's body and the bogus suicide note: they were blinkered by the thing that was most immediately in front of them. She sighed heavily. There were so many emotions she should be experiencing right now: bitterness, anger, betrayal. Anything but the sensation of impotence she was currently feeling.

The irony of this, given what she had seen Gail Trevelly write in her newspaper articles about Brandt, did not escape her.

Chapter Twenty-two

'You, sly old dog!'

It was a matter of minutes after the news breaking that Brandt was not dead that Jack found out. His second killing had ensured that murder was on everyone's lips on campus and the revelation of Brandt's faked suicide had spread like wildfire. Jack had guessed that, in their embarrassment, the police would have added little to the brief bit of information he had overheard in the student union bar, but he still wanted a chance to digest it in peace. Fortunately, Mandy hadn't been with him at the time, otherwise he would have needed to come up with a more convincing excuse for his departure than an overdue essay.

The admiration Jack felt as he re-read on his laptop the short statement on the news site he had accessed, was far greater than when he had found out that Franklin's claim that Brandt had merely been a pawn in his game was false. That may have served to redeem his hero but this now elevated Brandt to a god-like status.

Jack had never felt comfortable with Brandt's supposed demise. He had taken some solace in it being on his own terms, but it still felt like an opportunity wasted. To have something so good snuffed out in its prime seemed to Jack little more than cruel. Once again, he felt guilty for underestimating his mentor's brilliance, but that reaction was soon pushed away by the sudden realisation that Brandt would know of his actions.

Wherever Brandt had chosen to escape to, surely he would have received news of Jack's murders in Nottingham. The thrill this gave him was greater than anything he had experienced murdering those women, and much more so than the lustful, animalistic sex he'd performed with Mandy afterwards. But there also came the sense of great responsibility. No longer was he paying homage to his great teacher by way of honouring his glorious acts, what he had done was to perform in his image. Jack had always considered the shadow created by Brandt to be long, but that he was still alive to cast it added a certain pressure, giving him more to live up to.

As with many ambitious young people, understanding that the bar had been set higher only conspired to make Jack even more determined to clear it. Knowledge that Brandt would be seeing and judging his efforts, convinced him that he should not continue to delay his next task. If anything, Jack had been selfish. His reunion with Mandy had only served to strengthen the bond they had undoubtedly formed. His claims that he was falling for her, at the time said by way of an explanation for his bizarre behaviour, were becoming a self-fulfilling prophecy. They had also coincided with a feeling of becoming settled in his course of study. He may have only picked Politics and International Relations as a means of securing a place at the university, but Mandy's keen interest in the subject was beginning to rub off on him.

Yet all that was secondary to the true purpose of him being in Nottingham. Brandt's resurrection was a timely reminder for him not to lose focus and he would repay this kindness by ensuring that his next action would not just be soon, it would also be spectacular – a fitting tribute to his master. Coming to this conclusion may have been swift and simple, but establishing what exactly to do would be a greater challenge. The number of murders so far might have now made Jack a serial killer in his own right, but he still considered himself just a fledgling. He hadn't forgotten the problems he'd faced in Whitstable and how he had needed to cower behind some bins in Canterbury until someone came along who was sufficiently pissed that his job in killing them was made easy. Things had been much better since he had arrived in Nottingham, but he put down how much smoother things had gone, as well as the enormous increase in the satisfaction he had derived, to having closer followed Brandt's blueprint.

Jack considered whether recreating his murder in Milton Keynes would be sufficient. There were obvious logistical problems he would have to overcome but maybe that would illustrate the scope of his devotion. However, he quickly abandoned that idea. If he were to show himself truly worthy of the admiration from Brandt he now craved, he would have to do something bolder. But deviating completely from Brandt's own intentions wouldn't feel right, especially because he could never truly be sure that he would receive approval for something completely different.

'Got it!' he declared triumphantly to no one other than himself. The path set before him now seemed so clear, as to appear obvious. The only way to be certain that Brandt received his actions in the manner intended was to complete something he had tried but had been unable to achieve.

Jack leaned back on his chair, basking in the brilliance of the idea. It would prove to everyone, himself included, that he was truly worthy. Now he just had to figure out how he was going to manage what had eluded Brandt. This was going to be tricky, but he knew that it would make the result all the more satisfying.

He would start with a little research on the internet.

Chapter Twenty-three

'After you Kath,' Brandt insisted, indicating that his new companion should make her way through the door.

'Why thank you, kind sir,' she said, offering a slight curtsy that made them both laugh. 'Shall I prepare us a light supper and we can treat ourselves by watching it in front of the telly? If I'm quick we can catch the news before that programme you like comes on.'

'Perfect,' replied Brandt even though he was still pretty much stuffed from lunch.

The first few days since Brandt had moved in with Kath had been a little awkward. It had not been deliberate on either of their parts, but it seemed both had become very used to living on their own. Especially given the unusual nature of their relationship, it took a little while for them to find an equilibrium.

From Brandt's perspective, he still felt uncomfortable with the level of generosity shown towards him; it was certainly something he wasn't accustomed to and he tried too hard to be both considerate and a help around the house. Kath, on the other hand, had been so keen to ensure that her motives continued to come across as altruistic that she might as well have been treading on egg shells.

Things had come to something of a head yesterday when Brandt had noticed on Kath's kitchen calendar that she was meant to be hosting a book club meeting. Brandt didn't want to confront her because it might come across as pushy, instead drawing his own conclusion that, for all her generosity, she was worried what people would think of her. He didn't like the idea she was ashamed of him and that her fellow conservative, middle class, middle aged women would think he was taking advantage of her well-meaning but naively placed sense of kindness.

However, it seemed that Brandt hadn't done a very good job of hiding his feelings and eventually Kath had challenged him on his moody demeanour. The past few months had seen him lie so often that he wasn't sure he understood what it was to be truthful anymore but, with her not accepting his claim that he was just tired, no doubt because she was still being over-sensitive herself, he told her about what he had seen on the calendar.

Once Kath had explained that the very reason why she had cancelled the meeting was because she hadn't wanted Brandt to think she was reading more into their arrangement than there was by her appearing to show him off to her friends, there followed a healthy and frank discussion where it seemed their attempts to be considerate were only serving to make things more awkward than if they just behaved as normal.

To try and draw a line under their less than smooth start, and by way of thanking her for giving him a place to stay, Brandt had suggested they go out for the day. The weather was unusually warm and sunny for that time of year, and he hoped that being away from the house would allow them to develop their friendship on a more equal footing.

Brandt hadn't thought much of Rhyl, with the efforts of the local council to improve the seafront undermined by the tired town centre where the down-market nature of most of the shops that remained matched the demeanour of the locals. Llandudno, however, was entirely different. Kath had deliberately taken a coastal road so that, when they crested the brow of a particular hill, the bay in which it stood was suddenly revealed to them.

Bathed in the sunlight from the clear blue sky, it looked immaculate; the neat row of white townhouses following the coastline, most of them independent hotels, leading to a pier at the top, gave it a Victorian picture postcard feel. That beyond the town rose mountains and cliffs, serviced by a cable car, only served to make the view even more stunning in Brandt's eyes.

Closer inspection did not reveal any cracks in the façade, with the properties' owners no doubt having to keep them well-maintained in order to successfully compete in a very seasonal market. They parked adjacent to the beach and Kath suggested they cross into town to get some refreshments. Dismissing the chain coffee shops, they settled on a quaint little tearoom, far less pretentious than Mr Jones' and, after Brandt's insistence, they both had a slice of a lemon sponge to go with their hot drinks.

Much as he enjoyed their little stop off and feeling Llandudno's shopping district had avoided the tiredness that now blighted so many of Britain's coastal towns, Brandt was keen to get back to the seafront. With the late autumn sun's arc through the sky relatively low, once free from the loom of the buildings, they found themselves able to sit on a bench on the promenade for a time without becoming chilly. Brandt could feel his skin soaking up the Vitamin D and he breathed deeply in the nourishing sea air.

They chatted intermittently but both seemed equally comfortable allowing the silence to better enable them to hear the gulls overhead and the gentle lapping of the sea against the shore. Even the sight of the wind turbines on the horizon couldn't spoil what was, for Brandt, a perfect view. Benidorm's beach may have been far sandier and its water a much more enticing shade of blue than the murky brown of the Irish Sea, but this felt far more real. More than that, it felt like home. In that moment all the struggles that Brandt had been through suddenly became worth it; if nothing else, but to bring him to this point.

Somewhat with reluctance they agreed that they couldn't just stay there all day and made their way down to the pier. Brandt could imagine it teeming with families in July and August. The world had changed so much in his life time and, as far as he was concerned, little for the better, but the thought of the children pestering their parents for money to go on the selection of fairground rides was a comforting reminder of his own childhood. People didn't need their iPhones and eReaders and Ultra High Definition televisions playing hundreds of channels through their satellite receivers. They were just poor substitutes for what really mattered: companionship and friendship.

With thoughts of the important things in life, he dragged Kath into one of the amusement arcades. Avoiding the computer games, he led her straight to the 2p coin pushers, after changing a pound into a pot of coppers. Brandt could tell she was equally excited by the slice of nostalgia and they laughed away whilst feeding their money greedily into the machine and debating whether they used to be called penny falls or ha'penny shoves in their day. For one dreadful moment Brandt feared he might have undone all his good work by letting slip a detail that directly contradicted his claim to be from another country, but Kath seemed so caught up in trying to tip over a particularly precarious ledge of coins that she seemed not to notice.

Their grudging exit, following the depletion of all their loose change, was soon forgotten as they both found an immediate urge for lunch. The over-the-top consideration for each other's feelings, which had been such a feature of the past few days, had been abandoned as they entered into a good-natured argument as to what to have. Despite both presenting an equally strong case for their preference, Brandt won through with his insistence that collecting fish and chips to sit down and eat back on the promenade, with the sea in front of them and watching the cable cars climb the cliffs to their side, could well provide the highlight on an entirely wonderful trip.

The only thing that would have made their lunch any better was if it had been wrapped in newspaper rather than served in a tray. Not that the lack of traditionalism dented their appetite. With Brandt regretting his insistence on finishing his and Kath claiming she wouldn't need to eat again for the rest of the week following hers, they spent the next few hours pottering around and slowly digesting.

The sun was beginning to set far too early for either of their liking and they had trudged back to the car and headed home. Within a few minutes, they were back amongst the Welsh mountains and Brandt felt extremely lucky to be living in an area with such contrasting topography – any single element far more interesting than where he and his wife had set up home.

It was still with a feeling of true contentment that Brandt eased himself down onto the squishy cream leather sofa and turned on the television. Whilst he waited for the six o'clock news to start, he turned down the volume, so he could listen to Kath pottering around the kitchen – a sound he found extremely comforting.

But Brandt's sense of wellbeing was short lived. No sooner had the BBC's announcer introduced the news than he was greeted with his own face staring back at him. Although fearful that, at any second, Kath might walk in with the tray of whatever light tea she had prepared, he increased the sound, so he could find out why the hell he had become the lead story.

If his mind hadn't been in so much shock, he would have known that there could only be one possible explanation. Instead he sat there slack jawed as he listened to how the body, his body, had been exhumed and forensically identified as belonging to someone else.

When he had come up with the idea of faking his suicide, it had only been to buy himself enough time to escape. He had known that procedure should see his subterfuge exposed but, as the days turned into weeks and months since then, he believed he had got away with it. An extremely welcome slice of good fortune; it had allowed him to confidently establish his new identity, knowing that not only were the authorities no longer hunting for him, but neither would the general public expect to see him.

Why now? What had led the police to make this untimely and, for them, deeply embarrassing discovery? With his brain starting to catch up, the explanation became obvious. Brandt's ambivalence towards the person recreating some of his murders evaporated in the knowledge that it had now put him at risk. The cruel irony of it coming on the day when he had finally found true peace with his own continued existence, was all too clear.

His mind wanted to lead him to ponder how another person must be feeling; much as the news had come as a surprise to Brandt, he could only imagine what a tremendous shock this must be for Johnson. But consideration for her would have to wait, he had a much more pressing issue to deal with.

Kath.

He had to protect her, not just for himself, but the enormous damage it could do to her to find out that the man she had aided in his hour of need, now her lodger and, he hoped she considered, a friend, was someone depicted by the press as a vicious and evil serial killer.

'Shit,' he muttered, hearing her footsteps in the hallway. Fumbling for the remote control, he managed to change the television programme before she stepped through into the living room.

'What's wrong?' Kath asked, pausing awkwardly by the door.

'It's nothing! I just... I just wanted to find us something nice to watch before you came in.'

'Oh,' she said, shaking her head in puzzlement and putting the tray down onto the coffee table. It might only have been meant to be a light meal, but she clearly had gone to some effort. There was a bowl of dressed salad, a plate of meats and various accompaniments, including bread rolls and home-made coleslaw. 'I thought we said we were going to watch the news first?'

'Oh yeah!' Brandt laughed nervously. 'About that... Well, it's been such a nice day I thought it would be a shame to let something depressing spoil it.' Kath looked unconvinced. It hadn't taken him long to realise that her devotion to keeping up with the country's affairs was only bettered by her addiction to EastEnders and Coronation Street, soap operas which Brandt firmly detested, not least because his own wife had been so committed to the former. 'The world seems such an unkind place these days that I just wanted us to continue to live in our little bubble for a while longer.'

'That's really sweet, Greggy,' she responded, sitting down next to him. 'I never knew you were such an old romantic.' Her smile instantly faded, and her wide eyes told Brandt that she was worried her words were a step too far.

He only had a moment in which to act. He wasn't so much concerned that the wrong decision would somehow lead to her accessing the news that night, but he still had tomorrow to think about. The first thing she did each day after rising was to make the short walk down to the newsagents to get her favoured paper, which she would then read over breakfast. Even her desire to make Brandt feel at home hadn't interrupted this crucial part of her routine, and he had been made to eat in silence whilst she studied the sections she found most interesting. Any efforts at striking up conversation had been met by single word responses and he had even tried to hint at her unusual, almost obsessive behaviour, by questioning why she didn't choose to have it delivered and save herself the hassle of going out to collect it. Her reply that she couldn't trust it would be with her by the time she ate was enough to confirm that her behaviour was fully ingrained.

There was really only one thing for it. The only way he could ensure that tomorrow started differently for her. The voice returned, telling him that this was all part of the trap she had laid for him. That she really was just like that woman in the caravan in Benidorm. Moreover, it claimed that even if he wanted to, the unfamiliar surroundings and the worry about what was happening back in Nottingham would see him unable to perform.

It may only have been to spite that pernicious parasite lodged in his mind, but Brandt came to the conclusion that he wanted to. All the news headlines had done was to accelerate a process that had already started. Today had been wonderful; a perfect example of the joy companionship can bring and what better way to cement that than through greater intimacy.

Brandt leaned forward to kiss her. She pulled away, but he could see from her expression that it was through apprehension rather than reluctance. He offered what he hoped was a reassuring smile and moved in again. She went to resist once more. 'You don't have to do this,' she whispered.

'I know I don't,' he replied simply, trying for a third time. His attempt was met with a moment's more hesitation but this time it was followed by her leaning in towards him. Their lips touched softly and tentatively at first, but then becoming firmer and more passionate.

It was good, wonderful even, but not enough for Brandt. He wanted to feel her skin beneath his hands but to start groping at her on the sofa, like some lustful teenager, would feel like a betrayal of the tenderness of their union. He leaned his head back to break the kiss. He could feel her mouth trying to follow him before she realised what was happening. But any fear of rejection she once held, was noticeable by its absence as she slowly opened her eyes.

'Shall we forget tea and head straight upstairs?' Kath purred, standing up and holding out her hand.

Chapter Twenty-four

'This is no good,' Johnson muttered, picking up her phone. She had been feeling uneasy all week but now it was Friday she needed to find out more.

'Hardy, it's me,' she spoke into the phone as soon as it was answered.

'Look, ma'am, what is it?' This was typical of DC Hardy, reluctant to speak to her but unable to avoid respecting the position she had once held.

'I told you to keep me up to date with what's going on. What have you found?'

'Nothing major, unfortunately.'

'So, what do you have?'

'Ma'am, I'm really sorry but Fisher directly forbade any of us speaking to you about the case.'

'What the hell?!' To be honest, Johnson wasn't terribly surprised. That sort of move was just typical of that weasel. Rather than accept he needed some help, he just wanted to bury his head in the sand and was ordering the rest of the team to do the same.

'Er, yeah,' Hardy said, the awkwardness evident in his tone. 'It seems like he didn't appreciate your visit to the station.'

'But that wasn't my choice, Potter called me in,' she replied as innocently as possible.

'That's as may be, ma'am, but he didn't like what you had to say to him.'

'Whatever,' she huffed. It seemed like Fisher couldn't take what he dished out. 'And I bet finding out he had fucked up with Brandt's body did nothing to improve his mood. How's Potter been with him since? Tell you what, don't answer that, just tell me where you are with finding out who is doing these murders.'

'Look, I really can't say… I could be in the shit for just speaking to you at all.'

'Oh, come on, Hardy, don't be such a pussy!' She tried to make her jibe sound little more than banter between colleagues. 'Just tell me that people believe it is the work of a copycat and not Brandt himself…'

'Well…'

'Jesus Christ! Don't any of you get it? It makes no sense for him to fake his suicide and then do the very things that would make people suspect he wasn't dead.' Johnson could sense that she was heading down the road of the argument she'd had with Potter. Much as she wanted to discuss swipes of blood, she resisted. 'Surely you see that?'

'I guess so… but it doesn't really change anything, does it?'

'Why not?' Johnson was taken aback by this claim.

'Well, whoever it is, we just have to work on the evidence until we find them.'

'Holy shit, Hardy, please tell me you're doing more than that?'

'You what, ma'am?' Hardy hadn't been able to disguise the hurt in his voice.

'I said, please don't tell me you're all just sitting around waiting for the next murder to happen in the hope that the killer will leave you some nice juicy clues this time?'

'Of course not!' he shouted, affronted by the accusation.

'So, what are you doing then?' It hadn't been her intention to use this line of enquiry to get the information she needed, but it seemed to be working anyway.

'Well, there's tomorrow of course…'

This was good. The increased anxiety Johnson had been experiencing was because of their proximity to Saturday, the day of the week Brandt had favoured. She might have been convinced that all this was the work of someone else, but the fact remained that they were doing this as some sort of sick tribute to him. Therefore, it made sense for him to start using the same day as well as the same locations and type of murder weapon.

'Visible presence, yeah? All leave cancelled so everyone's out and about?'

'Yes, ma'am.'

'And where will the bulk of the force be concentrated?'

'I really shouldn't say…'

'Hardy!'

'Around the railway station.'

'Good,' she replied, hanging up the phone. With the alleyway and the river having been used, this was the most likely next destination. Perhaps Hardy was right. Maybe it didn't matter so much that they weren't as convinced it was the work of a copycat killer. In their complete misunderstanding of what Brandt would do, they had inadvertently come to the same conclusion she had: that the most likely place to be hit tomorrow was the scene of Brandt's very first attack.

When she had been tracking Brandt the first time, she hadn't felt comfortable just waiting for the next dead body to turn up. Back then, they had an enormous disadvantage in that it could have been literally anywhere – something Brandt's actions in other parts of the country had shown him at great pains to illustrate –but the station would be ideal. Even if it wasn't, that Hardy had confirmed there would be a significant undercover police presence, meant only someone with the skill of Brandt could hope to carry out a stabbing there and manage to slip away unnoticed.

But something still didn't feel right. It was as though there was an alternative place for the killer that was equally as good, if not better than the station.

Chapter Twenty-five

Jack awoke, immediately knowing this day would be different to any other. It was as though he had been building up to it his whole life. He expected to feel nervous, but he was excited to prove his worth. Perhaps Brandt would want to meet him to congratulate him on what he achieved and to thank him for doing what he could not.

The time leading up to the weekend had been a tricky balance between completing the research required to ensure today would be a success, and paying Mandy enough attention that she didn't become suspicious.

The stroke of genius had been falling asleep in the chair the night before. He had originally thought he would have to fake it but all the late nights on the internet whilst Mandy slept had taken its toll. When he woke up a little later, she was sufficiently concerned by this apparently unusual behaviour that he confessed he was struggling with sharing the small single bed. It had the desired effect of Mandy suggesting they restrict their sleeping together, although not the sex she was keen to point out, to only a couple of nights in the week. Satisfied, Jack had gone back to his own room where, despite knowing such a big day lay ahead of him, he managed eight hours of uninterrupted, nourishing slumber.

Nevertheless, it hadn't just been about getting rest. Jack needed to be left in peace the following morning so he could finish his final preparations. He would be out by the time Mandy would think to knock for him, but he had already taken that into consideration and had hidden in his room a gift for her he was going to claim he had gone into town specifically to buy. That should serve to immediately smooth over any difficulties with his mysterious disappearance and hopefully make sure she was feeling open minded for the kind of sex he anticipated wanting in the euphoria of completing this most challenging of tasks.

Jack had been anxious to get going as soon as he woke up but had to wait patiently until the appropriate time. It wasn't that he would be unable to do it any earlier, but it just felt right to arrive at a specific point in the morning. By the time he left his room, the campus was already starting to get busy, but he saw this as good. Today he would be taking more risks than in the rest of his murders put together, and he drew comfort from the fact his initial movements would just seem to blend in with what everyone else was doing that morning.

Except they nearly didn't. Just as he rounded the corner from his particular corridor, Mandy was stood at the pigeon holes by the porter's office, checking her mail. He froze with indecision despite knowing that if she were to turn around at that exact moment, she would spot him. It wouldn't mean that his plans would have to be cancelled but it would represent a more than unwelcome complication. With each second bringing his girlfriend closer to finishing, he gave himself two choices. He could turn around and work his way out the back of the college or just walk right past her and hope he completed the gauntlet before she noticed him.

Jack chose the latter. Today was all about being bold and, besides, if he did hear her calling his name from behind him, he could claim he hadn't spotted her in his sleepy daze and was just popping to the student shop to get some supplies.

He breathed a sigh of relief as he pushed open the double doors and walked into the fresh air. He had made it through unscathed and saw this as a sign that whatever unforeseen challenges might face him whilst completing his work, he was more than capable of meeting them.

Once safely out of the university grounds, he could block all other considerations from his mind and focus purely on the path ahead. Whereas he fully intended enjoying the act itself, the thing he was most looking forward to was getting the newspaper tomorrow and imagining how proud Brandt would be as he read the same article. Perhaps he would try and make contact with him. Jack understood that Brandt had been quite a formidable detective and although Jack had been careful in covering his tracks, part of him hoped that he had left a clue somewhere that he might follow. Perhaps they could murder someone together? Master and student fulfilling their destiny.

Heading back to the station felt like something of a pilgrimage for Jack. He might have been living in Nottingham for a number of weeks now, but the last time he had been there was his daytrip during the summer holidays.

It may have only been a couple of minutes' walk away from the very centre of the city, a place he had visited a number of times, not just at night to enjoy its bars and clubs but also during the day with Mandy, but he had never been drawn to the station. However, as he exited the Broadmarsh Shopping Centre and could see it further down the road on the left-hand side, it now felt entirely fitting.

Going there was like completing the circle and his arrival on a Saturday just before 11.45am had been timed to perfection. It was at this exact moment, on the same day of the week in early spring that Brandt had committed his first act. Jack knew from experience how the dump of adrenaline would have heightened the conflicting emotions of excitement and apprehension.

But Jack felt calm. Unlike Brandt that day, he was now a seasoned killer. Although he knew that his actions would be thrilling, he had learned sufficient control to keep his powder dry until the moment of impact.

Seeing the sheer number of people in and around the station helped him to understand why Brandt had been unsuccessful. All his other locations had afforded him sufficient time and seclusion to ensure his victims died from their wounds, whereas in the case of Sarah Donovan he'd had just one opportunity; one swift pass to deliver a killing blow.

Walking slowly along the pavement but at a pace he hoped wouldn't appear suspicious, Jack wondered what Brandt had made of his own failure. Did it still haunt him that his choice of destination had been too ambitious for his first attempt? Jack imagined it did, but he hoped that his actions today would go some way towards providing his hero with a degree of closure.

He lightly brushed the outside of his jacket, in the precise spot where he knew the knife would be resting in the lining. It had felt rather special to finally possess the same kind of weapon Brandt had used, but now the blade had been fed with the blood of others, it had taken on a special quality. Jack almost considered it to be alive.

With mere metres to go until he would arrive at the spot where Sarah Donovan fell, Jack could feel his hand creeping inside his jacket.

Chapter Twenty-six

The vibration of his phone ringing in his pocket caused DC Hardy to let out a small yelp of surprise. Fortunately, he was not in earshot of another colleague. Glancing around to make sure no one had noticed that the man who was, just a moment ago, casually resting against the wall forming the intersection between the railway station's sliding doors, was suddenly now alert, he allowed himself a quick glance at the phone's screen. He avoided the temptation to swear under his breath. It was Johnson. Not that he welcomed any of her calls these days, this one was most inopportune, and he pressed the red reject button before, a moment later, switching off his phone entirely for good measure.

He couldn't afford any distractions and needed to remain alert, whilst at the same time not appear to anyone observing him that he was doing anything more than waiting for a companion to arrive.

'Hardy. Report in.' The command came through the receiver placed in his right ear, with that side of his head kept angled towards the wall.

'Here, guv, nothing to report,' Hardy responded under his breath with the powerful but tiny microphone just under the lapel of his coat transmitting every word clearly.

'Stay sharp now.'

He might have taken it as an indication that DI Fisher had seen his recent indiscretion, but he knew it was more likely because 11.45am was approaching. They had been in position all morning, but it seemed fitting that their target would strike around the same time as the other stabbing.

Hardy's job, and that of the other undercover officers strategically placed at certain points in and around the station, was becoming increasingly difficult as the crowds of people continued to grow. Unless someone was acting very suspiciously, the chance of them spotting him and intervening before he pounced was slim. The knowledge of this did not sit comfortably with Hardy but he knew it would be of no use going on the radio to share his concern with Fisher. He knew what the response would be, not least because Fisher hated his decisions being questioned, no matter how respectfully and sensitively, but Hardy had already foreseen this problem when the plan had first been formulated. He had spoken to him in private and said that a visible police presence was far more likely to prevent an attack from happening because it would act as a deterrent.

Fisher hadn't needed to respond, the contempt in his eyes had been enough to tell Hardy he was aware of that but what was the use in stopping something from happening if it didn't bring them any closer to catching the man they were hunting? That Hardy could see the logic in this didn't help the disquiet he felt at knowing there was a very real possibility someone was likely to be seriously, perhaps fatally wounded just metres from where he stood.

'IC1 male approaching north entrance. Short dark hair, young, slim build, black jacket, blue jeans.'

The chatter over the radio had been like this all morning and this must have been the twentieth such call to alert. Hardy recognised the voice and knew that this particular person had been picked up by the officer stationed just outside the bookies. A swift glance at the unkempt man casually smoking outside the shop, seemingly taking a quick break from blowing what little money he had on another horse race or in the slot machines, allowed Hardy to see his lips moving. He followed his line of sight towards the person in his description. One thing was certain, it wasn't Brandt, and even his slow pace was enough for Hardy to understand why he had been highlighted. The man was young, hardly a man at all really, and young people tended to walk with more purpose. Of course, he might just be particularly early for his train but there was something about his manner that seemed odd.

Almost straight away Hardy realised what it was. The notion that a person swings their arms in time with their movement is often incorrect in reality. Hardy had seen countless people walking along with their hands rigidly dangling by their sides. But what marked this person out was that his left arm was moving whereas his right wasn't. Hardy could now see why. The lad was faintly caressing the side of his jacket, as though something special was contained within.

Under the circumstances, this was enough to alert Hardy to the possibility this could be their target; especially given the time of day it was unfolding. He moved forward, knowing that a single word over the radio would see armed officers emerge from multiple locations within seconds and take this guy down.

That's it, Hardy thought to himself as the lad stopped caressing his jacket and began reaching inside. He would need to wait to see what was withdrawn. He needed to be certain that he wasn't just pulling out his phone or something equally innocent but as soon as he saw that first glimpse of steel he would act – the codeword already on his lips.

Chapter Twenty-seven

As Jack slowly moved his hand inside his jacket, the temptation to just whip out the knife and start stabbing away indiscriminately was strong. Surely one of the blows would see someone die and allow him to achieve what Brandt had been unable to.

Instead he withdrew his hand and pulled the jacket's zip up the remainder of the way to his chin. The wind whipping down Carrington Street had conspired with his slower walking pace to allow the cold of the late autumn day to penetrate his layers of clothing.

Coming to the station at the correct time had always been part of his plan but only in so much as it marked the start of his true journey. This had been where it had all begun for Brandt, and Jack was going to achieve what he hadn't managed to, but not by killing some random passer-by in the exact same spot that Brandt had chosen. It wasn't even as though the playing field would have been level for Jack. He may not have specifically seen any police around the station, but he was sure there would be plain clothes deployed. Brandt had been able to target somewhere so bold because no one had been looking for him at that stage. Jack had missed his chance to kill here as soon as he murdered his first victim in Nottingham. The police may not have been able to catch him so far, but he was certain they would be attempting to anticipate his next move.

He just hoped to God that his true destination was more ambitious than they could have imagined. It certainly had felt an enormous step up as he had been planning it and it would do far more to impress Brandt than killing a stranger, even if the location would have held some meaning.

'The one who got away,' he murmured under his breath, jumping into the taxi at the front of the rank. He offered the driver a destination within a short walk of where he was really going, but sufficiently far away that no one would establish the link, and settled back in his seat to allow his body a quick rest before the task ahead.

Establishing her address had been easier than he thought. He knew her location would be a closely guarded secret given what had happened, and the expectation was confirmed by her social media accounts being locked down on the tightest privacy settings. Jack had expected he would need to find a way to hack in but had been gifted a simpler solution by those who knew her not being nearly as cautious. He supposed he could understand their complacency when they had believed that Brandt was dead, but they hadn't sought to hide their indiscretion once it was revealed he was still at large.

Now out of the taxi, and having paid in cash just in case, Jack walked along the road that he would only need to deviate from once to arrive at the destination. The nerves quickly began to set in. The greatest trouble he had found was on deciding which day of the week to carry this out. Not only had Saturday the greatest resonance with the reason why he was doing this, but it was better to find she had gone out for the day than arrive knowing it was highly likely she was still at work.

As he approached the house, the sight of it provoked a cruel smile. As well as managing a lucky escape, she had clearly landed on her feet. But there was a reason for this: the detached property in which she was currently residing hadn't been paid for by her own meagre salary.

He knocked on the door in the manner he had practiced. He didn't want it to sound like the casual, almost resigned to failure, rap of someone trudging from door to door trying to flog something or convert the occupants to whatever bizarre brand of Christianity floated their boat, and run the risk of it being ignored. He went for the purposeful bash of a harangued delivery driver, paid by the item rather than the hour, and who was liable to lob your precious package over the garden gate if you didn't open up within five seconds.

A flicker of movement from behind the frosted glass confirmed to Jack that he was in luck. The question now was who was going to answer. He had planned for either person, as well as how to successfully abort if he could hear the sound of them entertaining guests.

Good, Plan A then, Jack thought as the door opened to reveal a man. He recognised Josh Ramage from the article the local newspaper had run a few weeks back. Jack had seen it within hours of it being published online, when it had come up as part of his daily routine for searching for anything Brandt related. Sarah Donovan's personal details might have been locked down, but it seemed Josh was quite the man about town. Naturally Jack hadn't expected him to be stupid enough to leave his home address lying around, but a trawl through his Instagram posts soon gave him enough photographic evidence to work on. It seemed he was particularly proud of his new company car, a black Mercedes C Class coupe, and had uploaded a photograph of it gleaming on his driveway, much as it was now. From that, Jack had been able to identify the door number and, a few hours later, after spending the intervening time on Google Street View, he matched the image of the house with the relevant street name.

'I have a parcel for Mrs Donovan. Is she in?'

Josh turned back towards the interior of the house and opened his mouth as if to call his wife. He closed it again upon realising that it was not only strange that he simply wasn't being asked to sign for the package but, from what he had seen, the man wasn't holding anything either.

However, it was too late because Josh's action had been enough to allow Jack time to withdraw his knife from the jacket. He had planned on driving it into his chest, but Josh's exposed neck was suddenly all too tempting.

The slash didn't open his throat like the movies suggested it should, but the power of the delivery was enough to provoke a spray of arterial blood. Josh instinctively put his hands to the wound and the action was sufficient to allow Jack to bundle him inside and slam the door.

The commotion caused Sarah to emerge from the back of the house and Jack had a quick decision to make. Should he take the time to finish the man off or make a grab for her before she had an opportunity to run?

Instead he did neither. Quickly pulling his right arm around his back in order to conceal the blade, he put on his best concerned face. 'Mr Donovan, are you alright?'

Clearly he wasn't, and the sight of her husband writhing on the floor with blood pouring through his fingers was enough to bring Sarah closer. Jack bent down as if to try and provide assistance and when she copied the motion he sprung up, hauling her to her feet with him.

With her back pulled into his chest and the knife pressed hard enough against her neck to puncture the skin, he buried his head in her long blonde hair, so his mouth could get close to her ear.

'Where did he stab you?' Jack panted.

'What?' Sarah cried out.

'I said, where did he stab you?' He raised his knee to jab it into her side to indicate what he meant.

Before Sarah had a chance to answer, Jack could feel his standing leg being pawed at and he yanked her to the side, so he could better see what pathetic endeavour to assist his wife Josh was attempting. With both feet firmly planted on the ground again, he studied with curiosity the dilemma the downed man was facing. He couldn't helplessly watch as his wife was butchered, but removing his hands from his throat was only speeding up his blood loss and making his own death more certain.

Jack paused for a moment to consider if he would do the same for Mandy under similar circumstances. He didn't like the idea of anyone hurting her but was sure his own sense of self-preservation would kick in. However, he remembered reading that the copper had sacrificed himself in order to save Johnson.

Giving a shrug that Sarah felt through her own body, Jack knew that now wasn't the time to be pondering such things and raised his leg again. But this time it wasn't to knee her once more to get their conversation back on track. Instead he brought his heel down in a forceful blow that was met with a sickening crunch as Josh's head fractured. Jack was about to repeat the action to finish the man off, but it was clear Josh was slipping into unconsciousness and his hand fell from his throat.

Jack left him with his still beating heart continuing to pump out blood from his exposed wound in rhythmic, pulsing waves. He would have enjoyed remaining there watching the combined effects of him bleeding out and his heart stopping.

But he still had work to do. What he had witnessed so far was just a side show to support the main event. Although turned away from view, Sarah must have realised what had happened to her husband and started screaming. With the knife still pressed against her, he could have ended her outburst immediately but didn't want to be rushed. He may have come here with a specific task in mind but that didn't mean he couldn't enjoy himself along the way.

He half shoved, half dragged her into the sitting room and was glad that the property was detached, and that the weather meant no windows were likely to be open. He threw her down onto the sofa. It served to jolt the screams from her, but she immediately tried to get up again.

'Josh!' she called, fighting unsuccessfully against her stronger assailant. After the fourth failed attempt, she slumped back down and remained there.

'What do you want?' she demanded, rage emerging to overtake the fear.

Jack pulled the footstool across, so he could sit directly facing her. 'I want you to calm down,' he replied simply, as though this was the most reasonable request in the world. He could sense her about to lunge forward again, and he held out the knife in the hope she would realise that to do so would see her impaled.

'Good,' he said finally, satisfied that he had quelled her resistance for the moment. 'I need you like this, so we can have a proper chat.'

'But Josh?' Sarah exclaimed, glancing towards the doorway.

'Forget about him,' Jack replied firmly. 'You should be more concerned about yourself.'

She snapped her head back to him, the look of fear returning once more and joined by tears rolling down her cheeks.

'I want you to show me.'

'Show you what?' Sarah's voice was now little more than a whisper and punctuated by sobbing.

'Where he stabbed you,' he responded, waving his knife in the direction of her stomach.

'You mean… you mean Brandt?'

'Atta girl! And who said blondes were dumb, eh?'

Sarah looked at him incredulously but the fire in his eyes was enough to tell her he was deadly serious. Without removing her gaze from him, she twisted her body to the left and lifted up the bottom of her shirt.

Jack stared awestruck at the somewhat innocuous looking two-inch scar. He knew that surgeons were good at repairing damaged tissue, but he equally understood why Brandt's blow had not been sufficient to kill her. But it wasn't that which entranced him. Seeing it, even more so than being in the presence of Sarah Donovan, provided him with a far greater connection with his hero than being at any of his murder scenes. At that moment, he wanted nothing more in the world than to touch it; feel the very spot where Brandt had plunged in his blade.

He saw Sarah wince as he leaned forward, his free hand outstretched. Yet as he touched her skin, her body only gave the merest of involuntary jolts.

The sensation on his fingertips was glorious. The scar tissue itself was deliciously cool in contrast to the skin around it, and almost impossibly smooth. Jack considered whether he was finding the experience erotic but surmised that this was more akin to an entomologist discovering a new species of insect. Not that his visit hadn't awoken the same desire as before to get back to Mandy and spend the remainder of the day exploring her own body sexually.

'Well, that was lovely, Sarah. Thank you for your time but I have somewhere I need to be.'

He could see the look of confusion that his words provoked soon replaced by one of hope. Allowing a cruel smile to form on his lips he simply waited until she realised that their business wasn't fully concluded.

'I would ask you what it was like to actually see the great man, but I imagine he was gone before you even realised what had happened to you. I wonder whether I will ever get to meet him one day... Of course, he would be taking a huge risk in wanting to thank his greatest fan but perhaps this might compel him to do so.'

Jack didn't wait for Sarah to question what he meant by that. With her back still exposed, he dived forward with the full intention of burying the knife in the exact place he had been caressing moments before. But two words stopped him in his tracks.

'I'm pregnant.'

Jack sat back and coldly regarded her. This must be some form of a trick. He remembered seeing something on television where people who were abducted kept talking about their families in the hope that it would humanise them in the eyes of their captors and make it harder for them to inflict harm.

'But you're not fat.'

'I'm only twelve weeks but, look, I'm starting to show already.' Sarah twisted back around, and Jack could see that her stomach wasn't flat.

'Could be that you've just let yourself go a bit since you got married.'

'We had our first scan on Thursday. I have got the photo in my handbag if you'd like me to get it.'

Perhaps it was the reasonableness in Sarah's tone or the hope that was evident in her eyes that caused Jack to feel aggravated. How dare she try and throw a spanner in the works? How dare she think that just because she'd managed to get herself knocked up it would changed anything?

Jack shrugged. 'That's unfortunate.'

'I'm sorry,' she stammered, worry edging back into her features once more.

'This wasn't meant to happen.'

'It's not too late to stop this,' she said, delicately placing a hand on his knee.

Jack laughed; it was loud and full and, most of all, cruel. 'No, you stupid woman, none of this was meant to happen. You getting pregnant, getting married, this house,' he said, looking round the living room. 'None of this! You were meant to die outside the station.'

He didn't wait for a reply and lunged again; this time he wouldn't be stopped. As he drove the knife into her again and again, he considered how the earlier sensation of touching the wound inflicted by Brandt paled by comparison.

Chapter Twenty-eight

The need to keep Kath away from the news may have stopped but the sex hadn't. The days following their trip to Llandudno had been the best Brandt could remember. Better even than when he had met Susan because they didn't have the small matter of work to get in the way of their rapidly developing relationship. Their physical union had shown a hunger, absent from both their lives for so many years, but it was their connection on an emotional level that was the stronger indication of their potential compatibility.

Brandt had been worried this would prove difficult, considering he had needed to avoid discussing his past, fabricated or otherwise. However, and in much the same way that Kath had not sought to pry in their earlier conversations, she seemed satisfied to focus on the present, and was reluctant to expand on any unwitting reference to her deceased husband. This very much suited Brandt even if he was curious whether her reticence was borne out of respect for him, for no one liked to be compared to their lover's previous partners, or if she was seeking to keep buried some form of secret there.

Having finally ventured out of the house the previous night to share a dinner at the surprisingly good Chinese restaurant in Betws-y-Coed, it would be their first day in public since they had gone to Llandudno. They were both keen to avoid the kind of formal introductions that would inevitably lead to awkward questions, but they knew there was a fair chance they might bump into people Kath knew. As things currently stood, and without the knowing looks and raised eyebrows from judgemental others, what they had together remained personal and pure; something they wished to hold onto a little longer. They had also admitted to each other that they wouldn't know what to say if pressed about the exact nature of their relationship. Although they both knew that neither of them was getting any younger, experience had taught them that sometimes it was just best to enjoy the moment and accept things for what they were, rather than getting bogged down in how things might be.

So, as they washed and dressed, full from a hearty breakfast that had followed a lie-in not involving much in the way of sleeping, they discussed where they might go. Brandt's limited funds and reliance on public transport had seen him explore little of the region since his arrival in North Wales and, with the rest of the day promised to be fine, Kath suggested they take a nice Sunday drive out towards Snowdonia, stop off for some lunch and, if they felt they had time, come back via Conwy Castle.

This sounded perfect to Brandt and, as they set out on a twisty but flowing mountain road on which Kath drove with the confidence of someone who had spent their life on similar stretches of tarmac, he reflected on how wonderfully different his life was. Even if it wasn't for the fact he had found true companionship, the setting which he could now call home was so far removed from what he had experienced before as to allow him to pass off his previous existence as an, admittedly long, bad dream.

But this illusion lasted for less than half an hour.

Brandt hadn't yet got around to sharing with Kath his contempt for the majority of radio, and was actually finding the recognisable but insipid sounds of Radio 2 far from bothersome as they wound their way up and around to the Llanberis Pass. Kath hadn't been out for her morning paper since the day Brandt had become more than just a house guest, but he hadn't felt the slightest apprehension as the cheerful disc jockey switched over to the more sombre news presenter at the top of the hour.

It may have only been a quick update ahead of the main programme at lunchtime, but Brandt heard enough to know something was seriously wrong. Hearing a name so familiar, and yet one that had appeared so different, shook him back to reality with such force that he had to ask Kath to pull over, so he could get some fresh air, for fear he may otherwise vomit.

Fortunately, and despite his deliberately polite protestations, Kath had assumed Brandt's sudden change of disposition was the result of her driving being too enthusiastic. And yet this had only removed the most immediate of issues. How was he going to get through the rest of the day without the shocking revelations sufficiently altering his humour to arouse suspicion? What he really needed was time and space to think but he could not, would not, allow whichever sick fuck was committing atrocities in his name to endanger what he had managed to build up with Kath. And yet what had happened would need addressing. His ambivalence towards the copycat murders, a state of mind that had largely remained despite them leading to the exposure of his faked suicide, was now gone. The description of Sarah Donovan's killing was so brief as to almost be non-existent, but that didn't matter to Brandt. It contained one crucial detail: she had been expecting a baby. Brandt wasn't sure whether, at the time of stabbing Sarah, he had intended for her to live, but he remembered being happy when he had heard she was recovering in hospital. Not only had the person who was acting in his name sought to alter the course of history that Brandt had set, but he had taken an innocent life. He knew that people had described his own victims as innocent, but they weren't. They were adults: complicit participants in the society that had allowed itself to become fractured. But a baby, an unborn child, something Brandt had yearned for himself to no avail for so many years, had done nothing to contribute to the ills that blighted modern Britain.

The rest of the day had been excruciating for Brandt but had gone as well as he could have hoped. His initial thought that he would try and end it early, claiming his sudden feeling of sickness was symptomatic of him coming down with some bug or other, had to be dismissed for what he needed to do once they were back at the house. He had known Kath would understand, be concerned even, but to then have to ask if he could use her laptop rather than be tucked safely into bed would seem odd. It wasn't as though he expected her to suspect the real reason for his apparent malaise, but there was every chance she would take the change as him having second thoughts about what had developed between them over the past few days.

Therefore, for things to appear normal, Brandt had been required to continue with their day as planned which, in this context, had meant being exceedingly cheerful and enthralled by where they went and what they saw. He knew from his experience with Franklin, especially when he had been courting their friendship in order to gain the information about DCI Johnson he had required, that, even away from working in the police, he could put on an act. Nevertheless, today had been much harder because he had been constantly dogged by the darkness with which he viewed the recent events in Nottingham threatening to destroy his humour; feigned or otherwise.

So, it had been with tremendous relief that he had finally arrived home and Kath had accepted his suggestion that she run herself a bath to help warm up after the surprisingly cold castle battlements they had scaled. She had demurely enquired whether he wished to scrub her back but seemed equally thrilled that Brandt had been so enamoured with the day that he requested her laptop password, so he could plan their next, similar, trip out.

Safely logged in and with a series of tabs open about Wales' various tourist attractions he could easily switch to if she finished her bath early, Brandt set about accessing the dark web in search of the same software he had used in Spain to hide his IP address.

Having spent the day fighting the urge to just send the text from his phone, now that Brandt had the chance to message Johnson safely, he found himself both nervous and unsure what to write. He had known that the fire at her house might not hide his escape forever but had been certain he would never be communicating with Johnson again. In many respects he felt obliged to enquire how she was, no matter how crass and disingenuous she might receive it, but he resolved that it would be wiser to keep things as simple as possible and stick to the true reason for his contact.

– It wasn't me.

Brandt had sat with the mouse pointer hovering over the send icon for minutes. He didn't doubt that the message was the best representation of how he felt, but he kept going over the implications of the need to send it. If nothing else, it provided a connection with the past he had worked so hard to sever. It wasn't as though he was expecting anything other than bitter hatred and scorn to be flung back at him, but he couldn't allow the atrocity in Nottingham to go unanswered.

With the sound of the plug being pulled from the bath, he finally plucked up the courage to make that final, vital click that would see those simple words fly almost instantaneously across to Johnson. He would have liked nothing more than to have spent the evening waiting to see if a response came through, but he would have to leave checking his emails until the morning. He would insist that he make Kath breakfast in bed as a thank you for the trip out and, whilst hastily knocking up something for them to eat, he could have the laptop next to him in the kitchen.

'Hold on a second my dear, I'll come through with some fresh towels!' Brandt called in the direction of the bathroom, getting up from his seat with a last wistful look back at the computer.

Chapter Twenty-nine

Whilst Brandt had been obliviously enjoying his lie-in with Kath on that Sunday morning, Johnson had been making her way to the police station. She had considered going in the previous evening as soon as she had heard the news, but figured it was better to let them get to grips with the full scale of what they were facing. She also felt that to achieve what she required, Potter would have to be softened up by a sleepless night and the urgent phone calls from the top brass the next morning.

Johnson may not have been invited this time, but she was sure she wasn't going to face the ignominy of waiting for someone to let her into CID. She phoned DC Hardy as soon as she arrived in the car park and he had required far less convincing to come out and meet her than she had been expecting.

'Thanks for this,' she said, getting out of her car as soon as he emerged. There was no point rewarding his help with berating him for his role in the failings of his superiors. Not that Johnson felt completely absolved of all responsibility herself for what had happened to Sarah Donovan. Yet she had come closest to seeing that the railway station wasn't the killer's next destination and, whether fortunate or not, she wasn't the person in charge of the investigation.

At least not at this point.

'No problem, ma'am. Are you here to see the DSI?'

'Yes. How is he?'

'To be honest, I've hardly seen him. He's been holed up in his office most of the night and whenever I've passed by, he's been on the phone.'

'And Fisher?'

'Well…' Hardy paused, unsure exactly how to respond to this. 'I guess you'll see for yourself in a minute.'

'Indeed,' replied Johnson thoughtfully. 'I guess I will. I assume he doesn't know I'm here yet.'

'No, ma'am, I just slipped straight out as soon as I got your call. On that note, when we go in do you mind if I…?'

Johnson laughed. Under normal circumstances she wouldn't have been able to resist mocking Hardy, or anyone for that matter, for their cowardice but today she might need all the allies she could get. 'No problem. I'm sure I interrupted you when you were in the middle of something important that you need to get back to straight away.'

'Thanks, ma'am.'

Nothing further was said between them as they first went into the duty area and then up the stairs towards plain clothes. Once there, Hardy got his wish and managed to let them both in and slip away before Fisher noticed who had arrived to throw a cat amongst the pigeons. The man who had been heading up the team in Johnson's absence, with his back to the door, was deep in conversation with another detective. It only took Fisher a moment to read the surprise on the face of the person who, just a moment before, had been listening carefully to what he was being told, for him to swing around and see Johnson.

She had no intention of engaging with him and instantly moved in the direction of Potter's office. But Fisher had one distinct advantage. Johnson might not be willing to run and give the impression she thought she was doing something wrong, but he had no such qualms. With the long loping stride offered by his lanky frame, he was in front of her before she had even made it halfway across the office.

'What do you want?' he demanded, hatred dripping from his voice. There were to be no games or trading of petty insults today. Things had got far too serious for that.

'If you don't move within the next two seconds, I'm going to put you on your arse right here in front of everybody,' she hissed venomously.

Fisher didn't move and, without further discussion, seemed quite happy to remain there, blocking her path indefinitely.

Johnson thought about reissuing the threat but knew that to do so would just weaken it. As far as she could see, she had two choices: either she carry it out and knock this prick out, or leave and hope she could catch Potter on the telephone. Decision made, she took a step away, so her swing would have enough time and space to gather sufficient momentum. She had already closed her hand into a fist and was pulling it back, observing the look of shocked disbelief in Fisher's eyes, when a shout from ahead of her caused her to stop.

'Stella! I thought I might hear from you today.'

'Coming, guv,' she called, offering Fisher a vicious smile as he moved to one side.

'Lucky escape,' he said, low enough to be out of Potter's earshot.

'For you perhaps,' she muttered in return.

Johnson entered the office and closed the door firmly behind her. In most circumstances, she had resisted Potter's attempts to get her to sit down, but she needed to show that whatever breakdown they had suffered in their working relationship over the past few months wasn't irreparable.

'Look, if you've come to tell me what a shit job we're all doing then you needn't bother. I've had phone calls to that effect all night.'

It wasn't just the rare use of profanity that shocked Johnson, Potter rarely spoke in other than couched phrases about pressure from the top brass.

'Actually, guv, I wasn't but I do think it's a far worse situation than any of us realised.' She could see Potter's eyebrows raise at this rare moment of humility. 'I can imagine how much stick you're getting for Sarah's murder being predictable and that steps weren't taken to ensure her safety.' She raised a finger to stop the response that his open mouth suggested was about to follow. 'But whilst you're dealing with that, the important question is not what happened but what is going to happen next.'

'Go on…' This was the standard non-committal response from Potter for something he had yet to hear enough of to make his mind up about. Johnson had long learned to read the expression behind the bland instruction. She could see that in all the tumult since yesterday, he hadn't even begun to consider what the killer's next move might be.

'Well, I guess the big question is whether he is going to stick with Nottingham or, as Brandt did after three attacks, move further afield.'

'You still don't think this is Brandt then.' Half question, half statement and with none of the surety of their previous discussion as to the likely identity of the attacker.

Johnson now had a difficult decision to make. For all manner of reasons, she was not about to lie to Potter and claim that she knew that the last attack was going to be on Sarah. Rather, the issue was whether she would exaggerate her sense that the station wasn't the right call enough to elevate herself. Concluding that the situation was far more important than her own sense of propriety, she decided she would.

'Yes, and if you had believed me then you wouldn't have gotten into the same situation yesterday.' The words tasted bitter in her mouth, so she continued rather than let them linger too long. 'The very reason why you didn't think to provide extra protection for Sarah yesterday was because it was not something Brandt would do. We both know that if he hadn't intended for her to live when he attacked her, he had ample opportunity to finish off the job before now. If nothing else, look at how he managed to get to me. Twice.'

'Do you think he'll come for you next?'

'No!' Johnson responded, putting her head in her hands. 'That's the complete opposite of what I think! I'm saying that if it was Brandt and he was doing this to somehow tie up loose ends, he would have come for me first.'

She took a deep breath in an effort to calm her voice down. If Potter tired of their conversation, there was nothing stopping him from just kicking her out of his office and the police station altogether.

'Think about it: of everything he tried to achieve and failed to do, is his greatest regret going to be me or her? So, what I'm saying is,' she continued before he could answer the question, 'that if nothing else, yesterday proves this isn't Brandt.'

Johnson waited, watching Potter digest the information carefully. His expression became open, which suggested he was coming around to her way of thinking but then, abruptly, he shook his head. 'Okay, let's just assume, for argument's sake, that I believe this wasn't Brandt's doing. I don't have the luxury of being able to focus on one possibility and dismiss the others, especially if your claim is true, that such a thing led us to getting it wrong yesterday. The fact is that it could be Brandt because he is still at large and so we have to move forward, whilst considering every possibility.'

'And that's why you need me, guv.'

'I hope you're not suggesting you offer yourself up as bait,' Potter said incredulously. 'Again!'

Johnson laughed, openly and heartedly. Much to her surprise, after a few moments Potter followed. The tension that had built up between them, not over the course of the last few minutes, but in the months since she was first attacked, began lifting. More than any apology or attempted justification for the way they had treated one another, the simple act of finding something mutually amusing in such an awful situation served to highlight the strength of the bond they had grown before all of this mess. What Johnson had found funny was that Potter knew her well enough to both jump to such a wild conclusion as to her intentions and, at the same time, be utterly appalled by the idea. She assumed that he had laughed too because he realised she would have expected him to say the exact same thing.

'No, guv, not this time,' she said when they had both calmed down. 'And I would like to point out that I didn't intend the first one.' She found it hard not to succumb to the thought that flashed through her mind that she was making light of the situation that led to McNeil's death.

'And the second?'

'Well, that was just unfortunate timing,' she responded with a knowing smile, before taking on a more serious expression. 'In all honesty, though, I never want to get into a situation like that again. What I'm saying is that you need me. Here. Back at work where I can lead the investigation. You can worry about keeping all the options open and so forth, whilst I can focus on catching that sick bastard.' She could see that Potter was attracted to the idea but was otherwise unsure. 'Look, let me just ask you one simple question. Who does Fisher think killed Sarah?'

'Brandt.' The wholly predictable answer was immediate.

Much in the same way Potter didn't deem it necessary to qualify it or offer any justification, neither did Johnson feel the need to respond. She had done all she could, and it was now up to Potter to make the correct call.

Nevertheless, even though she had shown him all her cards, there was one final thing to add into the mix. They both turned the instant they heard the knock at the door. Under other circumstances, it would have tickled Johnson that whoever it was, in complete contrast to her, was waiting patiently for the invitation to enter.

'Come!' Potter barked impatiently.

'Sorry, guv,' Hardy said, stepping into the office. 'Sorry, ma'am,' he added, which Johnson took as more than mere courtesy given he had been aware that she was here specifically to see the DSI. 'I've got the report back from the forensics.'

'And have you shared this with Fisher yet?'

'No, guv… I thought you might like to see it first.'

'Very well,' Potter said, holding out his hand to receive it. He waited until Hardy was just about to leave and added. 'I'll tell Fisher, once I've looked over it.'

'Very good, sir,' Hardy responded with a deferential bow of the head before closing the door.

'Shit load of DNA was there?' Johnson said as Potter looked at the sheet in front of him.

'Yes, but that's not the question you want to ask.'

'So, what's the answer then?'

'No, it's not Brandt's and no, it doesn't match to anything on file.'

'I see,' she said evenly. It was hard to feel triumphant under such circumstances.

'Look, Stella, I have a number of things I need to sort out. Can I give you a call later today? It'll be tonight I would imagine.'

'Sure thing, guv,' she replied, standing up. She stepped out of the office to see Hardy at his desk with Fisher looming over him. She couldn't hear their conversation, but it didn't take her much to work out that he was pressing Hardy into revealing the details of the forensic report.

'I'll be seeing you,' she called over cheerfully, grateful to do what she could to buy Hardy a little more time. As it transpired, a little was all he needed.

'DI Fisher, step in here please,' came the order from over Johnson's shoulder.

She tried to infer from Potter's tone the exact nature of their meeting but knew that the DSI always tried to be discreet when dealing with a colleague in front of their subordinates. As she left CID and headed down the stairs and towards the exit to the car park, she reflected that, no matter how the phone call with Potter that evening went and what the future for them held, she was glad that today had done something to repair their relationship.

* * *

The contentment Johnson felt soon faded as the hours passed by and she found herself imagining what it must have been like for Sarah's parents to hear the news. To think they would have only just got over the trauma of the last attack and believe she had begun to rebuild her life. Had they known she was pregnant? Johnson couldn't work out which was worse, not having known or having the joy they would have felt snatched from them. And there was also Josh. Josh had been central to Sarah's recovery and, no matter how little Johnson had warmed to him in her dealings with her future husband, she wouldn't have wished anything like that on him.

But what she found strangest of all as she observed the sun going down on what surely would be one of the last warm days before spring, was how she had yet to fully come to terms with the news that Brandt was still alive.

Her thoughts had been centred around what that meant in terms of the person currently killing women in Nottingham, but now that she had made her plea to Potter and was simply waiting for the result, she could begin to explore her own feelings on the matter. The more she thought about it, the more she wondered why he had allowed her to escape. For there was no longer any doubt in her mind that this was what had happened. It wasn't something she would ever share with anyone, because she knew they would point to the fact he had been unsuccessful with his first visit to her house. She wouldn't want to have to get into the details again of how it was only thanks to McNeil's intervention that she didn't find herself raped and murdered.

But what she feared most was that she might not only be accused of somehow wanting to make excuses for Brandt, but that in some small way, the accusation might be valid. Despite everything he had done to her and everything she had been through since, there was something about this new killer that she found even more distasteful. Originally, she supposed it was the lack of imagination where, not only was he a deeply disturbed individual, but an uninspired one at that. However, the killing of Sarah had taken this to an entirely new level.

She couldn't begin to fathom what drove this person to follow Brandt's depravity but unless Potter gave her the news she required, any of her musings would be purely academic. The anxiety over the past 24 hours, along with the fact she hadn't been to the gym that day meant she had little appetite, but she fixed herself some dinner, if nothing else but to use up some time in its preparation.

Having poured a glass of wine to go with the pasta dish, she settled down in front of the television. Just as she was lifting the fork to her mouth for the first time, her phone beeped. Her initial thought was that she must have somehow missed Potter's call whilst in the final throws of assembling her meal, and was surprised it wasn't a message to tell her that she had received a voicemail.

Such a simple message and, to the casual observer, innocent, but the implications for Johnson were massive. *It wasn't me.* It mattered little that she knew it wasn't, the real question was why he wanted, perhaps needed, her to know that. And why now? What was it about the murder of Sarah Donovan that had led to him raising his head? Of course, it might have something to do with the fact that this was the first attack since it had been discovered his suicide had been fake, but Johnson knew it was more than that; it was quite probably the fact that Sarah had been pregnant. On the day when Johnson had visited his ex-wife, Susan had spoken at length about their unsuccessful efforts to have a child, and the effect it'd had on Brandt.

She would make a decision whether to respond and what with, once she had heard from Potter. With her supper now cold and losing what little appeal it had held, she concentrated on drinking her wine instead.

By the time the phone rang, she had reached the stage where she was deciding whether she should slow down or risk getting to the point where she would be unable to resist opening a new bottle.

'Stella. I know I said it would be the evening but I'm sorry it's taken so long.'

From Johnson's experience, commencing a call with an apology wasn't someone starting off on the back foot but was a pre-cursor to them following it with some bad news. 'Not a problem, guv,' she lied, noticing how easily the form of greeting she had always used once again sat so comfortably on her lips. 'Busy day I guess.'

'It was and with much to arrange. It was for that reason I couldn't call you any earlier.'

'Yes?'

'Well, to cut a long story short, we would like you back.' This was the news Johnson had been hoping for from the very moment she had heard what had happened to Sarah Donovan. Yet, and no doubt not helped by the slight fogginess in her mind caused by the alcohol, she wasn't sure how best to respond. 'I need you back,' Potter added after a few moments of silence.

'Do the team know?'

'I wanted to make sure you were on board before making an official announcement.'

'Come on, guv, you know what I'm asking…'

'If you mean Fisher, then yes it's sorted.' Another silence, but this one was entirely deliberate on Johnson's part. She wanted to know what Potter meant by sorted but didn't want to have to ask. 'That was what took most of the day to arrange. He's decided to switch constabulary.'

'Guv?' All sense of playing it cool had gone out of the window with this revelation and her tone was both shocked and desperate to know more.

'Yes. It turns out there's still a shortage at Thames Valley after Franklin and so on. I tried to get him the acting DCI post to cover the person who was promoted to DSI in the interviews that followed Franklin's… er… death. But it was a bit more complicated than I imagined.'

'I bet they'd heard of Fisher and weren't too keen,' she offered, unable to hide her glee.

'Something like that perhaps,' he replied coyly.

Johnson supposed there was no point pushing him any further on the circumstances of Fisher's transfer but, given that what Potter had said already was uncharacteristically candid, she decided to try her luck with one final question.

'How did he take it? Fisher, I mean.'

'How do you think?' Potter replied rhetorically. 'Let's just say he was left with little choice. I wasn't lying when I said the top brass had been on my back. I need you, Stella, and I need us to catch this sick bastard quickly.'

Johnson thought that he had pretty much summed up the situation and there was little more to add at this point. 'I'll see you first thing in the morning, guv.'

'Get some rest, Stella,' he said, signing off.

You're going to need it, she thought, finishing off his sentence. And that was what she intended doing. She would head to bed in a couple of minutes but in the meantime, she would finish off her glass and attempt to deal with the other issue of the evening. If she didn't respond to Brandt, she knew that her mind would not allow her to sleep, no matter how much wine she had consumed.

With the bottle drained but no message yet sent, she made her way out to the balcony. The act of smoking, as much as the nicotine itself, always managed to allow her to think more clearly. Deliberately eschewing a coat and promising herself that she would not be allowed back inside until the job was done, she sparked up her cigarette, perched on her plastic chair and stared at the open, but as yet blank, email.

A couple of minutes later and with the night time chill already causing her to shiver, Johnson punched in her simple reply and sent it before her analytical mind started sowing seeds of doubt.

— *I know.*

Chapter Thirty

'Darling, have you got lost down there?' Kath called softly from upstairs.

'Sorry, just a couple more minutes,' Brandt replied. On reflection, he had been up for quite some time, and had done little in terms of putting together their breakfast, having gone straight to the laptop, convincing himself that he would then prepare the food whilst considering any response he had received from Johnson. But his initial euphoria of finding his message had been answered was met with incomprehension of its true meaning. Of all the various replies he had anticipated, it hadn't been one as simple as this.

— I know.

Even that in itself was ambiguous. Was it that she had known all along that the murders weren't his doing, or was it only after the forensics had come back about Sarah's murder? Moreover, what was the subtext to her answer? He didn't dare hope that it was meant as some form of reassurance and yet why else bother to reply? She would know by now that there was little point trying to trace his IP address so why not just ignore him unless she wanted to strike up a conversation.

Brandt knew he had to be cautious with this. He would not allow the fact he had managed to outwit Johnson in the past to lull him into a false sense of security. She had shown her resourcefulness in tracking him down in Benidorm and the stakes were much higher now that he had seemingly found true happiness with Kath.

He started buttering the toast, having resolved that the best thing to do was nothing at this stage. He had opened the line of communication, which Johnson had accepted. If there was going to be anything more than that, now she needed to take the initiative. Brandt had something very specific he wanted to offer her, but he had to wait until she realised she needed it first.

Satisfied that things were going as well as could be expected under the circumstances, he decided that marmalade on toast constituted a pretty meagre breakfast in bed and started to whisk up some scrambled eggs.

Chapter Thirty-one

'Right, settle down everyone and let's get started.' Johnson was used to her team following her instructions, but it often took a while to get everyone seated for the Monday morning briefing. Under normal circumstances, people were busy swapping stories about what they had got up to at the weekend or, as had been the case over the one just finished, what they had missed as a result of having to work. Yet today, Johnson's words were more out of habit because everyone was already silent and looking at her expectantly.

She allowed herself a slight smile. She hadn't expected to feel quite as nervous as she had driving in to work, and had tried to reassure herself that her few months' absence was small in the context of the many years she had spent in CID. She need not have worried; she could tell from the majority of the expressions that they were pleased to see her back.

Not that she expected it to be entirely plain sailing. There were those on the team who were close to Fisher, even before her absence. Fisher might have been many things, but he knew how to build up a sphere of influence and he was bound to have treated them favourably whilst he was in charge. Johnson was determined not to worry about it until she was back up to speed and would take her time in deciding whether to take a soft approach with them or to squash them quickly. Their behaviour and general demeanour would help her choose what it was to be.

She had long felt certain that her career in the police was something now in the past, but as regarded the people in front of her, many of whom she had selected and nurtured in the few years she had been DCI, she knew that this was where she was meant to be. It would have been better if her return had been under happier circumstances and she knew that this honeymoon period wouldn't last if the results didn't materialise. DSI Potter was under a lot of pressure; the strain of which had been enough to prompt him into taking bolder steps than fitted in with his usual traits. Whilst that had been to Johnson's benefit, she also knew that he would be expecting her to mastermind the turnaround in the department's fortunes the top brass demanded.

'I'll keep this brief as we all have much to do and I want to catch up with each of you individually over the course of the morning to find out where we are with every element of the investigation. You will all have heard the news from forensics that the person we are hunting is not Jeffrey Brandt. I don't know for how many of you this news came as a surprise but let me tell you one thing, there is a clear distinction between following a gut instinct and leading yourself blindly down an alley.' She paused to let these words sink in, staring directly at each of Fisher's cronies. That most of them chose to drop their gaze before she moved on to the next person gave a clear indication of how likely they were to toe the line without her specific intervention, and also the validity of her assessment of how things were being run.

'What I also need you to understand is the important thing here, the only thing, is to catch this killer. We are professionals in a hierarchy who are trained to follow orders, but everyone's opinion is valid. If, in the course of your investigation, you come up with a theory, I want to hear about it. I may not agree with it and I may not choose to run with it, but I need to know it. From what I understand, we have no credible leads at this stage and what that means is that all options are still on the table.'

'By the end of today I want each of them identified and explored so we can start to take an evidence-based approach to elimination. For whilst we don't want to go down these narrow alleyways again, at the same time we won't get anywhere if things remain too open. And to illustrate that point, I still want us to focus on Brandt. He may well not have committed the act but, until we can establish that there is no direct link between him and the attacker, I want that explored. We already know he was a bit of a loner, so finding out whether there was anyone else he was close to, who is either being directed by him or has independently chosen to act in his name, should be relatively straightforward.'

'This leads me onto the second thing I need establishing today. Even if there isn't a direct link between Brandt and the killer, I want to know whether there is evidence of any inside knowledge. By that I mean, is there anything about the three murders that suggests specific knowledge that wasn't in the public domain? This person is trying to either recreate what Brandt did or to achieve what he thinks Brandt failed to. In the former instances, I want to know how closely they were recreated. For example, I know that a swipe of blood deliberately placed on the victim's arm was something of a calling card for Brandt.' She hesitated, wondering whether she should say the next bit, or would that be pushing them too far? No, they had to know that their mistake wasn't just in blindly following Fisher, which many of them would still put down to respect for one's superiors, but in failing to spot something as obvious as this. 'This is how I knew it wasn't

Brandt after the first killing.' Another pause to look carefully around the room. They needed to know that she was the expert here and, more than anything, her own personal experience with Brandt and the losses she suffered were not going to get in the way of her doing the job of which she was capable.

'But the point is this, even if we find out our guy is only going on what he would have been able to find out in the newspapers and on the internet, that in itself gives us plenty to go on. Without the full picture, he would have been filling in the gaps and so, just as I want to know where things exactly match with what Brandt did, I also want to know where they don't. It is these differences that will allow us to build a profile of who this guy really is, in addition to what we already know about people who develop the sort of fanaticism we are experiencing here. To that end, I want more done to look on forums and social media to see the sort of support Brandt might have out there. I don't expect you to find the killer on them, but it will at least give us an insight and, you never know, they may have done some early posting before they got to the stage where they decided they would take their support of Brandt to the next level.'

Johnson took a deep breath. This had been a much longer speech than she had planned but there was much to organise and, truth be told, she was rather enjoying herself. 'Oh, and one other thing before I let you get on with it: we're likely to be pretty stretched for the time being so don't be afraid to call on support from uniform if you just need an extra body and don't require the specialist skills of another detective. If you get in that situation, I suggest that PC Barnes might be worth a try.' In reality, Johnson had barely given a second thought to Barnes, the young recruit who had accompanied her when she had first returned to work following Brandt's attack on her and Potter had been trying to do everything to keep her away from the proper case. Yet she still felt guilty for leaving the station the following morning, when they were meant to be making a follow up visit to the man shot in St. Ann's, without at least saying goodbye. At what was a very challenging time for her, she had appreciated his good humour and sensitivity with avoiding asking her the sorts of questions that were on everyone else's lips. More than that, she could see the foundations of a good copper within him and, in much the same way as she wouldn't allow her experience with Brandt to warp her judgement, she wasn't prepared to have what happened to McNeil prevent her from nurturing young talent.

'Hardy, you're up first,' she called as everyone started to file out. She doubted anyone knew of the contact she'd had with him during her absence, but she still appreciated his act of rolling his eyes and muttering, *why me?* He was complicit in some of the mistakes that had been made but that still didn't stop her being grateful to him for his help, whether at times grudging or otherwise. Moreover, she wanted an opportunity to gain a bit more of an insight into the office politics before tackling some of the trickier members of her team.

Chapter Thirty-two

Brandt's answer to a question that'd disturbed him for the last couple of days had suddenly become clear. Not only did it explain why there was no follow up email from Johnson, it was the best possible news in terms of bringing her to the conclusion he needed her to reach.

There it was in black and white. Johnson had returned to work and was heading up the investigation into the recent murders in Nottingham. This was bound to have been a sanctioned leak to the press and Brandt knew exactly why they had chosen to do this. That they were under a lot of public pressure was obvious, and what better way to try and get some positive reporting for once than to make it known that their star detective was back on the case. For Johnson really was headline news; all the more so because of the mystery that surrounded her after her refusal to engage with any of the, no doubt lucrative, offers to sell her story. The irony of this given her own manipulation of the press in the past didn't escape Brandt, but that was all water under the bridge, and he doubted that the decision to make the press aware of her return was hers. Far more likely it was DSI Potter's. Brandt knew from his few dealings with Potter in the past that he liked to play with a straight bat but, equally, he could imagine what enormous pressure he would be under at the moment and this would buy him a couple of days' worth of goodwill from the top brass.

But more significant than any of this was what it revealed about their current investigation. It told Brandt in no uncertain terms that they weren't close to catching the killer, otherwise they would be simply trying to ride out the current storm in the knowledge that they would soon have some more legitimate good news to share.

The question was how desperate Johnson would need to be to reach out to him. The answer was simple, considering everything Brandt had put her through: very. And even then, would she really seek his help? Really? That was surely far too much to expect. No, he would have to do more to open up the line of communication if there was to be any chance of that happening.

As Brandt typed, with Kath pruning the rose bushes in the back garden, he steeled himself for the inevitable reply. All he was doing at this stage was sowing a seed – one that Johnson would utterly resent and would try and rip up from the ground. But maybe, just maybe, if the police continued to be unsuccessful in their pursuit of the copycat killer, it might germinate and take root.

– Let me help you.

Satisfied he could do no more, and with the rest now relying solely on Johnson, he collected his coat, put on his shoes and joined Kath in the garden. One of the many things he admired about her, and was no doubt a result of living her whole adult life in Wales, was that she never let the weather dent her enthusiasm. And Brandt had to admit whilst stood on the patio, in those few moments before she would notice his arrival, the steady rain and strong breeze was invigorating rather than depressing.

175

Chapter Thirty-three

The positive start to the week soon faded into frustration. On the face of it, they were making progress and, with the whole of the team following Johnson's instructions from Monday's briefing, the things that she wanted established had been achieved. The problem was that none of it was leading them to anything specific.

Whilst she wasn't prepared to rule it out entirely, there appeared to be no direct link between Brandt and the killer. And that was before Johnson received the email from him that was, frankly, baffling. She didn't know the motivation behind offering to help her and she was too busy to spend her time thinking about it. In any case, it was better than having to worry that, however unlikely, he might be contemplating trying to find her for a third time with the intention of finally finishing her off. There had been a moment when she had considered that his offer had been because he knew the identity of the killer and, in a similar way to how he had manipulated Franklin, was looking to use it to push some kind of agenda. But the evidence didn't fit the notion and she reminded herself that she wouldn't allow her personal feelings towards Brandt cloud her judgement.

Johnson didn't do what she should have done and report it. It wasn't like before, where she was intent on keeping things to herself because she was on some kind of vigilante crusade to snare him herself. Rather, she didn't want anything to distract the team from their current focus. Clearly Potter would have to act on it but, deep down, he wouldn't thank her for the information. Johnson didn't know what she was going to do with Brandt once this was all over, but he would just have to wait, despite how callous she knew this made her considering that it was only a few short months ago he had murdered McNeil.

Having found out there was nothing about the killings not already in the public domain, except for the location of Sarah – one of the team showed how it wouldn't take too long to figure that out from Josh's Instagram account – they began trying to build up a profile from what was distinct about his method of killing. The trouble was that to everyone, Johnson included, it didn't really narrow down the field of potential suspects. Things were made worse by the fact that the elements he had copied from the person who had inspired him had been deliberately designed by Brandt in the first place to be so general, like the use of a ubiquitous steak knife, as to give the police little to go on.

As the week wore on, Johnson found herself working more closely with DC Hardy. Her association with him was no longer through a need to find a relatively friendly face, but the more time she spent in his company the more she realised how far he had grown as a detective from the timid but intelligent person she had first appointed a year or so ago. She tried to block out any thoughts about the similarities between him and McNeil, not just because there was no attraction there on either part, but to do so would be too painful.

Hardy possessed the fortunate blend of being both thorough and insightful. He didn't allow his methodical approach and his eye for detail to prevent his mind taking a leap of faith in trying to establish some form of link that wasn't entirely obvious. That proved crucial in a time like this because, when working the evidence didn't lead anywhere, Johnson had to sometimes rely on coming up with a theory which they would then test by seeing whether the evidence could be made to fit.

But try as they might, the evidence either was simply not there or too general to discount enough of these theories to enable them to focus on something in particular.

* * *

'If you think there's someone who could do any better…' Johnson responded with more than a little petulance during her Thursday morning briefing with DSI Potter.

'Look, I'm not saying that, but I had just… hoped that we would be a little further down the line than this.'

'I know, guv, and, believe me, I feel exactly the same way too.' She sighed. 'Look, we'll keep examining and re-examining everything, but I think that, at the same time, we need to start looking ahead to the weekend.'

'You mean, in case there is another attack?'

'Yes. It's not as though there is the same pattern to the timings as we had with Brandt but…'

'Where do you think he is?' Potter interrupted.

'Guv?'

'Brandt, I mean. I know this is a bit off on a tangent, but you must have wondered where he might be.'

Johnson forced herself to think for a moment rather than blurt out an immediate response. She was considering whether the question was quite as innocent as it had been presented. Potter had never been one to play games, preferring instead to take a more direct approach, and there was no way he would know about the emails. But sometimes Johnson herself had stumbled upon something vital whilst asking an innocent question and finding her suspicions raised by receiving an unexpected response. She had to be careful not to make her effort to cover up what little she did know about Brandt fall into the unintended trap of seeing her say something he deemed out of character.

'Yes, I have, and I think he's abroad,' she lied.

'Oh. And why is that?'

'He would have thought that his only chance of escaping back into Europe would have been in the immediate aftermath of the fire.'

'Go on…'

'Not that I like bringing this up again, but he would have expected the body in the house to have been formally identified by dental records. Therefore, it would have made sense for him to flee the country before he expected that to happen. Furthermore, given the couple wouldn't have been reported as missing yet he could have crossed back into France using the same method as he had entered England with.'

'Hmm,' responded Potter, digesting all of this. Finally, he nodded. 'Okay, good. Now, where were we? Oh yes, Saturday.'

'Yes, guv, we have to consider that another attack may be imminent.'

'But where, Stella?'

'That's the thing. With hindsight, last Saturday may have been predictable but it's certainly not this time around. He's done Brandt's three attacks in Nottingham, but there's nothing to say he won't just revisit them again so we need police out in each location.'

'I'll phone the DSIs in charge of each of those,' Potter responded, reaching for the phone on his desk. Johnson could see the hope in his eyes that a bit of the pressure might be taken off them if the killer elected to switch areas.

'Of course, there is another possibility,' she added, waiting for him to replace the receiver in its cradle. 'He might decide now is the time to branch out on his own. But that might not be a bad thing because it could help us better identify which elements of the killings are of his own design rather than simply trying to follow Brandt's example. Also, without Brandt's unique experience, he might slip up with the location he selects, and we might be able to trace him from CCTV or whatever.'

'Fine. Let's just hope that if he does decide to go rogue then he sods off and does it somewhere else.'

Johnson uttered a laugh that she hoped Potter wouldn't realise was false and went back to her office. She could completely understand why he felt that way, but the last thing she wanted was the complication of having to work with other constabularies. The thought put her in mind of the press conference following the murder in Milton Keynes. It was there she had met Franklin and had seen the delight in his eyes at the media circus finally stopping in his town. They may never know the extent of his involvement in what Brandt did but even if, as Johnson suspected, it was little, she didn't feel a great deal of sympathy towards him. Not that she couldn't see the similarities between Franklin being happy that the notorious serial killer had visited his patch and Johnson not wanting the copycat to stray from her territory. And yet there was one crucial difference that separated them: Franklin wanted it for his own personal gain whereas her motivation was purely from a desire to bring this reign of terror to an end.

Chapter Thirty-four

'I guess it's now or never,' Brandt muttered to himself as he logged on to the computer. He had resisted the urge to check the night before, even though he knew that day would prove crucial in terms of whether there was a chance that Johnson would accept his offer of help. If nothing else, Kath was becoming a little put out by his, seemingly newfound, interest in the world wide web.

He didn't know if Johnson had truly expected another attack the Saturday following the murder of Sarah Donovan and her husband, but he did know that they would have been on high alert in case there was one. With all the pressure they were undoubtedly under, they couldn't afford any room for complacency.

Whilst Brandt had been nervous to finally meet Kath's friends, at least it had been a welcome distraction from pondering what was going on elsewhere. The day went well, and he believed the comments about what a nice couple they made not just been born out of politeness. More than that, he had genuinely enjoyed the company of a larger group and it was with a tinge of regret that he reminded Kath they had agreed not to stay out too late. He could tell from her reaction that she saw his keenness to get home was because he had something intimate in mind, but he was not displeased and, after insisting they catch up with the day's news, he duly obliged satisfied in the knowledge that nothing untoward had occurred in Nottingham.

— Are you looking for redemption?

Judging by how late Johnson had sent the message and the sort of long and frustrating day she would have experienced, he doubted she would be out of bed for a few hours yet.

Not that he had an instant response in mind anyway. He supposed he shouldn't be too surprised that she hadn't chosen to say yes or no and instead was enquiring as to his motivation. But redemption was a bit strong. The fact he was sat there pondering it for so long made him realise Johnson was hardly likely to have just rattled off the first thing that came into her head either. It was entirely possible she knew that he would be shocked by the question and so it would have been deliberate on her part. To say she was likely to be wary of him would be an understatement and why would she expect him to answer a simple question about his motivation truthfully? As a consequence, she could be trying to provoke him into revealing the reason why he was offering to help her by suggesting something it clearly wasn't.

— No.

Sometimes the best response was the simplest. He might have thought differently had her question come through immediately after his last email, but something had changed her previous stance of ignoring his offer. That could only mean that she was at least leaning towards acceptance and so all he now needed to do was to keep on leading her down that path.

— Well you can't have it. Not after what you have done.

The ping of the incoming message was surprisingly swift, and Brandt had expected to need to find another excuse to use the laptop later in the morning. This was good because it meant if he kept up the momentum, they might enter into a conversation that led to a conclusion. Of course, he needed to be careful in his haste not to write something he later came to regret, but Johnson was in the same boat and her speedy response was the first show of emotion.

> — *You assume by referring to redemption that I now see my actions as wrong.*

Bold, but perhaps it wouldn't do any harm to establish a certain amount of control. No matter how aggrieved Johnson may feel, Brandt still had something she wanted.

> — *You killed McNeil. And nine other innocent people.*

Brandt found it interesting that she chose to just refer to his name rather than the nature of his relationship to her but, more importantly, he was sure that this was a test. Johnson was using this to establish whether there could be any basis on which they could form a working partnership. He didn't want to retract the power of his earlier statement but to revel in the death of the man she had grown close to was likely to see this exchange terminated prematurely.

> — *It was not my intention to kill McNeil.*

> — *But you meant to kill me.*

The immediacy of her reply not only implied that she found his response acceptable but his thoughts about it being a test were correct. And yet Brandt suspected that this new message was the real trial. If she caught him out on what she believed was a lie then, again, it limited his chances of her accepting his help.

> — *I did the first time.*

He waited nervously and wasn't sure that every moment that passed without an incoming email was a good or bad sign. Even if Johnson hadn't wondered how she had managed to escape the fire in the weeks that had followed, surely the revelation that Brandt had faked his suicide would have caused her to reassess whether anything that had happened in her house that evening had been as it seemed. In addition, he hoped that his answer would do more than just indicate the sincerity in his offer to help identify the copycat killer. The subtlety of this confirmation that he no longer wanted her dead would do far more to allay any fears she may hold about her personal safety than any direct reassurance he tried to offer her.

'Damn it,' he muttered, hearing Kath stirring upstairs. He needed to see this through without being disturbed by her. His hopes that she might shower before coming down were dashed when he heard her bare feet padding along the wooden floor boards of the landing.

Brandt knew he could find a reasonable explanation for being on the computer so early, but he couldn't afford to have her trying to look over his shoulder. Instead, he picked up the laptop and went into the seldom-used dining room, taking a seat facing the doorway.

'Morning love,' Brandt called cheerfully as she passed. 'There's plenty of tea in the pot,' he added so that she wouldn't choose to linger too long.

'You're up early,' she said, carrying on into the kitchen.

'Yeah, slept like a log and just woke up fresh and raring to go.'

'What are you doing in there?'

'Well, call me silly but I was just doing a bit of daydreaming. I was looking at holidays next summer just in case I manage to pick up a job in the new year. I hope you don't mind.'

'Feel free, just make sure it's somewhere warm. Can I pour you another cup before I crack on with knocking us up a spot of breakfast?'

'I'm fine, thanks,' Brandt responded, trusting that the conversation was now over, and he would be left in peace to finish his important business. Kath was neither the greatest nor the fastest cook in the world and he estimated he should have a good 10-15 minutes to wait for Johnson to reply.

With the clashing of pots and pans indicating that it would be a while yet until she called him in to eat, the ping of an incoming email finally sounded.

– How do you propose to help?

Chapter Thirty-five

Johnson was relieved to find CID quiet when she went in that Sunday afternoon. It seemed that everyone, Potter included, had taken the one positive out of yesterday which was that they could spend a rare few hours with their family and friends. All except DC Hardy, that was.

'What are you doing here?' she asked, trying to make any inference of an accusation sound like mere concern for his wellbeing.

'I could pose you the same question, ma'am. Didn't you say that you were going to take the day off unless something cropped up overnight?'

'Yeah well, I just thought I would pop by and catch up with some paperwork,' she replied casually, already heading toward the confines of her office.

She hadn't expected Hardy to follow her in. 'Can I help you with any of it, ma'am?'

Johnson allowed a small smile to form on her lips. *Yeah, sure. Pull up a chair and help me send across all our confidential and highly sensitive documents to a serial killer. You know the one, the chap that nearly raped me and then killed McNeil. Yes, that's it, the one who tried to burn my house down with me in it.*

'Nah, it's alright. It should only take a few minutes and, besides, don't you have somewhere better you can be on a Sunday afternoon?'

'Well, as it happens, I was planning on going to the pub to watch the football.'

'Sounds fun,' she lied.

'Why don't you come, ma'am? It's just a couple of the boys from here and a few from uniform. Should be a good match.'

For one dreadful moment, she wondered whether this was his way of trying to ask her out. But a quick study of his face, with its open expression, and not to mention its obvious youthfulness, was enough to convince her she was just being silly and, despite everything, a little arrogant. 'Thanks, but I am overdue a session at the gym. Another time maybe.'

'Sure thing, ma'am,' he said chirpily, heading back to his desk.

A few minutes later, and having gathered what she could electronically, Johnson contemplated how best to do this. She could create a drop box and provide Brandt with the password but, and she thought this may just be a sign of her age, she didn't feel comfortable with the idea of all these files existing somewhere on the internet just for some spotty teenage hacker to find it. Not that the alternative of sending it through in a series of emails seemed any better.

With them all neatly arranged, ready for her to click the send button on each, she considered the full implication of her actions. This wasn't just crossing a line, it was leaping straight over it and giving it the finger as she went. Not only was a substantial stretch in prison assured if this came out, there was nothing to say that this wasn't Brandt's new way to get at her.

It wasn't as though he hadn't tricked her before, and all he would need to do this time would be to forward on the emails to internal affairs and that would be that. But whilst her brain was screaming at her to reconsider, her gut was telling her that it was a chance worth taking. Not only had Brandt proven that he favoured a more hands-on approach to dealing with people with whom he held a grudge, but there was something about his answers to her questions that morning that made her think his offer to help was genuine. Perhaps in some warped way he did think that helping her catch this killer would provide him with some form of redemption. Regardless, she felt she owed it to Sarah Donovan to take whatever risk was required to catch her killer.

'Whatever it takes,' she whispered, tears beginning to form in her eyes at the cruel irony of those all-too-familiar words. McNeil's sister had spoken them to her at the funeral and now fate had conspired to see her enlist the help of the man she had hunted across the continent in order to catch a different murderer.

'I'm off now, ma'am!' Hardy called as he got up from his desk.

'Wait!' Johnson shouted back. If left on her own she would agonise over the difficult decision she had to make for the rest of the day. Sending these emails was not to say she couldn't try and catch Brandt again at a later date. Regardless of her personal feelings and what she still owed to McNeil, there was a more pressing concern.

'The enemy of my enemy is my friend,' she muttered bitterly as she left her office.

'What's that, ma'am?'

'Oh, nothing, Hardy. Thanks for waiting. Thought you might like to walk me back to my car.'

'Sure thing, ma'am.'

Chapter Thirty-six

'Let me cook you dinner.'

'What?'

'Dinner, silly. I want to cook you dinner. These last few weeks have been really special, and I wanted to say thanks.' Mandy held up the shopping bags to indicate that the decision had already been made and he had better accept her offer, and graciously at that.

'Erm, sure. Come on in,' Jack replied rushing over to his bed to try and flip the duvet over the sandwich packet, its contents consumed less than an hour before. Lack of appetite or not, he liked just how grown up it all felt. A few short months ago he was living with his parents, working at that café and trying to pluck up the courage to ask someone out for the first time in his life. Now here he was, in his own place and with his girlfriend about to prepare them a meal. All very mature.

And yet that wasn't the only thing that made Jack feel grown up. He had completed his transition into manhood by successfully following in Brandt's footsteps. The journey back after killing Sarah Donovan had been the longest in his life. Although the sirens his ears strained to hear never materialised, he was sure someone would notice the blood splatters on him that he had tried so hard to conceal. Arriving at his room and being able to get washed and changed did little to allay his fears, especially when news of what he had done surfaced before the day was out. He really should have thought to close the victims' front room curtains so that when their visitors arrived, whoever they were, they would not have seen Sarah's lifeless body through the window.

The deep anxiety had lasted for most of the following week, but it conspired to strengthen his relationship with Mandy. Certain that at any moment the police would storm in to arrest him, he was determined to make the most of the little time he had left. Not only had he spent as many occasions with her as possible, but on the Sunday night as he lay awake once more listening out for the rush of footsteps down the corridor, he roused Mandy to tell her he loved her. It wasn't so much her response that she loved him too that gave him the greatest satisfaction, more that in the moment of saying it he realised he truly meant it.

In the days that followed, he pondered whether the absence of an urge to kill was like that of an alcoholic waking up after a particularly heavy bender and vowing not to drink again, and whether once he had recovered from the effects of what had happened, he would be compelled to resume his habit. But as the longest, and in a bizarre way the best, week of his life moved into the weekend and he started to believe he had got away with it, his thoughts hadn't turned to planning another murder.

This had pleased Jack because he could focus his efforts on his blossoming relationship with Mandy and ensuring that he did enough work to feel confident of passing his end of year exams, thereby ensuring he could remain at university. He hoped when they moved out of halls in their second year, they would be able to get a place together, just the two of them.

Not that Jack's happiness and focus on the future didn't stop him wondering why he no longer felt inclined to continue the thing that had been his sole reason for coming to this part of the country. Brandt had gone on to kill elsewhere and, although Jack hadn't been sure he would seek to switch location himself, he had believed that once he had replicated Brandt's Nottingham murders, he would look to branch out on his own. The single question in his mind as he planned how to get to Sarah was whether he would tie up the only loose end that remained: DCI Stella Johnson. The ease establishing where Sarah lived wasn't the key reason why he targeted her first. He knew that killing her would be far easier: Johnson was a copper, which was intimidating enough, and she had managed to foil Brandt twice.

Jack had known from the moment he had arrived back in his room following Sarah's murder that he would never go after Johnson; a resolution that didn't wane as his immediate fear of detection wore off. Even if he somehow managed to work out where she was now staying, he knew that it would be a step too far. He may never be truly certain why Brandt hadn't managed to kill Sarah, but if he'd wanted Johnson finished off then he would have to do that himself. With the news that Brandt was still alive, there was no longer the need to continue his work and Jack could settle on finding his own path in life, and preferably one that was far less dangerous.

Not that he wanted to forget the past. It had brought him to this moment of pure contentedness, where his girlfriend wanted to show her love for him by cooking a special dinner. And should he ever need reminding of everything he had gone through in order to get to this point, he need only retrieve his steak knife and relive that glorious moment when he had plunged it into Sarah's exposed flesh.

'Shit!' Mandy cursed loudly, rousing Jack from his thoughts. She was sat in the middle of the room, with the contents of her shopping bags strewn around her.

'What is it?' Jack asked, genuinely concerned.

'I forgot to buy the wine!'

He gave a hearty laugh full of contentment. If a reminder was needed how far they had come, then their biggest concern being that Mandy had forgotten the wine was it. 'Don't worry, I think I still have a few more beers in that box down there,' he said, pointing to an untidy heap of random items under his desk.

'No, Jack! We're going to do this properly. I went to the actual supermarket and everything. Be a love and nip to the shop and get us a bottle.' She fixed him with a glare that dared him to refuse. 'And don't go buying any of that cheap three quid shit. The purpose isn't to get drunk but to have a nice accompaniment for our supper.'

'Accompaniment for our supper,' Jack mimicked, good-naturedly. 'If only your left-wing anti-capitalist mates could see you now!'

'Oi! If you want to eat all this nice food rather than wear it, I suggest you piss off to the shop right now!' Mandy shouted, lobbing a packet of organic tomatoes on the vine at him for good measure.

Jack arrived back half an hour later to find Mandy trying to get out of the communal kitchen whilst holding a plate in each hand. 'Get that for me, will you?' she asked as Jack reached for the door. 'I was starting to think you'd done a runner.'

'The shop only had cheap shit, so I had to go to the off-license outside Uni.'

'There's a good boy. I may well house train you yet!' she said, offering him a wink. 'I've left all the stuff in the sink for now. Do you think the other people in the block will mind?'

'Nah, fuck 'em. They're messy enough themselves.'

The pasta dish Mandy had cooked may have been relatively simple, but it was a wonderful dinner. With the desk pulled out, she had sat on the wooden chair and Jack was forced to reach up from the much lower lounge seat. As they ate their food and drank their over-priced wine, they fantasised that they were sat at a nice restaurant somewhere in Italy.

'I guess we should think about cleaning up,' Mandy said reluctantly once they were finished.

'Ah, shame, I forgot about that.'

'You're not at home now, posh boy, where you can just click your fingers and the maid will come in and clear away the dishes and do the washing up.'

Jack opened his mouth to protest but then closed it again. He supposed it was fair retaliation for his earlier comment about Mandy's bourgeois attitude towards wine.

'I'll wash up and you can dry,' he said, getting up and chucking her a pristine tea towel from the unused set his Mother had packed him off with.

Despite Jack's earlier bravado, they were relieved to find the communal kitchen was empty and with no signs of anyone having been there in the meantime. As promised, Mandy had neatly stacked everything in the sink and Jack rummaged through the cupboards looking for the bottle of cheap washing up liquid that someone had left ages ago.

Having finally retrieved it and with Mandy waiting expectantly by the draining board, he started removing the sink's contents, so he could fill it with hot water.

'You seem to have used every pot and utensil I own,' he teased pulling them out one by one for effect.

Suddenly, it felt like his heart had stopped dead in his chest.

He was holding the steak knife.

Mandy must have noticed his hesitation. 'I tried using a butter knife, but it only squashed the tomatoes rather than cut them. If your mother remembered to buy you tea-

193

towels she really should have thought to also get you a set of…'

'You went through my drawers?' Jack interrupted incredulously.

'Don't worry, I didn't find any pornos,' Mandy laughed, clearly not yet sensing the change of mood. 'I thought you might have a pair of scissors or something; anything with a half way sharp edge I could use.'

'You went through my drawers?' he repeated, his tone now less of shock and more of accusation. He regarded the serrated blade and his fears were confirmed when all he could see was a slight smear of juice from a tomato and a milky smudge that had presumably come from slicing the mozzarella.

All traces of blood were gone.

'I'm sorry,' Mandy replied defensively. 'Although which is weirder, the person who hunts around for something to allow them to prepare dinner or someone who keeps dirty steak knives in a separate drawer to their cooking utensils?'

Jack didn't respond; couldn't respond. He could feel the rage building inside him. After everything he'd done, this nosey bitch had taken his one memento of what he had achieved. The steak knife had been his trophy, something to be celebrated and revisited when he needed reminding of the extent of his capability and, thanks to her thoughtlessness, it had been reduced to the by-product of a decidedly average meal.

'Jack,' she said, twisting him around so he was facing her. The silence had clearly given her time to think as well. 'What are you doing with a dirty knife in your drawer anyway?'

He swallowed down the anger. Regardless of what a disaster this was for him, it could not be rectified by berating her. Sarah's blood was gone and there was little point adding to his loss by scaring off Mandy. Worse still, the more he made of this situation, the more she was likely to find his attachment to the knife suspicious. With that in mind he needed to answer her question.

'Well, you see,' he said offering what he hoped appeared a coy smile. 'I took it that night we first went for dinner.' Jack could see her look of concern start to be replaced by one of confusion. 'I didn't know if it was going to lead anywhere but I… I had such a good time that if it wasn't to be repeated then I wanted a… a keepsake from our time together.'

Mandy let out a nervous laugh. 'Okay, that's just totally weird. And more than a little gross I might add. I was ages scrubbing off the remnants of your steak before I could use it, by the way!' She stopped to study him more closely and Jack tried to read what was going through her mind. 'I suppose,' she finally added, 'that it's kind of cute in a strange sort of way. But now that I know how odd you are, now's the time to confess if you took any of my used underwear from the laundry pile when you scarpered off early the next morning.'

'I swear, I didn't,' Jack responded with a laugh he didn't feel inside. He might have been relieved that he had managed to smooth things over with Mandy but that didn't remove his main concern. Would he continue to feel differently now he had nothing to remember his achievements by?

Chapter Thirty-seven

Brandt closed the laptop lid with a satisfied sigh. He didn't like to admit it, but he was enjoying doing some detective work, albeit remotely. Now having been on both sides of the fence he could see how comparable the thrill of the chase was between someone identifying their next victim and the person tasked with catching the murderer. The only real frustration with having to rely solely on the information that was fed through to him, was that he couldn't then act on his findings. Nevertheless, it hadn't taken him much studying of the available evidence to start to build up a picture of their quarry. It wasn't just his first-hand experience of killing, Brandt had progressed in the police force because of his ability to put himself in the mind of the person he was hunting. Perhaps it was that over-exposure that had begun to lead him down an alternative path but there was no point dwelling on that now.

That Johnson had also demonstrated a similar quality hadn't escaped Brandt. He may have managed to stay one step ahead on more than one occasion, but she had got far closer to him than anyone else. It wasn't just for this reason he was going to make her work for the breakthrough she so desperately craved. He considered it a bit like looking after a dangerous breed of dog. One of the things you were never meant to do was to feed it before you ate your own meal. As soon as it started to think it had the upper hand, it would seek to exploit that. Similarly, if you didn't feed it there was every chance it might view you as surplus to requirements and turn on you.

That Johnson remained a wild animal was in no doubt in Brandt's mind. Given the slightest opportunity, he was sure that she would end this uneasy alliance and track him down. Not that he was seeking to string this out: the very reason why he had risked contacting her is that he wanted this killer caught before he could commit more abhorrent acts in his name, but he didn't want to give away his true value too quickly. If nothing else, it would spoil his fun.

'Kath dear? Do you fancy a walk to the pub tonight?' he called along the corridor as he headed to the sitting room. 'What's the matter?' Brandt asked as soon as he found her.

'Oh, it's nothing, why don't you head on down without me?'

Brandt took a seat in the armchair opposite. 'The only reason why I suggested it is because I thought you might like it. I certainly don't want to go there without you.' He was excellent at spotting when someone was lying, as well as holding something back. Equally, he also knew how best to draw the truth out and, with Kath, a considered and measured approach was more effective than tackling it head-on.

'Perhaps an early night would do me some good,' she replied flatly.

'Cracking idea!' Brandt declared with enough enthusiasm to ensure she felt he had misread her intentions.

'No, I didn't mean it like that!' Kath responded firmly.

Confident the trap was set, it was now time to spring it. 'Oh,' he said, putting on his best crestfallen expression and getting up as though to walk out. 'I'm sorry. I guess I have been getting a little carried away with… you-know-what since we got together. It's just… oh never mind,' he said sadly, reaching the door.

'No, Greggy, wait!' Kath called out.

Bingo! Brandt thought, turning back to look at her.

'Hold on, there is something. Please, will you sit down?'

'Sure, but whatever it is I want you to know that I didn't mean to upset you and I promise not to do it again.'

The hesitation once he was sat down as well as the uncertain look on Kath's face indicated that she was still unsure whether she should raise her concern.

'We mustn't hide our feelings from one another,' he prompted gently.

'Well, I suppose that's it in a way,' she began finally. 'I'm a little concerned how much time you're spending on the internet.'

Brandt had to work extremely hard to stifle a laugh and hoped that he had successfully masked it with a fake cough. 'The internet?' He supposed he shouldn't be too surprised. Although he had told Johnson he would restrict their contact to twice a day, once in the morning and then again in the evening, now he thought about it, the regularity would seem in contrast with his claim that its use was for casual purposes.

'Yes,' she replied awkwardly. 'I'm not some kind of IT specialist, but I do read a lot in the news and I understand that these things can become quite addictive.'

'These things?'

'Pornography,' she whispered, as though the very mention of the word would soil her.

This time no amount of coughing would be able to conceal Brandt's mirth. He knew that it would work contrary to his efforts to resolve things with Kath, but he was helpless to resist.

'You think I'm on there looking at… inappropriate images?' he asked as soon as he calmed down.

'I hear the web is riddled with it!' Her haughty tone and Daily Mail attitude really was making her show her true age, but there wasn't the slightest chance Brandt would dare point that out to her.

'Well, that's probably true,' he conceded. 'But I promise you I'm not accessing pornography. I can show you my browser history if you like.'

'I've also read that it can be easily doctored.' However, this was presented more as a statement of fact than a suggestion that Brandt would have done this. Nevertheless, he had to admit that she was pretty clued up about things and he was glad that, as well as always disguising the IP address when contacting Johnson, he ensured that he opened plenty of pages pertaining to whichever topic of research he was claiming to be completing.

He got up from his seat and knelt down beside her, pleased to see that she didn't try and pull her hand away when he grasped it. 'I promise you Kath, I don't have the slightest interest in seeing anything like that. I have you now and that's all I want.' He regarded her carefully, hoping that the tears he could see welling in her eyes were a good thing. 'Years ago, I had given up hope of ever finding love again, much less developing a physical relationship.'

He waited as she stared down at him, wondering whether adding anything more would help or serve to undermine what had already been said.

'Perhaps we should have that early night after all,' she eventually said.

Chapter Thirty-eight

'He better have something good for me,' muttered Johnson, stalking back to her office. No sooner had she arrived at the station than Potter had wanted to meet with her. It turned out that the top brass and the media weren't the only ones pushing them for a result. There were reports that Fisher was kicking up a bit of a stink over at Thames Valley. Rather than take his transfer with good grace, it seemed like he was attempting to ingratiate himself with his new colleagues by bad mouthing everyone back in Nottingham. In many respects, it was to be expected; what wasn't was that he was finding himself something of a receptive audience. Whilst Franklin may not have been the most popular of DSIs, many of the people there resented what they had seen as an attempt by Nottingham to push the blame from Brandt to Franklin. Rather than Fisher admit his ultimate culpability in this, he had been using it as a way to get back at Potter and was now claiming his very speaking out about it was the reason why he had been moved elsewhere.

Not that Johnson had got away scot free in all of this. Fisher was claiming that her insistence that Brandt had nothing to do with these latest murders was down to

Stockholm Syndrome. Whilst accepting these accusations were just the bitter feelings of an incompetent little twat, the combined effects of his mudslinging was that Nottingham CID was under even more pressure to deliver a result, and time was running out. The top brass were even starting to call into question Potter's decision to reinstate Johnson to head up the investigation. It seemed that the winds of favour changed direction fast, given that little more than a week ago they were leaking the news to the press in order to gain a little bit of respite from all the negativity.

As Johnson sat down at her desk and entered the password for her computer, she could see how this was likely to play out. If things remained as they were, or worse still there was another murder with no immediate lead to the killer, at some point in the next couple of weeks someone would visit Potter in an unofficial capacity and ask him whether he had ever considered taking early retirement. He would baulk at the suggestion and they would tell him that he should perhaps take some time to consider the generosity of the package on offer. The only drawback, they would contend, was that it was time sensitive and he had 24 hours in which to accept, otherwise it would revert to the standard, and much less lucrative terms. Johnson liked to think that Potter would tell them where to stick their early retirement, but he would also know what would happen next if he refused. The man would simply shrug and suggest that he shouldn't be so hasty and explain that the offer would remain on the table for the time period stated.

The following morning would come a call from someone from the top brass, most likely the person Potter believed himself closest to. They would claim they were phoning in an entirely unofficial capacity and would make all the right noises of understanding whilst he sounded off about what was happening. What they would then do is confide in him that they couldn't consider themselves a friend if they did not share with them the rumour they had been told. They would couch it suitably vaguely to allow deniability should Potter decide to kick up a fuss, but would say there was a concern of improper conduct that was sufficient to see internal affairs interested. He would depart by offering his strong advice, as a friend still of course, that Potter accept the offer made to him the day before.

Johnson had been in the police long enough to know that if internal affairs dug around anywhere for long enough, something would crop up. It wouldn't matter whether Potter heeded the writing so clearly daubed on the wall – the upshot would be the same. Within a relatively short period of time and either because he had retired or been suspended, pending further investigation, he would no longer be DSI. And the first order of business for the new incumbent would be a reshuffle of the team which would see Johnson marginalised so that the best she could look forward to was the kind of bullshit case Potter had placed her on when she had first returned to the station. If she wanted a generous pay-off, she would have to go hunting for it because they would rather see her wither away somewhere than risk the sort of publicity the news of her departure might bring.

And yet she didn't find all of this completely depressing. When committing the highly illegal breach of security that saw her share the case files with Brandt, she had tried to convince herself that the ends would justify the means. Her discussion with Potter only confirmed that this was an enormous risk worth taking.

But that was only if Brandt's help led them to the killer.

> – *I need you to stop messing around and tell me exactly what you've got.*

Johnson knew that he was likely to derive great satisfaction from her first message of the day. She didn't believe he was trying to patronise her but, for whatever reason, Brandt seemed intent on treating her more like a mentee than a partner in this. Rather than tell her what he thought of the evidence she had sent him, he was resorting to questions that were designed to make her think. At the best of times, she had been an awkward student to those who attempted to teach her, always wanting to work at her faster, more furious pace.

Clicking away from her personal email, one she had set up specifically for communicating with Brandt when she had discovered his direct involvement in Franklin's death, she decided that she could do her bit to speed up communications. She would knock off early so that she would be at home and on her laptop for when Brandt logged on this evening. That way she could ensure there was more of a dialogue than passing messages like ships in the night. If needed, she would tell Potter she was revisiting the crime scene in the morning to allow herself enough space to converse with Brandt undisturbed then as well.

Chapter Thirty-nine

Brandt wasn't surprised that his email that evening elicited an immediate response. Her impatience was demonstrably clear and Johnson being the woman of action he had come to know, he had expected little else than her now undivided attention. That she would have to think on her feet lest she risk losing their communication also pleased him.

> *– Let me put it in simpler terms for you. What sort of a person seeks to copy others?*

> *– Those who lack imagination?*

> *– Not true! The very thing they are doing is imagining themselves in the shoes of the person they are seeking to replicate. Try again…*

> *– Impressionable?*

> *– Much better. Good in fact. Now run with that for a moment.*

> *– Could be someone who is vulnerable. Perhaps they have been damaged by something in their past.*

— True, but that could be anyone. Which is of no help. Try and think broader. What people are most likely to be impressionable?

— The young.

— Bingo!

— Is that it?! You could have told me that without getting me to send you all the files.

— Yes, I could... but I didn't KNOW it was someone young at that stage.

— Go on...

Brandt let out a small titter of pleasure. He was enjoying this. Not only had he found his analytical mind was a prominent muscle that had needed little attention in order to get back into perfect shape, but to display it, parade it even, in front of his fiercest critic was providing him with a source of great entertainment.

— How did his killings differ from mine? For the moment let's leave out the unfortunate business with Sarah Donovan.

— The main differences were in the nature of the stabbings themselves. As you will have seen from the photographs, they were less focused.

Brandt smiled. He had nearly forced her into a compliment and he wasn't going to let her get away with being quite so vague. *Less focused?* He could imagine how frustrated she would be at his deliberate obtuseness.

— Yours were more targeted.

— And his?

— Less controlled. More sporadic.

— More vicious? Tell you what, you don't need to answer that. Ah, the exuberance of youth!

– How can you be so certain?

– Well perhaps we could dismiss his first act in Nottingham as the product of all that nervous tension. Leading him, if you like, to overdo it a little.

– But your first wasn't like that…

– No, but we'll come to that later. Instead, let us visit Sarah Donovan's house.

– What about it?

– It displayed a certain confidence wouldn't you say? And I don't just mean in terms of going around to a house this time, knowing that her husband was also likely to be there. Tell me about the manner in which he dealt with Mr Ramage?

– Well obviously you've read the report so I assume you're asking me what I make of it. It shows a confidence, not just in that he was prepared to take on Josh, but how effectively he dispatched him.

– Yes, no over exuberance there, just a nice little slash to the throat followed up by a solid stamp to the head.

– There's no need to sound so proud of it…

– Tsk-tsk Miss Johnson, and we were starting to get on so well. Instead of petty jibes why don't you focus on the contrast between that and poor Sarah…

– Okay, so you've made your point. He is far less controlled than you were because he chooses to be. And that means he must be someone young?

– Put it all together and it does. There is no agenda here which suggests a lack of life experience. That there seems to be no sexual motivation either also suggests that he may appear on the outside as someone who is well-adjusted. Perhaps he even has a girlfriend.

And like all ambitious, intelligent young people he soon grew tired of following my example and wanted to go beyond what I did. For if he were just some unimaginative traumatised loser who you originally depicted him as, he would still be painting by numbers and sticking to replicating what I did rather than what he thought I had been trying to do.

— So, what is he going to do next?

— Have you ever considered he might come for you?

— Do you really think so?

— No. Perhaps he might have done before Sarah but if he is to kill again then it's going to be something different.

— Like what?

— I haven't got the first idea what. But that's the point. Sarah Donovan was the transition to him breaking his ties with me. There's a chance he will consider himself finished for that is the folly of the young. One minute's obsession is replaced the next moment by something new and more exciting.

— So that's it, he's just stopped now?

— I didn't say he HAS stopped, I said he might have. Regardless, there's no point trying to predict what he will do next because it is unpredictable. His next kill would be new and distinct because it would no longer be tied to me. It would be like hunting for a new killer again.

— So how the hell do we stop him?

— By focusing on the past rather than the future.

— Go on...

— If only I could but, unlike you Miss Johnson, I have plans this evening. But whilst I'm out enjoying myself don't consider yourself left without anything to do. If you read back through the thread of this conversation you might find you no longer require my assistance. Ta ta x

'Are you out of the bath yet, dear?' Brandt called up the stairs.

'Yes,' came the irritable reply. 'I'm already dressed and unless you do the same in the next five minutes, we're going to be late.'

'Shame,' Brandt muttered under his breath. His email exchange with Johnson had made him rather hope he would find Kath still with just a towel wrapped around her.

Chapter Forty

The thought of that murdering bastard out enjoying himself wasn't the main reason why Johnson found herself restless that night. It wasn't even the fact that he would know she would be deeply irritated by it. It was the smug way in which he had left her dangling. Without doubt they had made progress but rather than either reveal the full extent of his insight into the killer, or simply say he'd had enough for the evening, he had cryptically suggested she would find the rest of the answer buried in their conversation.

She might have believed him to be telling the truth, but it didn't stop her feeling a fool as she read and reread the email chain. What's more, revisiting what he had typed only served to make her feel more resentful of the nature of their relationship. Whilst he had been online, she hadn't had time to dwell on the patronising comments and the thinly veiled slights. Take, for example, his insistence of calling her Miss Johnson rather than DCI Johnson or even just plain Stella. Not that she would ever call him Mr Brandt, much less Jeffrey. He was keeping things suitably impersonal and she had to remind herself that this was just a temporary arrangement and whatever pleasure he was deriving from having her as a captive audience for his puerile insults was worth it given everything at stake.

With the clock informing her it was well past midnight, she went to bed; more out of defiance than belief that she may actually get some sleep. It therefore came as something of a surprise when she woke up to find the first rays of dawn pouring through the window. However, it would seem that her brain hadn't completely switched off because she woke up with an idea in her head. She could feel herself starting to lose grip of it, in much the same way one does a dream that had initially seemed so vivid, but she managed to cling on just enough to cause her to immediately head for her laptop and the email thread from last night.

Scrolling down to the relevant place, she stopped over a specific part of her discussion with Brandt:

Well perhaps we could dismiss his first act in Nottingham as the product of all that nervous tension. Leading him, if you like, to overdo it a little.

But your first wasn't like that…

No, but we'll come to that later. Instead, let us visit Sarah Donovan's house.

What had her mind latched onto whilst she slept? Was it because of the last bit? But surely that could have just been because he was concerned it would lead them off on a tangent? If it was unimportant, then, why say *we'll come to that later*?

They hadn't got around to discussing it, but perhaps that was the point. He could have said we'll come to that in a moment or something similar, but later could mean another time.

Johnson wasn't convinced this was going to take her anywhere, but she had learned throughout her career that a lead was a lead and warranted exploring until such point as it was proven false.

If this was the section Brandt had been referring to when he said, *if you read back through the thread of this conversation you might find you no longer require my assistance*, then it had to be something to do with the difference between his first attack and the killer they were hunting. Aside from this new guy going for the river first, rather than the station, there was the obvious fact that Brandt's attack had only hospitalised Sarah instead of killing her. But then they'd already discussed how the viciousness of these new attacks weren't the result of first time nerves.

'Oh. My. God!' Johnson exclaimed loudly into the silence of her flat. That was exactly what Brandt had been getting at. It all seemed so obvious to her now.

Well perhaps we could dismiss his first act in Nottingham as the product of all that nervous tension. Leading him, if you like, to overdo it a little.

Johnson had gone along with this statement at the time because it was what she believed to have been the case. But Brandt had gone on to disprove it by illustrating that the lack of control the murderer continued to display wasn't through nerves, but was a chosen behaviour, as illustrated by the simplicity with which he dispatched Josh Ramage, someone who didn't represent his primary objective.

But that in itself wouldn't be enough to lead Johnson anywhere, were it not for something in that message she had overlooked. *His first act in Nottingham.* There it was, clear as day. Brandt was saying this guy was already a killer before he started his copycat murders in Nottingham. Why he thought this, Johnson didn't know, but it now made sense to her. The killings themselves displayed a confidence that seemed unlikely for his first time, and far less tentative than Brandt's had been on Sarah, but also it fitted the notion of a copycat. For this person to want to follow in Brandt's footsteps then it implied a certain degree of hero worship. Surely, they would have been scared that they may not be able to live up to the example of the person who inspired them so much? Therefore, it would make sense to dip their toe in the water first to see if they were capable. That's why Brandt was so dismissive of trying to draw a comparison between his first attack and the woman's murder on the River Trent.

Johnson knew that she needed time to think what her next steps should be in light of this discovery, but there was something she would do first. It was still early, and she wanted to message Brandt before he could send her anything. She would have dearly loved to see the look on his face when he realised that she had taken what he had believed was a cryptic clue and smashed it.

> *– I need to get in the office early today. I don't know when I'll be able to contact you next.*

Johnson sat there staring at the cursor blinking next to her full stop. Rather than make her feel powerful, she could see how weak it was. Suggesting that she didn't need him anymore was not only petty but quite possibly false. Until she had something concrete to go on, she couldn't be sure that she wouldn't require his help again and all this message would do is make him less likely to provide it. That Brandt liked to play games was already clear and she could well imagine him ignoring her for a couple of days to re-establish who really was in control here.

So, what if showing a touch of deference massaged his ego? There were much more important things at stake here and, besides, the sooner she could find this killer the sooner she could concentrate on locating Brandt again.

She hit backspace until all of the text was removed and began typing again.

> *– I'm in the office following up your lead. I'll let you know how I'm getting on. Feel free to share any further thoughts you may have.*

It made her feel sick sending such an obsequious message to a serial killer but she sent it anyway.

Chapter Forty-one

Brandt woke up to find the other side of the bed empty. He wasn't surprised he had overslept. He hadn't been lying when he had said to Johnson that he had been going out. It may have only been to the pub to meet some friends, and Kath's keenness to go he had taken as a sign that she had got over whatever concerns she'd had about him using the internet so much, but the email exchange had put him in a particularly good mood. He still had needed to be careful not to over-indulge but had allowed himself to drink enough that he felt a pleasant buzz as they walked back to the house in the cold night air.

A quick glance at the alarm clock told him it wasn't late and, in fact, earlier than Kath typically rose. He hoped he hadn't kept her awake with his snoring, an unfortunate side-effect of his drinking that Susan had resented so much. Kath could be a sensitive soul and he knew that the best way of ensuring it wouldn't hamper the day would be to tackle it straight away.

Brandt arrived downstairs to find her in the kitchen with the newspaper and a pot of tea beside her. Clearly, she had been up for some time if she'd already got dressed and had gone to the shop.

'I'm sorry I disturbed you last night.'

'What's that dear?' Kath asked, looking up from the article.

'I said I'm sorry about my snoring. You know… if it woke you.'

'Oh, that's fine,' she replied, going back to what she was reading.

'Perhaps it would be nice to go out today.'

'Yes, perhaps.'

Brandt didn't like the way Kath was acting. 'I was thinking maybe it was time we went back to the Welsh food market.' That was bound to provoke a reaction.

'If you like.'

'Something interesting in the news?'

'Just the usual.'

Brandt had enough of this. He didn't know why Kath was in a strange mood, but he had done his best to generate a bit of warmth from her and had more important things to attend to.

'I might check the headlines myself on the BBC website,' he said, wandering out of the kitchen. Hopefully she'd have a nice fry up cooked for him when he was done.

'Atta girl,' he murmured, reading Johnson's message. For a fleeting moment, he considered what a good team they might have made if she had joined his CID back in the day. He was also intrigued by the cheerfulness of her tone that went beyond excitement for getting a lead. She was trying to butter him up in the hope he would be more attentive. The reality was Brandt didn't need encouragement, he was enjoying this far too much.

> *– Good. Start with places like Milton Keynes and Canterbury.*

Even now he couldn't bring himself to type St. Albans, but he knew that Johnson would understand that he was referring to the other places where he had killed.

— I wouldn't go further back than six months, but it may be he didn't use the same method then. If that draws blanks you're obviously going to have to widen your search.

'What time do you want to leave?'

'Huh?' Brandt was startled by Kath's sudden appearance at the doorway.

'You mentioned going to the Welsh food market…'

'Oh yeah… er, you don't mind if we stay in after all, do you? I'm not sure I'm ready for all that yet and, anyway, the weather forecast doesn't look too good.'

'Fine,' she replied, leaving him alone again.

'And make me a fucking bacon sandwich,' he muttered under his breath. There was no way he was going out today now, and certainly not to visit that prick Mr Jones.

Chapter Forty-two

'What's got into you?'

'Nothing, I'm fine.'

'But you've been like this for days, Jack. Are you trying to avoid me?'

'Why would I?'

'I don't know, that's why I'm asking!' Mandy huffed. 'Fine, I'll see you at the seminar this afternoon.'

'Yeah, sure,' Jack replied, happy to be able to be alone again. He shut the door to his room and lay down on the bed. He could hardly blame Mandy for being so pushy, he had been different. He felt different. The discovery that the knife, his knife, was just an implement for cutting up one's dinner again had been even worse than he had feared at the time. With the news sites having moved on to discuss other events, it was as though the two things had conspired to make everything he'd done seem like a dream. He'd tried to get over it, but couldn't turn his mind to other things. Jack knew it was totally irrational, but he had even considered going around to Sarah's house just to make sure he hadn't imagined it all, and she wasn't inside playing happy families with her husband.

The solution to his problem had presented itself very early on but until now he had refused to entertain it. Even if he was prepared to risk killing again so that he could reinvigorate the knife once more, he had no idea who and where. He tried to remind himself that his first murder, on Whitstable beach, had been all his own doing but so much had changed since then. Not only had he lived up to the example set by Brandt but he had surpassed it with Sarah. Even if he could get to Milton Keynes or St. Albans, it would seem like a step backwards. Of course, there was always DCI Johnson, but that would take a huge amount of planning and he didn't feel that time was on his side. At the rate he was going, he was liable to lose Mandy and that was something he could not allow to happen.

Jack went to his drawer where the knife now lay, to all intents and purposes exactly the same as the other utensils his mother had bought him when he left home. He could barely stand to look at it and quickly snatched it up and put it into his jacket. The familiar feeling of it at the bottom of the inner lining was comforting and made him sure that he was doing the right thing. Thoughts of doing something that would trump what he had previously achieved and, once again, confirm he was worthy to stand in Brandt's shadow, could wait. If the taste of blood he received today was not enough to slake his thirst, he could then go on to find DCI Johnson or plan for something equally spectacular.

Jack smiled as he left his room. If things went smoothly, he could be back in time for the seminar and could seek to make it up with Mandy afterwards. Already he felt better than he had in days.

Chapter Forty-three

In a high-pressure environment such as CID, it was far from unusual to hear raised voices but there was something about this occasion that caused Johnson to come to the door of her office. Unlike Potter, she tended to keep hers open, that way none of the team would have the excuse they thought she was too busy for not sharing something important with her immediately.

Even before she looked across the expanse of the open plan desk area, she knew what it was that had caught her attention. DC Hardy, for all his blustering, was a mild-mannered man and she could count on the fingers of one hand the number of times she'd heard him shout. What was particularly concerning was that he was the sole person she had employed to follow up Brandt's lead. With all the stuff going on recently, the team was quite fragile, and she hadn't wanted to make a big thing until she was more confident that it was going to get them somewhere. However, she had learned to rely on Hardy and with it requiring a significant amount of leg work, she had briefed him on what to do without, of course, saying where the idea had come from. Thankfully checking for other murders around the country had sounded routine enough, and he had set about his task without question.

Johnson opened her mouth for her to shout for Hardy to get into her office, so she could find out what the hell all the commotion was about, but then she noticed he was on the phone. She marched towards him, glaring at any of the rest of the team who dared stop what they were doing to rubber-neck. Hardy spotted her before she arrived at his desk and his look suggested one of relief rather than fear.

'What's going on?' she hissed quietly.

He removed the receiver from his ear and covered up the mouthpiece with the palm of his hand. Perhaps now was not the time to point out that there was a mute button just below the keypad. 'I'm doing what you said, ma'am, and phoning round, but Canterbury are being rather... unhelpful.'

'You what?'

'When they seemed reluctant to share information I asked if they would like to speak to my commanding officer and then she just went off on one. I was just trying to calm her down, honest!'

Johnson shook her head, unable to take in what sounded to her like nonsense. She sighed. 'Okay, I'll deal with this. Patch the call through to my office.' On her way, she turned back and shouted: 'I want you to get onto the database and look up all unsolved murders in the past six months.' There was no way she was going to reward Hardy messing up the simple task she'd given him by allowing him to take a break.

Slamming the door with irritation, she marched round her desk and plonked herself in the chair. 'Hello?' she barked into the phone.

'Who is this?' Came the terse response from the other end.

'DCI Johnson. Who the hell is this?'

'Well, holy shit! Hi there!'

Johnson was so taken aback by the sudden change of tone that it took her a few moments to recognise the voice. 'DCI Marlowe?'

'Sure is! I didn't realise you were back, Stella.'

'You don't read the papers then?' Johnson replied, not unkindly.

'Too busy for that sort of thing. Look, I'm sorry about Harding or whoever I was just speaking to. I thought when he asked if he could refer me on, he was talking about DI Fisher.'

'Oh, you've had dealings with him then?' Johnson was intrigued but hardly surprised given what she had found out recently about Fisher and his political machinations.

'Yeah, you could say that…'

'And?'

'And what?' Marlowe laughed.

'And what did you think of him?'

'Are we speaking as colleagues or friends?'

'Friends,' Johnson replied. She had liked DCI Marlowe the moment she and McNeil had met her at Canterbury police station.

'He's a complete dickhead.'

'Yep, that just about sums him up. But tell me how come you know him so well?' Although Johnson thought that this was a little off topic, any dirt she might be able to dig up on Fisher could prove useful if Brandt was leading her down a dead end and they failed to get their killer. It might not be enough to stop the top brass following the path she had predicted, but it would be some consolation if she and Potter could take him down with them.

'To be honest, we've only spoken a couple of times. You know, follow up stuff about Brandt after you were… you were gone.'

'Oh,' Johnson said, utterly disappointed – Marlowe had seemed to have Fisher down to a tee. But it was nice speaking to someone friendly for a change and she was loath to see their conversation end so soon. 'About anything interesting?'

'Well, he was completely dismissive when I wanted to share with him the details of a murder here. It was as though he couldn't give a shit.'

'Murder?'

'Yeah, towards the end of September. What with everyone thinking that Brandt was dead we just thought it was a coincidence, but seeing as it was in the same spot…'

'What was?' Johnson interrupted, unable to hide her impatience.

'The same place where Brandt killed the girl. Don't you know about this?'

'No. That's why Hardy was ringing around to see if there have been any unsolved murders in the last six months in the places Brandt had visited.'

'Shit, I'm sorry, Stella, he did say something like that but, to be honest, I was a bit miffed anyway that he had been put straight through to me and then I thought he was ringing on behalf of that prick Fisher… You mean Fisher never told you?'

'Told me what?' Johnson asked, confused by the sudden switch of focus again back to Fisher.

'About the murder. Like I said, at the time none of us thought it could have anything to do with Brandt and was, most likely, just a coincidence but we wanted to pass it on anyway. You know, just in case.'

'Alright then,' she said with a calmness that in no way matched the thumping of her heart in her chest. 'I think you'd better start from the beginning.'

Chapter Forty-four

Brandt laughed when he saw the message. Although he had been certain they were on the right path, even he hadn't expected it to turn up something as good as this so quickly. Not that he was too modest to take the credit and, besides, the search parameters would still be unfeasibly large if it were not for his revelation that it must be someone young. Brandt was also laughing because of the irony of his bladder being so desperate for him to empty it. Having coaxed Kath into the garden, he had kept nipping inside to check his inbox, under the pretence of either needing to put on warmer clothes or, latterly, that he had to go to the toilet. He was worried that if he kept having to make excuses she would start to think he had something wrong with his prostate. Not that it mattered though, he could sense that Johnson was close to a result, and he would soon be able to return to giving Kath the attention she deserved.

He wanted to type his response before giving into his need to relieve himself, just in case Johnson had remained online long enough to be able to reply.

— If nothing else the timing of the murder suggests it could be a student, just before the start of the new

academic year. Have a squad car go to both universities to get their admissions departments to provide you with all the students with a Kent postcode, then prioritise first years from Canterbury itself.

'Christ, that was a close call,' he muttered to himself in the bathroom a few moments after sending the message. He hadn't planned on typing so much and he found himself barely able to hold his urine in as he rushed to the toilet. He uttered a small groan of pleasure as the powerful stream continued to hammer the bowl.

Chapter Forty-five

Jack was panting hard. His eyes were wild with panic as he looked back over his shoulder in the direction he had come. He knew he couldn't keep up this pace for long and allowed himself a few moments to catch his breath. He would dearly have loved to be able to take off his jacket and allow his body to cool but it was soaked in blood and he didn't fancy having to carry it if he needed to start running again.

'Shit!' He swore loudly as the man rounded the corner. What was up with this guy? Why couldn't he just shout out and then call the police like any other normal person if they stumbled across a woman in the midst of being stabbed? That she had then grabbed him in the confusion and pulled him into the steady stream of blood that was pouring from her had only made things worse.

As Jack set off again, he considered where to go. He had settled on a spot not too far from the university to carry out his murder, but he couldn't afford to head back home until he had lost this crazy guy chasing him. The surroundings might have been familiar, but Jack was still new to the area and hadn't explored the back routes.

However, he knew that he had little chance of getting away unless he tried something different.

He took the next left following signs for the Jubilee Campus. He had never been to this separate part of the university, but he trusted that if it was even half the size of the main one, he would have plenty of opportunity to evade his pursuer.

But to his horror the area opened out into a vast expanse of green space, with the buildings themselves still hundreds of metres ahead. Jack wasn't sure he could make it and, with a stitch now firmly rooted in his side, he started to consider the alternative. He could stand his ground and fight. He didn't know what had given the man the confidence to chase him, but Jack still had his knife and was more than willing to kill him.

Perhaps that would be the best thing, he thought. At least that way this guy wouldn't be allowed to provide the police with a description. Cursing himself for allowing fear to replace common sense, Jack stopped abruptly and prepared to turn and face his next victim.

What confronted him was more than an anti-climax. It would seem the man had viewed the back entrance to the campus with the same negativity, had concluded he would be unable to chase him down over such a vast area, and was now crouched, with his hands on his knees, barely ten metres into the site.

Jack was wracked with indecision. If he started running after the man, there was every chance he would now decide to flee. He had already shown he could maintain a decent pace and, the additional rest he had enjoyed combined with Jack's extra exertion, meant he was likely to be uncatchable. Of course, he could also choose to stand and fight, but this way Jack would have lost any element of surprise.

Disgruntled, Jack started trotting off in the same direction as earlier, only stopping to pull out the hood from under his jacket before he was close enough to the buildings to be picked up by CCTV.

He changed direction as soon as he was out of the man's eyesight, reasoning that even if he had somehow managed to call the police earlier, he would be back on the phone again to give them an update of his whereabouts.

This time Jack was headed straight for his own campus. He wanted to get back to his room as quickly as possible, grab some things and go and lay low for a while. He might not have much in his bank account, but he would dig out the credit card his father had ordered for emergencies and use it to withdraw some cash from one of the university ATMs. He could then go and find a cheap hotel somewhere until the coast was clear. No one except Mandy would be concerned by his absence, his tutors had long become accustomed to his inconsistent attendance, and he would text her to say he had gone back to his parents for a few days to sort his head out.

With an absence of sirens and his body temperature dropping to a comfortable level in the early afternoon of a typically cool late autumn day, he could feel his heart rate returning to normal. Now that the sweat on his head was also beginning to dry, all it required was for him to take off his jacket and bundle it up in his arms, with the knife safely stashed in its familiar resting place.

As he entered the main university grounds, he gave a giggle as he looked at his watch and realised that, if he rushed, he probably wouldn't be too late to be accepted into his seminar. But even if he had been inclined to sit through another snooze-fest there was no way he was going to run again that day if he could possibly help it.

His stance abruptly changed as soon as he had made his way up the long, sweeping drive. Right outside the front of the main building was a police car. Not only was it empty but they must have been there sometime because they hadn't passed him on the road up. He thought about fleeing there and then, but without access to funds from his father's credit card he wouldn't be able to get very far.

Jack tried to bring his racing mind under control. Even if they were here because of him, surely they wouldn't have established his exact identity yet. If he was careful, he could walk past his room a couple of times to see if the coppers were in there. Anyway, it was a risk he was going to have to take. He was just glad that Mandy would be busy talking shit about the cultural and political divide in post-war, pre-wall Berlin.

Aside from a few students shuffling along, the corridor leading to his place was quiet, but Jack still felt exceedingly apprehensive as he opened the door leading to the quintet of rooms, of which his was the middle one. Tiptoeing through and waiting to make sure there wasn't a slam behind him, he carefully put his ear to his wooden door. There was no sound from inside, but he still waited a little longer, just in case. Finally satisfied, he pulled out his key and slipped it carefully into the lock.

He was already half way into his room when a noise from behind caused him to spin around in fright.

'What are you doing here?' he yelled at Mandy.

'When you didn't turn up for the seminar, I told them I was feeling sick and excused myself.'

'Why would you do that?' Jack asked, still trying to recover from the shock.

'Because I'm worried about you,' Mandy replied earnestly, approaching.

'Just leave me alone!' he shouted, moving inside so he could close the door and shut her out. But she was already through before he could react quickly enough. 'What the hell?'

'No, Jack, not this time! I'm not leaving until you tell me what the fuck is going on.'

With Mandy glaring at him intently, he quickly considered his options. Clearly asking her not to worry

227

wouldn't work but nothing else was liable to see her leave. Unless…

'I'm sorry, I just don't love you anymore.' The words tasted as awful as they sounded but, as he fought to stop himself immediately retracting them, he could see from her expression that they were having an effect. Jack didn't know whether he could fix this at a later date, but his immediate concern was getting rid of her, so he could make his escape unimpeded.

'No,' she whispered, shaking her head slowly with tears starting to well up in her eyes; the sight of which broke Jack's heart. But then he could see her expression alter, the hurt to be replaced by something else. Rage – pure unadulterated rage.

'No!' she said again, this time a shout of fury, and she lunged at him.

Jack, so taken aback by this sudden and terrifying change, instinctively raised his arms to protect himself and closed his eyes for the impending blow. Mandy wrenched the jacket out of his arms and cast it aside. With the barrier now removed she pulled back her hand ready to strike.

She slapped him full across the face, dazing Jack, and was about to deliver another when something caused her to pause. 'Shit I'm sorry,' she cried, concerned that she had drawn blood. She was reaching to find the wound when she realised that her hand was similarly wet, and so too was the one on her left.

In that moment Jack understood what had happened. Whilst Mandy was still staring at her palms in disbelief he dived for the jacket. There was to be no way of explaining this, he needed to get out – to get away – but he had already seen what she was capable of and there was every chance she would follow him screaming blue murder.

There was only one way he could ensure her silence. He plunged his hand deep into the inner pocket, ripping the hole at the bottom wider so he could get to the knife. As soon as he felt the warmth of the wooden handle, he yanked it out and brandished it at Mandy. He was ready to see the rage rise in her once more and prepared himself to lash out, but all her face displayed was terror.

He urged the muscles in his arm to do what they must, but they wouldn't respond. The sight before him was one he had revelled in many times since he had arrived in Nottingham but this time it was different; this time it was wrong. This wasn't some stranger who stood before him offering greatness in the eyes of the hero he worshipped. This was Mandy, the woman he loved; the woman who had taught him that his life had a purpose beyond the reason why he had come to this part of the country. She had nearly got him to stop the killing and he had failed her.

'I'm sorry,' Jack whispered, his own tears now beginning to flow. These feeble words were meant for Mandy but also to himself for being unable to do the one thing that might yet save him. He dropped the knife and lunged for the door in one desperate movement.

Moments later, he was gone.

Chapter Forty-six

'I think we've got something!'

Johnson had been downstairs in the police station since the news of another attack had come through. It wasn't just because of what she had found out from DCI Marlowe in Canterbury, this time their guy had made a mistake. He had been disturbed in the act and, although it had been too late to save his victim, who died from multiple stab wounds before the paramedics arrived, they had been provided with a more than passable description.

'What is it?' Johnson demanded, pushing her way past two men in uniform to get to the radio controller.

'We've got reports coming of a disturbance up at the university.'

'So what?'

'It was picked up by the officers you sent up there. A woman is claiming she was threatened by a man with a knife.'

'Description?'

'Fits the one from the attack. She also has blood on her that she claims is neither hers nor the man's.'

Johnson worked hard to keep her emotions in check and remain professional. But that was not how she felt inside. She wasn't one for counting her chickens until they'd hatched, but surely this was it?

'Where is he now?' she demanded.

'Fled on foot but it sounds like he's only had a few minutes' head start.'

'Right, I want all available units over there now. I want him cuffed within the hour!'

Johnson marched upstairs to inform Potter. As she passed her own office she paused, wondering why she also felt an urge to tell Brandt. The enemy of my enemy is my friend. She shook her head vigorously. Whatever he was, he was certainly no friend. And yet when she had needed him to cut all the bullshit and help, irrespective of the games he seemed to enjoy so much, he did. So, was it a sense that she owed him? It couldn't be that and, as she had told him when she first responded to his contact, there was no chance of redemption coming.

Moving inside to sit at her desk she realised what it was. Although the hunt for Brandt resumed the moment the dental records were checked on the exhumed body, the only person who had got close to catching him, Johnson, would continue to be otherwise engaged whilst the new killer in Nottingham remained at large. Therefore, by choosing to help her he was speeding up the point at which he would consider himself in danger. For that reason alone, she would tell him. In the context of what he had done to assist her, he deserved to know that the chase would soon be back on and that their current state of peaceful co-existence was over.

Johnson had already worked out what she was going to type as she entered her password for the email account she had set up specifically for communicating with Brandt. She would merely inform him that a positive ID had been made and an arrest was imminent.

As she clicked on her inbox, there was an unread message. She smirked to think he was offering further instruction that was not needed and started to revise what she would send to him. Surely it wouldn't hurt to sound a little smug.

But the message wasn't from him and it didn't look like some random spam either.

— Whoever you are, keep away from my man!

'What the actual fuck?' Johnson murmured to herself, barely able to comprehend what she had just read.

Chapter Forty-seven

Kath Hardcastle had always tried to live her life as a woman of virtue and believed that telling the truth was the best course to take. But when you'd lived as long as she had, no matter how sincere your intentions were, there are inevitable exceptions.

Kath had thought she had found contentment, if not happiness, in the years that had followed the death of her husband, Mike. Her childhood may have been in the swinging sixties but her conservative upbringing allowed her few boyfriends before she finally settled down and got married. She had been apprehensive prior to the wedding and had confessed to her mother that she wasn't sure whether she loved Mike. Kath had not been prepared for the reaction that followed her uncharacteristic baring of her most closely guarded secret. Laughter. It hadn't been meant cruelly. Her mother had always been kind but was a product of an earlier time. Marriage isn't about love, it's about security, she had explained to Kath.

But Kath had grown to love Mike. It may never have been the whirlwind romance she had secretly read about on her trips to the library as a curious teen, but if she needed any indication of how much he had come to mean to her, then his death provided it. It had been entirely unexpected, and Kath had spent the following two years lost. And yet slowly she had begun to rebuild her life and found purpose for it by keeping to a schedule that saw her venture out each day and make new friends.

But then the mysterious guy from Eastern Europe arrived, Gregori. She realised early on that Greggy wasn't the correct pronunciation, but she had grown to like it. For all his good manners and keenness to serve, his face took on a brooding look whenever he didn't think he was being observed and the nickname helped to soften the darkness she sensed behind his eyes.

Not that she felt intimidated by him; she knew as well as the next person that everyone has a history, and he must have gone through some difficulties for a man of his age to find himself serving coffee and cake to well-off retired people in a far-flung part of the country. And that was before he hinted at the problems facing people in his native country since the break-up of the Soviet Union.

Even when fate conspired to bring them closer together, she had not sought to challenge his obvious reluctance to talk about the past, not least because the sense of betrayal she felt towards Mike meant that she didn't want to be pressed on her own.

Indeed, she had not allowed herself to get too carried away with the speed at which their relationship was developing. She just wanted to enjoy the moment and not be caught up in where it might lead. And there was much to enjoy. Kath found him handsome, perhaps not conventionally, but the obvious intelligence with which his mind worked was alluring. Not least were his linguistic skills and she was staggered how far his command of the English language had come on in such a relatively short space of time. His accent was all but gone and he had picked up the sorts of phrases and expressions that could now enable him to pass as a native to these shores.

And then there was the sex. Kath had thought her days of physical union were behind her, long before Mike passed away. She had been terribly nervous the night she and Greggy had first made love. She had come close to backing out but the way he looked at her, with an almost primeval yearning, convinced her to put aside inhibitions based on the effects of time and the, now distant, menopause. His ability to be so tender and sensitive one minute and then animalistic, to the point of rough, the next, allowed her to experience sensations long since forgotten.

But it hadn't all been plain sailing. That gnawing doubt that it was all too good to be true never went away and, worse still, had begun to grow. The seed that something was amiss was ironically planted on that magical day in Llandudno. She might have been able to dismiss that it had all seemed too familiar to Greggy had it not been for the obsession with the internet he had developed soon after.

His efforts to be considerate about it with things like getting up early, had only made her more suspicious. At first, she wondered whether he was using it to gamble. Given that he didn't seem to have an issue with alcohol, appearing to be able to take it or leave it, an addiction to betting would help explain the state of near destitution she had found him in. However, when she had checked her bank accounts to make sure he wasn't somehow stealing her money to fund his habits, she considered that he may be using the internet for other purposes.

Always an avid reader of the paper, the years since she became a widow saw her consume her favoured publication from cover to cover each day. From that, Kath was aware of sexting and revenge porn and the like from the numerous articles she had read on them, and believed Greggy when he claimed he wasn't downloading inappropriate images.

But then she heard him typing, and more than could be expected for things like entering web addresses. The suspicion that he was communicating with someone was confirmed when she overheard bursts of him tapping away at a keyboard, followed by moments of silence, before it started up again. She had encouraged him to let his hair down at the pub afterwards, in the hope he might crash out when they returned, and she could try and work out from the laptop exactly what he was up to but, if anything, the alcohol had made him more amorous.

Therefore, Kath had got up early the next morning under the pretence of going to the shop to get the newspaper and, when he didn't stir, she spent a frustrating hour finding nothing untoward on the computer. She knew when he did rise that she was doing a poor job of acting normally, but she was upset and fearful of what it was he was going to lengths to disguise. Any efforts to try and bury her concerns were lost when he changed his mind about them going out that morning – making excuses to keep going back inside from the garden. Even if he was contacting a family member, one of his children perhaps, that wouldn't explain all the secrecy, much less the need to maintain such a constant dialogue.

Each time he would leave her in the garden, she would sneak up to the back door and crack it open to hear what he was up to. She didn't hear him typing but she could tell by his footsteps that he was going into the dining room, where he now favoured setting up the computer. Knowing that eventually he would have to make good on one of his claims that he needed the toilet, she waited until she heard him go upstairs following a hasty flurry on the keyboard, and pounced.

Kath wasn't cut out for deception and intrigue and, when she found that it took her longer than expected to remove her outdoor shoes, she nearly aborted. But then she reminded herself that it shouldn't matter if he caught her. Not only was it her laptop he was obsessing over but, given his behaviour, she had every right to be suspicious. Nevertheless, she acted as quickly as possible, pausing only to scribble down the random letters and numbers that made up the email address of the person he was conversing with. Much as she would have loved to read through the messages and get a real sense of what he was up to, she figured this was enough to work with and was relieved to be back in the kitchen by the time he came back down the stairs.

She knew her iPhone had many more functions than she could possibly comprehend, but that one of them was the ability to email from it. It took her many minutes, whilst Greggy was thankfully still preoccupied in the dining room, for her to work out how to access her personal account on the phone but as soon as she did, she started typing her message to the mystery person.

It was only then that Kath realised that she hadn't even considered what it was that she should write, but her blood was up, and she typed in the first thing that came into her head, hitting send before her natural inclination towards caution intervened.

— *Whoever you are, keep away from my man!*

Chapter Forty-eight

'Guv!' Johnson shouted, her bursting into his office now so much part of the routine that DSI Potter didn't raise an eyebrow. The way he was feeling now, he wouldn't mind if she entered by ploughing through the wall with a bulldozer.

'Stella! I've been wanting to congratulate you. Where have you been?'

'I've got him!'

'I know, and well done. I've just been told he's been picked up. The dog unit found him cowering in a bush. A suitably inauspicious end, I would suggest!'

The news that the man terrorising Nottingham over the past few weeks was finally under arrest barely registered with Johnson. She had already known the hunt was as good as over and recent developments had seen her focus shift elsewhere to the main prize.

'I mean Brandt.'

Potter didn't reply and, under other circumstances, she would have found the length of time for the smile on his face to waver amusing. 'I've found Brandt,' she said to try and offer some clarification.

'I'm sorry?'

She could see him studying her as though he were trying to understand if this was a punchline to a joke that, in his excitement, he had failed to get.

'Guv, I need you to listen to me, okay? I have been in contact with Brandt for a number of days now.'

'But…'

'Please, Steven, hear me out first. I don't know why but, after the news about Sarah Donovan broke, he sent me a message.'

Already she could feel her mind start to tie itself in knots. At the inquest following the fire at her house she had said as little as possible, and had not mentioned that she had gone to Benidorm, never mind their email exchange where she had been posing as the reporter, Gail Trevelly. She knew that, if not now, at some point Potter would want to know how Brandt had managed to contact her but she would try and leave that for when she had more opportunity to think things through. Thankfully, it seemed he was going to respect her request not to interrupt because he hadn't tried to punctuate her pause with comment.

'He and I have been communicating since then.'

Again she hesitated. Even if she wouldn't feel deeply uncomfortable sharing the extent of the co-operative relationship that had temporarily existed between her and Brandt, after everything she'd been through, she didn't fancy having to share the credit for the success the station was currently enjoying.

Clearing her throat she continued: 'He's been disguising his IP address, but I maintained the connection with him in the hope that it might lead somewhere. And it has. It would seem that whoever he has got himself shacked up with has become suspicious and sent me a message. An unencrypted message,' she added, unable to hide her triumph.

'Jesus Christ, Stella. And where does it trace to?'

'I haven't had that run yet,' she replied evenly.

'You what?! Why the hell not?' Potter exclaimed.

'Because I needed to see if you were on side first.'

'Go on…'

'When this gets out, there are going to be inevitable… questions. Questions, guv, many of which I think are already on the tip of your tongue. I need to know that you will back me on this.'

She waited, watching Potter's reaction. A few short weeks ago he would have baulked at the request. In the many years she had known him, Potter had always played things down the line and was wholly against anything that was ethically questionable. He also wasn't one to like feeling he was being backed into a corner; but it was for this very reason that Johnson felt confident of success. No matter what a difficult position covering for her actions placed him in, it was nothing compared to the pressure he had been under from the top brass; in particular since Fisher started stirring things up. But today's arrest would not only see that pressure evaporate, he was also being given the chance to add to that the biggest prize of all. Britain's most notorious serial killer, former Detective Superintendent Jeffrey Brandt.

'What do you need?' he asked quietly.

'I just need you to say that we both thought it was a possibility that Brandt might make contact once it was made known he was still alive; that you gave me permission to work undercover to lure him into making a mistake that would lead to his capture.'

Johnson knew that this stance may seem pretty thin but, as with before, she doubted there would be much of an appetite to dig deeper and turn what was a moment of celebration for the police into a witch hunt.

'I agree on one condition…'

'What's that, guv?'

'We play this now by the book. I'm sure I needn't remind you of the perils of trying to arrest him yourself.'

'Don't worry, guv, I fully intend leaving it to the specialists. But…'

'But nothing, Stella, I'm not having you anywhere near this. Not after what… what happened to you before.' The almost paternalistic way Potter said this would have been touching, were it not that the same desire to protect her had led him to refuse her going back on the Brandt case following McNeil's funeral.

McNeil. He was never far from Johnson's thoughts, but she had to admit everything else that had happened recently had seen her somewhat preoccupied. Not that it had stopped her wondering why Claire never made contact again since the news about Brandt had come out. Johnson liked to think that Claire had believed that she had been through enough already in her efforts to avenge her brother's murder. But she suspected that it was just wishful thinking on her part, not least because she herself would never feel enough was done until Brandt was finally brought to justice.

And now was that time. Perhaps as soon as this was over, she would call Claire and share the good news herself. That way she would know that those three words she had spoken after the funeral, *whatever it takes*, had remained with her.

'But I want to go there so I can ensure that he is brought back to us for questioning. There's no way some other force is getting the credit for this. I might not be able to bring him down myself, but he's still mine nonetheless.' The firmness of her tone made it clear that this condition was not up for discussion.

'Fine, but you take someone with you. You're on official business now after all.'

Johnson nodded, with exactly the right person in mind.

'And just one last thing. I feel a little uncomfortable asking this, but how do you know he's not fucking with us again; fucking with you again?'

Potter's question felt like a large stone had been placed on her chest. From the first moment she read the mystery email, she knew there was a chance this was just another of his tricks. It wasn't as though he didn't have a track record of outwitting her. It was the timing, more than anything, that convinced her this may be genuine. If it had happened mere hours later, once he knew that the guy they'd been hunting had been caught, then she would have smelled a rat. As Johnson had reflected before, Brandt's success in helping her would only speed up the point at which she could concentrate on capturing him. Brandt's brilliance, if she would call it that, is that his mind worked with cool, rational calculation. It would make no sense for him to spring a trap now, unless the whole point was that it was illogical. If nothing else, the past few days had given him a greater insight into how her mind worked. What if his offer to help had just been a charade to enable him to better plan how he was going to trick her this time?

'Fucking hell,' she muttered, wondering whether she was allowing herself to be duped yet again.

'Stella?' Potter asked in concern.

She looked up at the DSI and realised in that moment that the alternative to springing whatever trap Brandt might have laid for her would be to do nothing. In comparison to that, even if there was a slightest chance that the email sent to her was genuine, then it was a chance worth taking.

'I guess we're about to find out!' she declared, marching out of Potter's office.

* * *

'Half an hour?!' Johnson shouted at Hardy a few minutes later as they descended from the CID floor.

'At best, ma'am. North Wales doesn't have many specialist firearm units,' he replied, having to take the stairs two at a time in order to keep up with the DCI.

'Can't they just send the local plod in?' But she knew the answer to that and, anyway, she'd rather risk having to wait than get there to find the place littered with corpses and Brandt nowhere to be seen. In any case, it would give them a chance to get nearer.

'Why couldn't he have been hiding out in Derby or somewhere else local?' Hardy offered, and Johnson could detect a hint of excitement in his voice.

'What's the weather like outside?' she asked, heading for where the keys to all the unmarked cars were.

'I, er...' Hardy mumbled.

'Dry but cloudy.' Sergeant Andrews called across from the duty desk.

How he knew, cooped up all day, filling out his log book, she didn't know. 'Rough temperature?'

'A balmy 7 degrees Celsius I'd say,' he replied, still seemingly engrossed in his writing.

'Perfect,' Johnson said, grabbing a particular set of keys.

'Er, why's that, ma'am,' Hardy enquired, spinning round to now follow her in the direction of the car park.

'It means we can go for the poise, precision and, not to mention, power of the BMW M4 rather than the all-wheel drive security of the Audi S4.'

'Oh,' he responded, clearly not understanding a word she had said.

'What car do you drive, Hardy?' she asked as they entered the car park, with the inky black of night already covering the sky.

'A VW Polo, ma'am.'

'The GTI?'

'Er, no, it's a diesel of some sort.'

'Then you'd better strap yourself in tight,' she said, flinging open the driver's door.

Chapter Forty-nine

What have I done? Kath felt sick to her stomach. The part of her that was convinced she didn't deserve the love of this good man was telling her that it didn't matter if he was chatting to other women online, as long it was her bed he was warming at night. Her more rational side was suggesting that she had every right to feel affronted, but she had gone about dealing with it in completely the wrong way.

If some brazen hussy was bold enough to cavort with a man she didn't know online, no doubt sending him naked pictures and videos of herself doing God-knows-what, she was hardly likely to back off just because someone told her to. No, the first thing she would do would be to message Gregori, her Greggy, and tell him what had happened.

Almost as soon as she had sent the email to this random stranger, Kath had regretted it. She had to do something to intervene before he found out. All this time she had been fussing about what an enormous breach of trust his behaviour had been, and she had chosen to deal with it by doing something equally as bad. There was every chance he would leave her when he found out, and she would be back to her hollow existence of planning her life around the various places in North Wales where she could get a nice pot of tea.

So, what to do? The first thing that had sprung to mind was to smash the laptop. But how could she make it look like some kind of unfortunate accident? She could say she was dusting and bumped into it.

But Kath knew that was a stupid idea; pathetic even. Acting in haste had got her into this mess. What she really needed to do was to buy herself some time to think. She would have to find a way to distract Greggy from checking his emails for a while.

Kath watched day turn to night through the gap in her curtains whilst he snored peacefully beside her. That she felt cheap for using sex as a weapon was nothing compared to the agony of indecision. She knew she had been lucky that he had slept as long as he had, and that he was bound to wake soon. Similarly, it was inevitable that he would seek to use the computer again before the evening was out.

With Gregori now beginning to stir from his slumber, she made her decision, even though she knew there was every chance she would come to regret it. Yet she had learned in the course of her life that the best way wasn't always the easiest. She would not compound her mistake from earlier by persisting with deception. As soon as he was fully awake, she would tell him the truth. It was the right thing to do and she would just have to hope that finding out from her rather than his... his lady friend might cause him to forgive her.

As she watched the man she loved slowly coming back to consciousness, she wondered whether this was the last time he would share her bed.

Chapter Fifty

Johnson and Hardy were most of the way towards Stoke-on-Trent before they managed to establish a direct line with the specialist firearms team moving in on the location they'd been given. When Hardy had first punched their route into the M4's sat nav it had estimated the total journey time to be 3 hours and 10 minutes. In only half an hour Johnson had managed to knock their remaining time down to 2 hours. She had rejected the most direct route for the one that would see the majority of their journey on motorways and dual carriages. That way she could keep her foot down and trust that most of the other drivers on the road would see the unmistakable pulse of blue from the light bar suctioned onto the carbon fibre roof and get themselves well out of the way before the BMW's snarling grill filled up their rear-view mirror.

'Sergeant, I want you to maintain open comms throughout. I want to see what you see. Understand?'

'Received, five minutes out,' came the clear, flat response.

The wait felt like an eternity.

Johnson was about to check whether a problem had developed with the line when suddenly the radio crackled back into life. 'This is Sierra Tango Three, opening constant line with Whisky Foxtrot One. Whisky Foxtrot One, are you receiving, over?'

'This is Whisky Foxtrot One. We are receiving you Sierra Tango Three. Proceed, over,' Hardy responded.

This was it. Johnson's speed was unconsciously dropping as she diverted some of her attention to the steady stream of information coming over the airwaves. She would have dearly loved to be there, if for nothing else than watching the SFOs in operation was a sight to behold. She could imagine them all sat calmly in the back of the speeding van, carrying out their final equipment checks before making ready their Heckler and Koch MP5 or G36 sub-machine guns. Even McNeil, who nearly found himself run over by the unit she had deployed to Sarah Donovan's place, had been otherwise impressed by the calm and efficient way they had stormed the block of flats.

How Brandt had wound up living up some dirt track on the outskirts of Betws-y-Coed, she had no idea, but was encouraged that the remoteness of the house itself gave him little chance of escaping by vehicle. A helicopter had been scrambled but was being kept back so as not to be heard before the officers on the ground arrived. It would be moved into position if their assailant were to flee on foot, where their infrared cameras were sure to pick him up in a matter of minutes.

The description of the property might have been perfunctory and merely there to highlight potential points of entry and exit but it was precise enough to allow Johnson to picture the ex-farmhouse. There was little chance their arrival would go unnoticed but the speed with which they disembarked and, with half the force flanking either side of the house, they would ensure that they maintained a sufficient element of surprise.

The steady thud of the commanding officer's boots was audible and there was only the briefest of pauses when they stopped before a single blow from the big red key, loud enough to cause Johnson and Hardy to wince, gained them entry through the front door.

From there on, it was all noise as each of the officers shouted instructions to the occupants as they swept the house quickly and methodically. The contrast to the calm hushed tones from before was distinct but it did not signify a loss of control, being as it was deliberately designed to intimidate and subdue. Over the steady calls of *Clear!* as each room was checked Johnson could hear a woman screaming.

'What is it, Sergeant?' Johnson demanded, as soon as she felt it safe to do so.

'IC1 female located and secured,' came the response, delivered without the slightest suggestion of breathlessness, despite the recent flurry of activity. 'No further occupants, over.'

'Repeat that last, over,' Johnson barked back.

'IC1 female. Sole occupant of property. Commencing search of the surroundings, over.'

'Shit!' Johnson roared, not caring in the slightest who heard this outburst. 'Proceed with search.' Not that they wouldn't anyway, but Johnson already knew that, somehow, Brandt had managed to evade her once more. 'I want that woman calm and ready to speak to me in one minute. Oh, and good work, Sergeant, over.' Her tone was enough to suggest the apparent gratitude in her last statement was somewhat forced.

'What now, ma'am?' Hardy whispered so his words were only heard by their intended recipient.

'I'm not sure,' she replied honestly. 'But I still want to get there as quickly as possible,' she added, clicking the left-hand paddle on the M4's steering wheel to kick it down a gear before she planted the accelerator pedal to the floor.

Chapter Fifty-one

'I… I don't understand,' said Brandt, his voice croaky from sleep. He didn't yet feel properly awake but, even though his brain wasn't processing properly what Kath was saying, he could tell from her tone that it was something serious.

'I'm really sorry, it's just that I was so… so jealous.' Her voice was now shrill with anguish.

'Sorry about what? Jealous?' He sat up and rubbed his eyes.

'You were just spending so much time on there and I started to worry, and I did bring it up, but then you told me not to worry, but I couldn't get it out of my head, and so I tried to find out, but then I couldn't, and so I waited and then you…'

'Enough!' Brandt barked, grabbing her shoulders in an effort to calm her down and get her to stop the incomprehensible babble. 'Just tell me what's happened,' he said, kindlier now that he had her attention.

Kath took a deep breath. 'First, I just need you to know that what I did was wrong but that I only did it because I love you.'

'Okay,' he responded impatiently. He still didn't know what she was talking about, but a sense of foreboding was gradually enveloping him.

'I sent her a message.' Kath had now gone completely the other way, replacing her raving with an inadequately short, unqualified statement.

'Who?'

'The woman you have been emailing…'

There was only one person Kath could be referring to, but it just didn't seem possible. Even if she had remained suspicious about his internet use, there was no way she could have found out about his contact with Johnson. At the end of each session, he left no trace of their conversation.

'How?'

'I guessed you were deleting your history or whatever, so I waited until you went to the bathroom.' Her cheeks were flushed with shame.

'Shit!' Brandt cursed loudly. He hadn't locked the computer when he went to the toilet, but he had only been gone for a two-minute piss and she was meant to still be out in the garden.

'I'm sorry, Greggy,' Kath wailed, tears running down her cheeks.

Brandt completely ignored this latest attempt to apologise; his mind was busy trying to think through the implications of what he had been told. It was bad, but not necessarily disastrous.

'And you emailed her straight away?'

'I'm so sorry,' Kath repeated burying her head in her hands.

Brandt yanked her arms away with such force that Kath immediately looked up in shock. 'Yes or no. Did you email her straight away?'

'Yes,' she blurted out.

'What did you say?'

'I… I told her to back off.'

Brandt laughed, it might have only been a brief outburst, but it was enough to raise a hopeful smile on Kath's face.

'And you didn't tell her your name or anything else – like where we live?'

'Er, no.'

'And what did she respond?'

'I… I don't know.'

Brandt sat back against the headboard, feeling decidedly better. He knew he should be angry about this clear breach of trust, but it was nothing as bad as it might have been and, besides, it was nice to have someone care enough about him to be jealous. Nevertheless, he was also aware that at some point soon Kath would be expecting an explanation as to whom he had been messaging and why. Perhaps it would be best not to let her off the hook too soon and allow himself some time to think of a plausible excuse.

'So, let me just get this straight,' he said in a more serious tone than he actually felt, given the wave of relief that was still sweeping over him. 'You've been worried about what I'm up to on the computer, so you waited until I went to the toilet and you had a sneaky look. You saw an email from a woman so you replied, telling her to back off, and you then crept away before I came back?'

'Yes,' Kath replied guiltily, lowering her head in shame.

Brandt smiled. This should be easy to cover up. Perhaps he could claim he was emailing his sister back home in Georgia to see how things were going under the current political regime, or some such bullshit he could make up about social unrest there.

'Well, sort of…' Kath added before he had finally made up his mind.

'What do you mean, sort of?'

'Well, I was so scared you would return and find me there. It had taken me so long to get my gardening shoes off but then the email address was just random letters and numbers and I…'

She was off again, and Brandt could already feel his impatience return, along with a pang of worry. 'Be clearer, Kath!' he scalded, provoking a jolt of surprise.

'I wrote her email address down on a piece of paper and messaged her from my phone.'

There were a few moments of silence whilst Brandt let these terrible words crash down on him. It was as bad as he had originally feared. If she had simply replied to the email she'd found, it would have been sent with the same IP encryption he had installed on the laptop. But she hadn't. She had sent Detective Chief Inspector Stella Johnson, the woman who had been tasked to stop his serial killing, whom he then stripped and tied to her bed before killing her boyfriend, only to then reappear at her house a few weeks later to burn it down with her still in it, a message that would take approximately two minutes to trace.

'What time is it?' he roared, finally leaping from the bed.

'I… I don't know,' she replied, leaning over to check the alarm clock. 'A little after five.'

'Shit!' It was hours since he had left the laptop unlocked whilst he went to the toilet. As if to emphasise the point, his bladder started complaining that it was full again. But it would have to wait. By some stroke of good fortune Brandt wasn't already staring down the barrel of a police-issue firearm, but he couldn't afford to push his luck a moment longer.

'Where are you going?' Kath asked, fresh tears beginning to fall.

He stopped for a moment to look at her. He would have expected to feel anger, but here there was just loss. Realisation of how much he had changed thanks to her only made the situation he was now in more painful. He had arrived in North Wales unsure whether his decision to fake his suicide rather than actually carry it out was just plain belligerence. Nevertheless, there was one thing of which he had been certain. This was to be his very last attempt to find a way of carrying on. All he had been looking for was an existence, and he had never dared hope that he might achieve something more than that, much less find a love to rival anything he had ever felt for Susan. But he should have known that after what he had done, there could be no redemption, even if it was just to make one person's life happier than it would otherwise have been. He had learned through past, bitter experience that if something seemed too good to be true, it was. He had no doubt that the love he and Kath shared was real but that, equally, he had been a fool to think it would last.

Brandt opened his mouth to speak to Kath but couldn't think where to begin. An apology seemed like an appropriate start, but to condense all he had done and now all he would fail to do into two simple words just seemed crass. The coward inside him suggested that she was hurt enough, and he should spare her the details of the awful truth but then, much to his surprise, his more confident side concurred. However, his argument was based on the idea that he would be a fool to throw everything away unless it was strictly necessary. It reminded him that it was many hours since Kath had sent that message to Johnson. Of course, the delay was likely to be down to Johnson just not seeing it straight away; Brandt knew better than anyone else what she was currently involved in and it was highly unlikely that she was sat in her office waiting for his emails.

Alternatively, could it be possible that she had seen Kath's message and decided not to act on it? Maybe she felt somewhat indebted to him for his assistance in tracking down the new killer in Nottingham. He shook his head, knowing how unlikely that sounded. But then there was another option, and one that meant he was not in immediate danger. Admittedly she had only provoked rather than intended their first meeting, but since then Johnson's actions towards Brandt had been entirely outside the realm of law. So, whilst there may only be a small chance that she no longer wanted him caught, there was every chance she would want to do so herself.

'Informed decisions,' he muttered.

'What's that?' Kath asked, her voice barely a whisper.

'Oh, nothing,' he replied dismissively. When Brandt had been in the force, he had always told his teams that the worst decision was indecision, but he would then follow it up by saying that the best decision was an informed one. Right now, he felt he was at the most crucial crossroads in his life and each direction could fundamentally change the course of the rest of it. As such, he would be foolish to select one without knowing more about the danger he faced.

He dressed in silence before turning to Kath once more. 'I need to go out now. I hope it's just for a short while and, if so, I promise that I will explain everything when I get back. If, for some reason, I can't return to you as quickly as I intend, I want you to know that none of this was your fault and, as hard as you may find it to believe, my love for you has been genuine.'

With that he turned and left, hoping against hope that he would be reunited with her in a matter of hours.

Chapter Fifty-two

As Brandt waited in the layby, he kept his eyes trained on the road ahead. Each approaching vehicle was announced by the sweep of its lights as it rounded the bend and, rather than feel relief when every single one continued without slowing to turn onto the narrow lane that led up to the house, he cursed the agony of his fate remaining undisclosed.

Now away from immediate danger, he was able to better comprehend his situation and understood there was no hope for him and Kath. If no one arrived that night, it wasn't as though he could simply go back to the house, make up an effective story for what had happened, and things could return to normal. The spectre of their life about to be shattered at any moment would always remain above them and it was better now to know what he was dealing with.

With the situation apropos Kath now tragically resolved, the question for Brandt regarded Johnson. If she came alone, he would be able to escape once more. As desolate as it felt to have to start afresh, and now without the woman he loved, he would try and take from this experience, as he indeed hoped Kath may be able to once she got over the pain of the revelation of whom she had welcomed into her bed, that happiness still remained out there if he was prepared to find it. As unappealing as it now seemed, many options would remain open to him as he sought to find a way of establishing another new identity in another location. His circumstances may be far more dire than when he had arrived in North Wales, but the difference this time was that he had the evidence of his experience with Kath to convince him that it wasn't a situation from which he couldn't recover.

And so, as the specifics of each vehicle slowly revealed itself through the gloom of night, Brandt continued to will that he would finally see the red Audi he had first spied emerging from Nottingham police station all those months before. He laughed as he considered the irony of the pain he felt at losing Kath. It wasn't just the copycat killer in Nottingham that had brought him and Johnson together once more, they were both experiencing the same sense of loss. Inadvertently, they had each denied the other the person they loved. Perhaps then, it wasn't too much to hope that she might finally seek to abandon her personal vendetta towards him and start to move on with her life. The arrival of her car would therefore not signal the end for either of them but the beginning of their new lives, where they could independently try and put all they've been through behind them. And failing that, of course, he could always seek to blackmail her into submission with the threat to expose her highly illegal sharing of confidential information, not to mention her myriad of other misdemeanours since he had first met her.

Brandt was so caught up in his thoughts of what might be, that he did not pay any attention to the unmarked Ford Transit speeding towards him, having already dismissed it as soon as it came around the corner for its lights being set too high for it to be a low-slung sports car. His mind didn't register the red glow emanating from its rear as it slowed to make the turn. It was only as he heard the crunch of its tyres on the unmade road that he was brought to his senses.

Johnson hadn't come.

The cold, calculating part of his mind was telling him that he needed to start the car and move off before the police helicopter would arrive. It would currently be hovering just a few miles away, and would soon be cleared to move in. He would also need to figure out how far he could travel before being required to ditch the car. He didn't believe there were any ANPR cameras around Betws-y-Coed but as he headed north, towards the A55 that runs horizontally across the coast, linking England to the port to Ireland of Holyhead, he would start to encounter them. The might of the British police, and all the resources available to it, would soon be on his tail.

But it wasn't the weight of this bearing down on him that had caused him to hesitate in switching on the engine. He knew the futility of trying to escape this time without the assistance of Franklin or under the cover of his faked suicide. It was the sense of betrayal that was threatening to clog his mind. He could understand Johnson using the advantage Kath had gifted her to come and finish him off, but to take something that had become so personal between the two of them and open it out to the wider world, felt like cheating. Clearly there were no rules as such to their game, but their experiences had set certain parameters that Johnson had breached.

Brandt let out a bitter laugh as he finally twisted the key. Now that he thought about it, he wasn't in the least bit surprised at all; in fact, he found it rather fitting. Sure, Johnson had gone outside the powers granted to her by the police, but that had only been to try and change the game in her favour. She had done it with the newspaper articles and she had flown solo in order to track him down to Benidorm. She had even gone rogue to catch the copycat killer in Nottingham by accepting Brandt's offer of help. But that didn't mean she had a predisposition to behave as a maverick – it was her pragmatism enabling her to choose whatever path presented itself to be the best. Given that Brandt had managed to outwit her on each previous occasion, her electing to follow protocol on this one was merely her switching up the game once more.

This time it had been effective because it hadn't been anticipated. Much like an idiotic zoo keeper who seeks to hand-feed a tiger through the bars of its cage, only to then be shocked to find he gets his arm bitten off, Brandt should have realised that Johnson couldn't be tamed. Rather than show that she wanted to do this on her own, she had merely demonstrated that she was prepared to do whatever it took to get him.

Hell hath no fury like a woman scorned.

And it wasn't as though there was anything he could do with all the shit he could divulge about her. That ship, and all the other opportunities he'd had to stop her, had now sailed and was never coming back. Within the quiet confines of Kath's Kia Sportage, Brandt's laughter reverberated. It seemed such a delicious irony that the reason why he, the notorious serial killer, had been unable to win out against the celebrated police detective is that he lacked the utter ruthlessness she did. If their roles had been reversed, would she have loosened his bonds, so he could escape the blaze that was about to engulf his house? Not a chance!

Chapter Fifty-three

As Brandt made his way in the only direction available to him, Johnson was feeling anything but triumphant. On what should have been a day for celebration with the catching of the person currently terrorising the streets of Nottingham, she now only felt the bitter pang of defeat. Her conversation with Kath Hardcastle, the woman who had emailed her earlier that day, had only compounded the sense of helplessness. It seemed she had known nothing of Brandt's true identity, much less have any idea where he was now. By the sounds if it, the only time when she had felt even the slightest bit in danger, was when the SFO team had burst through her front door.

Due to its apparent futility, the journey ahead now seemed much longer. It would be quicker to return to Nottingham than to continue ploughing forward to the place where Johnson had pinned all her hopes of finally catching Brandt.

'What's wrong, ma'am?' Hardy asked as they suddenly slowed.

'I need to pull over a minute,' she replied, flicking on the indicator as she approached the layby.

'Do you want me to drive?' he asked helpfully.

Under the circumstances, she couldn't find the will to offer her usual sarcastic response to such a suggestion. 'No, I just need to check something.'

As soon as the car came to a halt, she fished her phone out from her bag. She used the internet browser to access the email account she had set up for communicating with Brandt. Whilst she couldn't bear the thought of it, she had suddenly developed the need to see his final, jubilant message. She could imagine the glee on his face as he typed the mocking words that would confirm he had outsmarted her once again.

But there was no message.

It wasn't to say there wouldn't be one, but Johnson took solace in the fact that he must have been so thrown by the unexpected turn of events that he hadn't been able to afford himself the time to fully reassert his dominance. More than the scant comfort it gave, it also provided Johnson with the will to continue. Conversation with his woman aside, in his haste there might be some clue as to his next destination. And this time she had the advantage of having the police with her. She knew from experience that Brandt would use his unique insight into their workings to ensure he wouldn't slip up in that regard, but that he would have to consider such limitations would present him with many challenges.

Feeling reinvigorated, Johnson eased back onto the road with a quizzical look from Hardy she chose not to react to. If Brandt had escaped, then she would have to find a way of dealing with it, but until it had been established that the trail had gone cold, she would not allow herself to give up hope.

Johnson wanted to see the house for herself, no matter how uncomfortable it would have been to view the life he had managed to build up whilst hers had remained in tatters, but Kath Hardcastle had been taken to the local police station for questioning. Johnson rarely enjoyed entering someone else's patch, probably something to do with the way she often viewed visitors as intruders, but she found the constabulary there to be welcoming; a situation no doubt helped by Hardy's disarmingly good manners. It didn't take them long to be granted access to the detainee.

The interview room they found her in was plain like countless others up and down Britain, except for the few signs that were on display being written in both English and Welsh.

Johnson couldn't help but be intrigued by the sight before her. Whilst she hadn't expected Kath to resemble any of Brandt's female victims, and especially not the young ones, she was surprised by the contrast between her and his ex-wife, Susan. Admittedly somewhat older, this woman had done little to conceal her age and, to all intents and purposes, looked like a perfectly decent person who was accepting of her transition into the latter phase of her life.

'Thank you for volunteering to come to the station to answer some questions. We spoke on the radio earlier. I'm DCI Johnson and this is my colleague DC Hardy.' She waited to see if there was a flicker of recognition. 'I wonder, perhaps, if you might know who I am,' she prompted when there was none. Johnson felt uncomfortable with the public profile she had developed, but in this case, she thought it might prove useful.

Moments later she could see Kath's eyes widen, but the look of horror that accompanied it implied that it was more than mere identification of a face that had been on the news. 'No, it can't be,' she whispered slowly.

'What can't, Kath? What have you been told?' She hated it when details were revealed to suspects in an untimely fashion.

'Well, nothing really, except, of course, what you said to me earlier.' In some respects, the woman seemed remarkably composed, but Johnson knew that it could sometimes be the result of shock numbing their emotions.

'But?'

'I could hear a name being mentioned.'

'What name?' Hardy asked gently.

'I… I don't want to say it,' she said, bowing her head as tears started to fall.

'I'm sorry, Kath, for the record I'm going to need…'

'Not now,' Johnson intervened, silencing DC Hardy. She wasn't sure why she felt sympathy for this woman but perhaps it was because, in their own unique ways, they had both suffered at the hands of the same man. 'Tell me about the person you have been with.'

'He… he is kind… he is intelligent,' she began slowly. 'He… he just has this zest for life and…'

Johnson wasn't prepared for hearing how wonderful Brandt was. Hardy must have sensed her discomfort because he intervened, despite her having only just shut him down. 'No, we mean who did he claim to be?'

'He is…' Kath managed before shaking her head as though trying to remind herself of the present situation. 'He was Gregori.'

'Gregory?' Hardy asked.

'No, Gregori,' she corrected, emphasising the *o*. 'The surname was one of those long Eastern European ones. He is… was from Georgia.'

'Georgia?' Johnson was grateful not to detect even the slightest hint of amusement in Hardy's voice.

'So he said,' she replied with bitterness creeping into her tone. 'He said he didn't like to talk about his past and, to be honest, that was fine by me. I used to be married, years ago, but Mike died and then…'

'Have you got any idea where he might be now?' Johnson interjected.

Kath paused for thought and it was clear she wanted to help. If it was because she hoped that this was all some kind of mistake and Gregori might be returned to her, Johnson couldn't tell. 'I can't think of anywhere.'

'Where did he live when you two met?'

As soon as she gave them the address of the caravan park, Johnson nodded to Hardy that he was to go and pass the information on. However, she knew it wouldn't come to anything. Brandt was too smart to make a simple mistake like that.

'Tell me about places you two liked to go?' she asked kindly, as soon as they were left alone.

'He... he liked everywhere really. We were often out and about.' The way her voice lifted at the mere mention again of their life together was almost heart breaking.

'Give me an example. Somewhere specific that sticks out.'

'Well, er, I suppose there was Llandudno. We had a lovely day out there. It was the day we became... close.'

Johnson allowed Kath to prattle on about how they walked along the promenade and ate fish and chips together watching the cable cars beyond the pier take people up the cliffs. Waiting for Hardy to return so they could wrap this up, she allowed her a few moments more to relive the fantasy that Brandt had woven for her, before the full reality of the situation she found herself in came crashing down. If she thought things had been bad so far, it was nothing compared to what it was going to be like becoming the most talked about woman in Britain. Johnson had experienced a taste of it and could imagine the horrors that awaited her.

As they exited the police station and got back in the car, Johnson wondered whether the sympathy she felt for this woman was the same as with any of Brandt's victims. She was certain that Kath was entirely innocent, just another person duped by the promise of love, but there was a difference and not just because she was physically unharmed. When Johnson cut away the pain of hearing about their time together, it was obvious that what they had shared was more than Brandt manipulating the woman to serve his own purpose. Much as Johnson hated to admit it, there was a tenderness there. Perhaps his comment in the email about going out for the evening and enjoying himself hadn't just been a smug dig.

If nothing else, he had not sought to enact any form of retribution on Kath for her blunder with contacting Johnson. But regardless whether he had formed the same emotional connection with her that she had clearly formed with him, it still didn't bring Johnson any closer to finding him.

Unless she could figure out some way of exploiting it, that was. She might better understand now why he had not chosen to revel in his ability to escape Johnson once more, with his sense of his own personal loss a greater factor than any time constraints. However, that would make Brandt a wounded animal and she knew from experience how dangerous that made him.

Chapter Fifty-four

It had taken Brandt a long time to get there. He had gone as far north in Kath's Kia as he dared, before parking it discreetly down a quiet road in some anonymous hamlet with a name he couldn't even begin to pronounce. Satisfied that it would be at least the next day before it was discovered, he continued on foot. It was hardly a surprise that people weren't too keen to pick up a lone, male hitchhiker at this time of night, but he hadn't been too concerned; he still had ample time to get to his destination and his afternoon nap had endowed him with plenty of energy for the long walk ahead.

The outskirts of Llandudno were as plain, if not downright ugly, as any decent sized town in Britain. Brandt tried not to focus on any of it and risk spoiling his memory of the place, instead concentrating on keeping one foot in front of another.

Finally, he made it into the centre and he carried on until he recognised some of the shops from when he and Kath had spent the day there. Although where he was headed was further up, he couldn't resist detouring to the promenade as soon as it was available to him. Immediately upon exiting the side road and with the sea shimmering in the moonlight in front of him, he knew that he had come to the right place.

The area was deserted, for it was now well past midnight, but it did not feel eerie with the warm glow from the street lamps and the occasional light still on in some of the hotel bedrooms running along the length of the seafront. In the hours it had taken to reach there, Brandt had wondered how he would feel returning to the place where he had found true happiness for the first time in decades. He had wondered whether it would heighten his sense of loss; of what might have been.

But instead it made him smile. This place reminded him that everything he had been through, and every sacrifice he had made along the way, had been worth it. He would hold on to those memories, fleeting though they might be, as he continued on to his final destination.

He waited until he was almost at the pier, where he and Kath had laughed their way around the amusement arcade, before he pulled out his mobile phone.

Punching in the relatively short message, he knew that within minutes it would be traced to the nearest phone mast. That it would result in the police descending upon the area, awakening the few visitors who chose to holiday here at this time of year, did not concern him. The audience his text would find may be large but only one person would be able to determine its true meaning. For any notion that he had found his soul mate in Kath was a lie almost as big as the one on which he had based their relationship. With Susan now dead, there was only one person in the world who truly knew him, and it was to this person he was reaching out now. What she chose to do with it was up to her. He had learned to his recent cost not to try and predict her reaction, but that didn't stop him hoping that she would do the right thing.

Chapter Fifty-five

'Ma'am, we're going to need to stop for fuel soon.'

'Fine,' Johnson replied curtly. She knew the subtext to Hardy's observation was less about the need to find a petrol station and more that he believed their continual driving around was increasingly pointless.

Nevertheless, to stop, other than briefly at the Shell indicated up ahead on the car's sat nav, would be to admit defeat. If she were in Hardy's shoes, she would probably feel the same, but Johnson couldn't help holding onto the idea that if she thought hard enough, she would be able to figure out Brandt's next move. The rest of the police force out that night would be following the typical assumptions based on how the situation presented itself. However, she knew that Brandt was equally aware of these things and would neutralise their effectiveness. The fact that he had taken off in Kath's car and yet hadn't pinged a single ANPR illustrated that.

But rather than accept that it meant he could be anywhere, it spurred her on. Much as Johnson hated it, the fact was that the person she knew best in the world was Brandt. He was the man, not McNeil, who she woke up thinking about each day and was her last thought before she went to sleep. Speaking to Kath may have seemed fruitless but it had allowed her an insight into his current state of mind. And she would not give up until she combined that with her unique knowledge of Brandt to work out his trail. All she needed now was to find a clue to put her on the right path.

With the only sound the steady thrum of the petrol pump dispensing its contents as Hardy dutifully filled up the car, and with her eyes finally adjusting to the harsh contrast of the forecourt's sodium lights, she got it.

> – *You've won. You'll know where I'll be if you want to collect your prize.*

No name and from a number that her phone did not recognise, and yet this could only be from one person. Casting an anxious glance over her shoulder to make sure Hardy hadn't somehow heard the ping of the incoming message, she read its brief contents again.

Johnson let out an ironic laugh. To hear from Brandt again directly was more than she could have hoped for as she and Hardy had driven around aimlessly. But it was so typical of the man for his contact to be ambiguous to the point of irrelevant. The only place she could think of was her house, or what remained of it, back in Nottingham. Technically he could have made it there if he had managed to steal a car, its loss yet to be discovered and reported, but it wouldn't make sense for him to have managed to entirely flee the area only to then concede defeat.

Naturally, this could just be one of his games: his loss of Kath causing him to seek revenge on the person he believed responsible; and this time he would look to finish the job. It all seemed rather fitting, except for one small detail. He had abandoned the new life he had built for himself because he must have believed that his partner, his lover, had accidentally compromised its safety. Of course, he may have been trying to intercept Johnson before she could do anything with the information, but too much time would have elapsed between Kath having sent the email and his message now. No, if he had expected Johnson to act on it, as surely he must have, then he would know either she or the police were coming to get him. Either way, it wouldn't make sense for him to try and rendezvous with Johnson back in Nottingham. If she had come alone then it would be illogical to meet her anywhere other than somewhere around here, especially as he would also have the advantage of being on more familiar soil than her. Whereas, if he had expected that she would pass on the location from which Kath had sent her email, then surely he would expect her to also have the police track this message and intercept him.

With her head now aching from all the different permutations thrown up by Brandt's text, and with the sound of the petrol pump substituted by the tank's filler cap being replaced, Johnson knew she had a more immediate decision to make. What, if anything, to tell Hardy? She wanted more time to think things through before revealing the message to him, especially as she knew what his reaction would be. Hardy would be insistent that the number be radioed in so that it could be traced and, even if she could convince him otherwise, she knew she would be putting him in a compromising situation.

And yet without tracing it she didn't think she would be able to unravel the clue contained within. If it was really designed to be a trap, then what would be the point if Johnson was unable to fall into it? What an unfortunate time for him to over-estimate her capabilities. Unless, of course, he had somehow known that she had gone by the book on this one and had sent in the police ahead of her and, as a consequence, would have them run a trace on this too.

'Argh!' she screamed into the confines of the car's interior. The more she thought about it, the more she seemed to be tying herself up in knots.

The passenger door was flung open. 'Are you okay, ma'am?' Hardy asked hurriedly. 'I heard a shout.'

No more thinking; just do it. 'Quick, get in,' Johnson said, the car screeching off the forecourt in a flurry of wheelspin with him yet to fully close his door. 'Take my phone,' she ordered, thrusting it towards him whilst she tried to concentrate on successfully navigating the junction ahead. 'Call through a trace on the number associated with the last text message.'

Out of the corner of her eye, she could see Hardy's face illuminated by the screen as he swiped into her inbox. However, he didn't then immediately reach for the radio. 'Is this from… but how did he…?'

'Not now, Hardy!' she roared. 'Just call it through, I'll explain later!'

* * *

'The mast from which it was sent has coordinates 53.32 degrees north, 3.83 degrees west,' responded the anonymous and dispassionate voice a few minutes later. 'Llandudno centre.'

'Repeat that last, over,' instructed Hardy.

'Coordinates are for Llandudno, Conwy, North Wales. Over.'

'Thank you. Out,' he responded, replacing the handset. 'What now, ma'am?'

'Call it through,' she said, whilst trying to convince herself that this was the right thing to do. 'Then programme the sat nav for those exact coordinates,' she added. The local police were going to get there before them but she hardly expected Brandt to be sat beneath the phone mast with his wrists held out, ready for cuffing.

She could also use the journey to figure out how it related to his claim that she would know where he was. The first time she had heard of Llandudno was when Kath spoke about it at the station, but he wasn't to know that. There had to be something else to his message…

Chapter Fifty-six

Brandt hadn't needed a response from Johnson to know that she had received his text. From his vantage point, he could see the flashing blue lights as multiple police vehicles descended on the town centre. If anything, it added to the moonlit visage before him.

He knew it was only a matter of time before they finished sweeping the immediate area and would start exploring further afield, but whilst the darkness of night remained, they would not be able to see him on the cliffs above. Naturally dawn, still an hour away, would change that but by then it would be too late. He just hoped that he had given Johnson enough time to arrive.

Brandt buried his hands in his pockets and stamped his feet in an effort to keep out the cold. He was fortunate that the only coat he possessed was a warm one but it was proving insufficient, exposed as he was to the elements. Nevertheless, he didn't have to worry about the potential onset of hypothermia and distracted himself by continuing to watch the pretty patterns of the police as they continued their search.

The sight was mesmerising almost to the point of appearing to be the contents of a dream, but Brandt was brought back to reality by the sight of a pair of headlamps sweeping past the pier and onto the steep drive up to the entrance of the cable cars. Not that it ultimately mattered but he peered through the gloom to try and determine whether it was a squad car with its emergency lights switched off.

Then finally the bass tone of its high-performance engine drifted up to him and Brandt began to smile. He waited until it came to a halt and watched its two occupants get out. 'Up here!' Brandt shouted, the steady breeze carrying his salutation down the hill and causing them both to snap their heads in his direction, the swish of the ponytail suggesting the driver to be Johnson. The identity of her companion, he didn't know, but nor was he concerned.

The way she marched up the steep incline was impressive, but he reassured himself that he would have found it easier had he not already walked countless miles before arriving here. He spent the time it took them to approach pondering how she must be feeling. She was bound to be wary given their previous encounters but clearly not enough to bring the rest of the police force with her.

'Aren't you going to introduce us?' Brandt asked, as soon as she stopped, no doubt deciding that being 20 feet away was plenty close enough.

'Why have you brought us here?' Johnson demanded, ignoring his request.

'I think you know that,' he replied in an even tone.

Johnson didn't respond but simply stood there, hands on hips.

'I've had enough of this,' Hardy piped up after a few seconds of watching them posturing. 'Jeffrey Brandt, I am arresting you…'

'Stop!' Johnson roared, reaching out to pull her partner back.

'You see, she does know why we're here,' Brandt said with a smile. 'If you're not going to tell me, I think you should at least bring your friend up to speed.' He waited for a few moments and then shrugged theatrically. 'Play it your way. Time is tight, so I'll just assume it was because you had the phone's signal traced to Llandudno and then worked out that I would be pretty much in this exact spot. So, I guess the question really is how you knew…'

Johnson still would not allow herself to be baited even though Hardy's expression had changed from shock to one of curiosity.

'Fine, looks like you've had a wasted journey then,' Brandt said, turning around and walking towards the cliff edge.

'He's bluffing,' Hardy stated, without any real degree of confidence. 'At least let me call this in.'

'No, he isn't,' replied Johnson flatly.

'Go on…' Brandt called over his shoulder, dangling a foot out over drop below.

'When Brandt was in my house the second time, he confided in me that he used to fantasise about plunging off a cliff.'

'And what else did I say to you?'

'That death was a better experience shared.'

'Exactly,' Brandt responded turning back around, but without moving away from danger. 'It's nice to know you were paying attention.'

'So, this is to be my *prize*, is it? To watch you jump off and onto the rocks below?'

Brandt let out a long and loud laugh. 'No, of course not. Just like you knew me well enough to find me, so too I know you well enough to understand that you wouldn't view it as sufficient reward for your efforts, nor indeed adequate compensation for the… problems I have caused you.'

'No, I wouldn't,' Johnson whispered, clenching her fists.

'Tell me, have you met Kath yet?'

'Yes.'

'A wonderful woman, isn't she? Would it do any good to suggest that losing her makes us even?'

'Not even close.'

'Ah, as I thought,' he sighed. 'Well, then dawn is about to make its appearance, so I guess it's time for you to claim your prize.'

Johnson remained rooted to the spot. 'Why didn't you just run again?'

'For the same reason why I tried to fake my death when I burned down your house. I knew that neither of us could move on whilst you still believed me alive. By the time you discovered my subterfuge I had found another reason to live, but now she is gone. When I contacted you offering my help, you asked me if I was looking for redemption. I wasn't, but I can't help wondering whether you might be. I assume you got that killer in Nottingham today. Wasn't enough, was it?'

'No.'

'I guess there was a part of me that hoped you would decide there might be a purpose to me remaining in this world. But your actions tonight involving the police have shown me that you won't. You can't.'

'Whatever it takes,' Johnson muttered.

'Indeed,' Brandt responded wistfully.

'So, are you going to arrest him then?' Hardy asked impatiently.

'No, she's not,' Brandt answered. 'Are you Detective Chief Inspector?'

'No,' she whispered.

'What?' Hardy cried out.

'Do keep up, dear,' Brandt said, before turning back to Johnson. 'If it would help, we could always push him over first.' He paused for a moment. 'I'm joking of course... well, unless you're going to allow me one more for old time's sake...'

'Don't go near him, it's a trap!' Hardy warned.

'Look, I'm tired of running, almost as much as I suspect you are of chasing me,' Brandt said to Johnson. 'If neither of us can have a life whilst the other one lives, then one of us has to go.'

With the sun now creeping over the horizon and silhouetting Brandt, Johnson was unable to see his expression. She started walking forward anyway, understanding the truth in his words. Casting a final glance over her shoulder, she was relieved to see that Hardy remained rooted to the spot; his mouth open, aghast. Young and inexperienced he may be, but she knew he would do the right thing once this was over.

Fixing her head firmly forward, all that now mattered was the man before her. Brandt's arms were held out to the side, and the biblical pose in the dawn's early rays caused her legs to hesitate. But then she remembered how McNeil hadn't faltered at the last moment, and with his name on her lips, she continued on towards what awaited her at the cliff's edge.

The instincts she had honed over her career prompted her to watch for the first signs of movement, but Brandt remained motionless until she was so close that she could almost reach out and touch him.

'How does it feel for us to be face-to-face once more?' Brandt asked, his face silhouetted against the rising sun.

'There's never been an *us*,' Johnson replied bitterly.

'And yet *us* is all we've been left with,' he responded calmly, his voice almost soothing.

'So you're just going to let me push you, then?' Johnson's voice was now flat, but her heart was hammering in her chest.

'No, detective chief inspector,' Brandt said, allowing a small chuckle to escape him. 'That may be what you want but this is what you need…'

Brandt had no sooner finished the word than he took a single step backwards and plunged over the edge of the cliff.

If you enjoyed this book, please let others know by leaving a quick review on Amazon. Also, if you spot anything untoward in the paperback, get in touch. We strive for the best quality and appreciate reader feedback.

editor@thebookfolks.com

www.thebookfolks.com

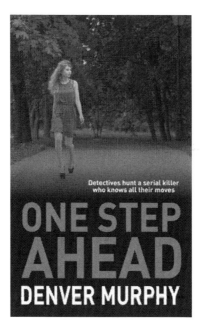

He spent his life fighting crime. Now he has a taste for it himself. His first attack is a stab in the dark. Next time, he'll kill. Knowing how the police work, ex-cop Jeffrey Brandt stays one step ahead of them. He will even taunt those trying to catch him. DCI Stella Johnson is responsible for finding him. Has she got what it takes?

Book II, available on Kindle and in paperback.

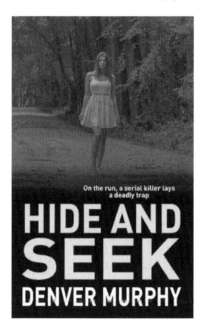

Having discovered Brandt's identity, the race is on to capture him. DCI Johnson now has a very personal reason to hunt him down. But Brandt knows she is coming. Can she evade the traps he has laid?